3 29001 00087 3449

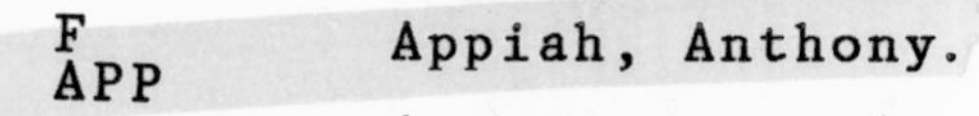

# Avenging Angel

# AVENGING ANGEL

Anthony Appiah

St. Martin's Press
New York

Library of Congress Cataloging-in-Publication Data

Appiah, Anthony.
Avenging angel : a Sir Patrick Scott mystery / Anthony Appiah.
p. cm.
ISBN 0-312-05817-9
I. Title.
PS3551.P558A97 1991
813'.54—dc20
90-28721
CIP

First published in Great Britain by Constable & Company Limited.

First U.S. Edition: August 1991
10 9 8 7 6 5 4 3 2 1

*David Glen Tannock was tired, 'dog-tired' as he said to himself, wondering all the while where this odd expression came from. He knew it was also a German idiom –* 'Hündemüde', *as his German master had taught him at Eton – so he supposed it must be an old idea; and, as his consciousness faded, he decided that he would canvass opinions at the Society's annual dinner.*

*This evening's paper at the Society had been interesting enough, so that the discussion had run on. But David had had slightly too much port after dinner and, by the time the paper was over, he was already suppressing a yawn. He had to get some sleep tonight; there was that one final exam to do tomorrow, before he settled down to May Week and the 'unexamined life'. On the way in, he had put a kettle on to boil in the gyp room at the head of the staircase beside his attic rooms. Now he heard it boiling, and he stepped out to make himself a cup of cocoa. It was an old nursery habit. Perhaps it would help him sleep.*

*Memorial Court had been still as he came through it, the pale brick bright in the moonlight; and as he had thrown open the window of his bedroom, he had wondered vaguely why everything was so quiet. It* was *the examination period, of course, and there were no doubt members of the College who were taking the opportunity to rest and study for their finals. Still, it struck him, even in his exhausted state, as somehow not quite right that the college was so peaceful. After all, even Clare has its shirkers. But his thoughts about the quiet reached not much further than the thoughts about the origins of idiom that followed them as he pulled on his pyjamas. And by the time he fell asleep, the origins of 'dog-tiredness' and the emptiness of the night had both faded from his mind. What David Glen Tannock dreamed of no one would ever know.*

*Of course, no one was to know of his etymological speculations or his worry about the stillness of the college courtyard, either. For when – at eight thirty the next morning – David's 'bedder' unlocked the door to the outer of his two rooms, what she saw, through the open door of the inner room, was the boy's body, cold and stiff under the flapping curtain of the window over the bed. And though, in thirty years of cleaning the rooms of 'her boys', she had never before seen one of them dead, she knew in an instant that David had dreamed his last dream. The smell of urine caught her nostrils as her eyes focused on the red blotches on his pale skin. When she mumbled, 'My gawd,' before she ran screaming to the porter's lodge, for perhaps the first time in her life, it was a genuine call on the Almighty.*

*Sometime between returning to his room and lying for the last time on that bed, David Glen Tannock had drunk the draught that killed him.*

# 1

There are ways and ways of reconstructing a death, and – so far as deaths that might be murders are concerned – I've tried most of them. I barely get to hear of deaths where 'foul play' is not suspected; nowadays suicide is a straightforward matter and they leave it to the ordinary work of the police laboratories to identify the poison, or write up the ballistics report when another shotgun finishes the life of its owner. But with 'Glen Tannock, Viscount David Charles, twenty-one years and three months,' I reckoned the only way to start was with his mind: we had nothing else, at the start, to guide us to the mind of his killer. In the first day after his death I gathered enough information to tell myself this and a score of other plausible tales.

The boy was clever, everyone knew that . . . and well-bred and good-looking. I knew he was clever because I had heard him speaking (and, more importantly, observed him thinking) at meetings of the Society, on the rare occasions I had attended recently as an 'Angel' – as we call those members who have passed beyond the real world of weekly meetings in Cambridge and entered the unreality of what parents and politicians mistakenly regard as the 'real' world. I knew he was well-bred not because he had ever mentioned his family at those meetings, but because his mother was a cousin of mine; I had seen him off and on as he grew up, and when he was deciding which college to apply to, I had urged him to break with the family tradition and go to Clare: I was an honorary Fellow, I dined there from time to time, and the Master, who was a nice enough chap, had been in my house at school. I had wanted David to go to Clare because, of all the younger members of my family, only my son Sebastian meant more to me: the college was the finest gift I could think to give him.

But even if I hadn't known him, the college file that I read in my room the evening after his death had his antecedents laid out as clearly as an entry in Debrett's.

His father was Charles David Hamilton, fifteenth Earl Ivor, a Scottish peer who managed the scarcely imaginable feat of being well-known and well-educated without alienating the vast majority of his noble friends who were neither. Lord Ivor was a popular figure on television, the sort of aristocrat whose mildness and good manners, combined with the effortless affectation of a middle brow, guaranteed that he could always be regarded as unthreatening. He sat on the boards of numerous, especially technological, companies; and he spent a few weeks of the year in his rooms at All Souls in Oxford, dining with the other Fellows and reminding them, quietly, of his immense erudition, his good will and his wit.

No one could dislike Charles. No one who knew him could fail to respect the noble lord's intelligence, or to recognize his kindness. In short, if David Glen Tannock was the perfect youth, he was overshadowed by an even more perfect father.

Somehow it was inevitable that David's mother, Lady Ivor, my kinswoman, was beautiful and charming and intelligent and kind, as she went quietly and gracefully about the work of a countess, opening hospitals and raising funds for orphanages, shattering men's hearts on her way from this opera to that fête to the next ball. There are few such families left for the *Tatler* to celebrate, and the Earl and Countess of Ivor played the role well. If the world knew less of their children – David, Viscount Glen Tannock and Lady Caroline Hamilton – it was because, in being so charmingly available to the press, they were able to make the newspaper editors of the British Isles their accomplices in keeping the terrible secret that their children were perfect also.

So when the death occurred, I, like everyone else, felt a special horror; not only was it numbing to lose David – my kinsman and, as I liked to think, my friend – it was strangely disturbing to witness the intrusion of something so appalling into the flawless perfections of the Ivor line. And since I was a Fellow of the college he died in, and a cousin with a little reputation for clearing up such difficulties, it was natural that Charlie should ask me to volunteer my services. I did not mention either to the police or to the Master of the college that I was, like Glen Tannock, a member of the Society, an organization whose paradoxically notorious obsession with secrecy had even, on occasion, been held to threaten the national security. If it were possible, I thought, I should like to keep the Society out of the matter: the last time we had surfaced in the press it had been in connection with the unearthing of another Soviet 'mole', and some of the Society's senior members were naturally less than keen for another go-round in the press.

Which is why I found myself trying to reconstruct in imagination the last thoughts of David, Viscount Glen Tannock; and wondering if, with his curious and intelligent mind, he had noticed the only thing that was unusual about the night of his death – save that he died on it: namely, the quiet.

The quiet certainly was unusual at one on a summer morning towards the end of exams; and it had been achieved by an engagingly direct method. The Senior Tutor, who lived in rooms that overlooked both the courts on the other side of the river, where David had his rooms, had announced at dinner that anyone who disturbed his rest during the examination period would be suspended, prohibited from taking exams and refused readmission. That old Finch had been in his cups at the time and acting rather substantially *ultra* his *vires* was not something that the undergraduates had had time to find out; and the Master's shock at this astonishing aberration was such that he had not thought at the time to rise and dismiss the Senior Tutor's remark as a jest. By the time he decided that this would indeed be the best thing to do, it was too late. To speak five minutes later would have been to expose the Fellowship to ridicule.

Now, David Glen Tannock had dined that evening at the University Pitt Club, as he once told me was his custom before meetings of the Society, because it enabled him to start a little earlier and finish a little sooner than he could either in college or at a restaurant in town. So he would not have heard the Senior Tutor's odd announcement; and by the late hour that he got back to his rooms, its effect would probably have meant that no one was around to communicate it to him.

If I knew David, his last thoughts as he fell asleep would have returned to the quietness: and, more importantly, if there had been anyone hiding in his cupboards or behind the inner door, even the slightest of their moves would have been audible. On such a night a murderer would have had to move slowly and wait long; wait until he heard the steady breathing of the sleeping Viscount. He – or she, since, as I occasionally had to remind myself, I had succeeded in my campaign to get the college to admit women *in statu pupillari* and as Fellows – would surely have had to be extremely circumspect.

*If*, that is, David Glen Tannock had been murdered. To find *that* out we should have to wait for the autopsy; and my first task on that first day had to be to make sure that I got the results as early as possible.

That turned out to be easier said than done. Fenton, who was also the medical tutor at Clare, would normally have carried out the post-mortem in his pathology lab at Old Addenbrookes. He had often regaled me with the gory details of his dismembering of a recent corpse. I should have had no difficulty in pumping him; none even in getting in to watch the proceedings. But Inspector Fanshaw, of the Cambridgeshire Constabulary, had told the coroner that the death had occurred at Clare in suspicious circumstances; and she had concluded that it would be better to leave the autopsy to Dr James Hagarty. Not that Mrs Braithwaite doubted Fenton's *bona fides*, but it seemed to her unwise, given the publicity that was bound to attend the death of the scion of so famous a house, to offer the press the opportunity even to speculate about a cover-up. Later, of course, I was thankful for her caution.

Jimmy Hagarty was famous in Cambridge for having missed the insulin in the blood of the last victim of the Grantchester rapist. If anything interesting had happened in the physiology or biochemistry of my young cousin, there was as good a chance as not that Hagarty would miss it. For *fancy* work in the way of forensic pathology, he was not, let us say, the first person you would think to call upon.

Granted, Hagarty had his points – he could be guaranteed to tell you if the deceased was poisoned with methanol or had syphilis. Unfortunately, there was nothing in this case to suggest that Lord Glen Tannock had consumed methanol – I had confirmed by way of a discreet chat over the telephone with the Pitt Club's manager that it was ethanol (in the form of a Pouilly-Fuissé of no special vintage and a '55 Warre port that I, at least, would have wanted to live to talk about) that his lordship had consumed with his dinner companion on the eve of his death; and, as for syphilis, interesting as it might be to discover so old-fashioned an infection in so old-fashioned a body, I rather doubted that it could have been a cause of death.

In the circumstances, therefore, Jimmy Hagarty was not quite the thing. Still, the coroner had dispatched him; the best I could do was to make sure that Fenton was at least present – with helpful suggestions and a curious eye – as the old boy set about butchering this elegant, aristocratic corpse.

I had heard from Charlie Ivor by nine a.m. By eleven I had reached Cambridge by the train from King's Cross, stopping in a coin-box at the station for a brief chat with the manager of the Pitt Club to confirm my expectations about David's last dinner. I went straight to the Master's lodge to sign in, so to speak, and asked if I could see the boy's room before the police messed it up irretrievably. While the Master was explaining to Inspector Fanshaw why the college wanted me in on the case, I called Paul Fenton on the phone. It was just after midday when I got through to him in his college rooms. He grasped the situation immediately.

'Oh Lord. Hagarty. Well, I'll just have to potter over and keep an eye on him.' I didn't even have to suggest it.

By the time I got off the phone, Dominic, Lord Wratting – the Master of the college – had persuaded a sceptical Inspector Fanshaw that it would do no harm to let me into David's rooms.

As we walked over to Memorial Court, the Master told me the story of the Senior Tutor's strange announcement and then fell silent. Only a couple of years ago, Dominic had taken, at his wife's suggestion, the title of Lord Wratting, when, as is the way in these matters, his turn to be Vice Chancellor had come round. Wratting is not a name I would myself have chosen, even if the manor of West Wratting had been in *my* wife's family in the seventeeth century, but it was a cosy enough reason for choosing a Barony and Dominic had always struck me as a cosy man. The ancient Harris Tweed jacket he wore looked as comfortable as his baggy brown corduroy trousers. After an elaborate search he produced from the depths of one his pockets a pipe that gave him, even more definitely, the look of a Lincolnshire poacher. I had half expected him to produce a rabbit or a brace of snipe. I wondered what Inspector Fanshaw had made of old Dominic.

I thought how strange and marvellous it was that he and I had known each other for more than half a century without ever having to become friends. I was grateful that he knew instinctively that I didn't want to talk about the boy or his death; and the thought of the hushed courts fuelled my imaginings of David's last hours. I needed to think it through visually, to imagine it all, if I was to make sense of his dying.

When we reached the rooms, the body was gone, of course, but the forensic types were still buzzing about with cameras and little plastic bags. In ten minutes I saw all I wanted to see. 'Did you take a sample from that cup by the bed?' I asked a fellow who was taking fingerprints on the window-sill.

'It's cocoa. I sniffed it.'

'Be a good chap and keep a little for the coroner,' I said, hoping that he wouldn't ask me why I was telling him his job. And then, in case he didn't quite get my message, I did one of those small irregular acts that my mother always warned me would be my undoing. While everyone was busy in the next room, I took out the clean handkerchief that I had shoved in my pocket as I hurried out of my house in London to the cab, and dipped it into the milky fluid in the cup. I sniffed the handkerchief. It certainly did indeed smell like cocoa. Then I returned the handkerchief to my pocket.

You never can be too careful. Even if the police did analyse the contents of the cup, they might be stuffy about telling me what they found. This way, I thought, I could, if necessary, keep up with the facts while the trail was still warm.

But the rooms gave few clues. An ordinary undergraduate set, perhaps a little tidier than most. I stepped out on to the landing and looked into the gyp room. There were the kettle, the cocoa powder, the sugar cubes, a glass jar of powdered milk. It looked as though this was where David had made his last drink.

*

As it happens, I needn't have bothered with the handkerchief trick. Paul Fenton called me in the Fellows' guest-room as I was dressing for dinner. 'Patrick. That you?' Taking my momentary pause for assent he continued. 'Open and shut case,' he barked. 'Anaphylactic shock brought on by a massive dose of penicillin. Turns out the boy had a known allergy to the stuff. Hagarty asked his doctor. Can't think what he was doing taking it.'

'How did it get into him?' I asked, wondering whether to explain to Paul that the reasonable assumption was that David hadn't meant to take a dose of penicillin of any size.

'Orally. Plenty in his stomach on top of his dinner. Rather good boozy dinner, too. Sometimes you get vomiting in these cases, but Lord Glen Tannock was able to keep his dinner down. Unfortunately the allergic reaction swelled up his air passages: angioedema, asphyxiation, death. Probably took less than a quarter of an hour from when he swallowed the stuff.'

'And when did he die?'

'At a rough guess, I'd say about half-past midnight; certainly somewhere between midnight and two a.m.' There was a pause. 'He was a very nice boy, you know, Glen Tannock. If someone had given him a half-mil. of epinephrine within a few minutes he would still be alive. It seems an awful bloody waste.'

For a moment neither of us said anything, acknowledging the truth in Fenton's last remark.

'Well, thank you so much for keeping me informed, Paul. I wonder if I could ask you one more question? I take it that the allergy would have been known to more people than his doctor. Would there have been a record in the college?'

'Good Lord, yes. Things like that would be in the boy's tutor's files.'

'And who was his tutor?'

'Oh, you'd have to ask the Senior Tutor; he'd know. What was he reading?'

'History.'

'Probably Parker or Adkins, they look after most of the historians. But you'll have to check with Alan Finch, as I say.'

'Well, thanks again, Paul.'

I had about a quarter of an hour before I had to go over to dine in hall. Time enough to write down what little I knew.

# 2

During the afternoon I had wandered distractedly through the Market Place and down Market Hill towards the Pitt Club. As I turned into Jesus Lane, Mr Caufield, the club manager who had presided when my own son had been a member nearly a decade earlier, was walking slowly towards me, dressed, as always, like an undertaker and looking more than usually mournful. We met outside the club. 'Good afternoon, Sir Patrick,' he said. 'It's a sad business.' And then he added what was becoming a familiar refrain: 'He was a very nice young gentleman, if I may say so, sir. One of the best of them.'

As we stood under the old portico, memories of my own days in the club, back before the War, in such a different Cambridge, flooded back. In those days only the extremest left-wingers thought it odd that the club, while officially, I suppose, open to any undergraduates, admitted only those from the better public schools; unless, of course, you were blackballed by a member of the committee. In the admissions book each autumn, page after page of Etonians and Harrovians and Wykehamists appeared and members scrawled their names in support. Occasionally it came into someone's head to oppose a nomination. If your school was less well known someone was bound to write 'Where?' or 'Never heard of it.'

Once or twice a week I had dined with friends in evening dress in the candle-lit dining-room and watching as Magdalene men, back from an afternoon's beagling, drank themselves into a state in which debagging undergraduates from less exalted backgrounds and dumping them in the river seemed a natural way to round off an evening. I had picked up a bloody nose once coming to the aid of a harmless classicist from Emmanuel, whom I knew slightly, when he was set upon by a pack of mindless upper-class drunks. From then on, I slipped out of the club on many an evening when the whispers and the unfriendly glances from a noisy table gave signs that I might be being sized up as a potential victim.

My feelings when Sebastian, my son, was admitted to the club had been more than slightly mixed. In his day the evening-dress had gone; but the habits of members had changed regrettably little. If anything, the nastier occupations were engaged in with the bravado of a class that knew its time had passed. I wondered what David had thought of these rituals. It's funny how much you realize you haven't talked about with someone once they have gone.

Caufield's voice drew me back. 'What can I tell you, sir, apart from what I told you on the telephone this morning?'

We went over the evening once again. Mr Caufield's grip on the facts was impeccable. David had dined at the club at seven with a friend. 'A Mr Buckingham, sir; Jeremy Buckingham, known to one and all as Hippo.' Hippo Buckingham was at Jesus, Mr Caufield thought; and I could tell from his tone that if one of the two 'young gentlemen' had absolutely had to die, Caufield would have rather it had been Hippo.

At a quarter past eight David and Hippo had left the club, saying good-night courteously to the staff and perhaps slightly tipsy – this was *not* Mr Caufield's contribution – from the wine and the port that had accompanied their rather hurried meal. David had told Mr Caufield that he would be bringing in a new member the next day, 'so that I could treat him – the new member, that is – as well as I treated Lord Glen Tannock. He always put things so nicely.'

'This will seem a mildly eccentric question, I am sure, Mr Caufield, but is any of the china from last night still unwashed?'

'I should hope not, Sir Patrick. But we could go and see.'

We wandered together through the massive kitchens of the club to the ancient sinks where the washing-up was done. There were a few glasses on the draining board, washed and sparkling, no doubt the traces of the last drinkers as the bar closed at ten thirty the previous night, but no signs of crockery. It probably didn't matter. Paul Fenton thought that the allergic reaction would have occurred in a quarter of an hour at the most. And the last time David had been in the club was more than three and a half hours before the earliest time of death.

'Thank you so much. You've been most helpful. I expect the police will be wanting to hear your story, Mr Caufield. Perhaps you might volunteer it to them by phoning them now.' And as

I said that, it occurred to me to ask one more question: 'By the way, I don't suppose that Lord Glen Tannock telephoned anyone while he was here last evening?'

The answer was: 'No.'

Well, as I say, you never can be too careful.

From the Pitt Club I walked briskly back towards the Old Court of Clare. I was planning to go up to the Senior Combination Room to use the telephone. There were several old friends I needed to talk to, and the sooner the better. My mind turned, as it had on the train, to the difficulties of investigating a homicide in one's own social circle. It was, of course, *because* I knew David, knew Clare, knew the inner workings of the university, that I was in a better position than any policeman to explore my cousin's death. But the fact is that when someone has been killed everyone is a suspect; murder is always out of the ordinary and the ordinary assumptions one makes about one's friends and familiars must all go by the board. Knowing someone may allow you to imagine motives others will not see; it can also blind you to those out-of-the-way weaknesses that prompt a man to kill.

Worse still, in the long run, is that no one you have suspected ever quite forgives you . . . and, once a case is solved, you never quite forgive yourself the breach of friendship suspicion represents. It had happened before, once, when I found myself in the unfortunate position of being at a house party where secret passions erupted into violence. A Siberian chill had descended on my relations with several old friends on that occasion, and the years had not turned the atmosphere more clement. It struck me as the most depressing of prospects that I might lose the ease of my regular sojourns in Cambridge. Still, it was David's death I was looking into: and I reflected contritely that these somewhat self-centred concerns hardly counted for much against the chance that I could bring his killer to justice.

As I walked back down Trinity Street, I found my eyes scanning the windows of Heffers as these bleak observations cluttered my mind. And I was momentarily startled to see, there in the window, piled high under a huge photograph of my wife, Virginia, a great stack of copies of her new novel, *Good*

*Intentions*. I was reminded of my vague sense of unease at her complaisant acknowledgement of my sudden departure that morning: and it came to me in a flash of guilty remembrance that I was due at a party to launch it in London that evening. The first call would have to be to her.

'Jinny,' I began. 'I really am sorry, but this business with David Glen Tannock put it quite out of my mind. I shan't be able to come to your party this evening. But you'll do very well without me.'

'Don't worry, darling. I'll take my revenge later. In the mean time, do tell. What have you found out?'

The answer, I had to admit, was not much. 'David dined early at the Pitt with a friend, whom I have yet to meet. He had a fair amount to drink but was certainly quite *compos* when he left the club at about a quarter to eight. And three and a half hours or so later he died of anaphylactic shock after taking a dose of penicillin, to which he knew he was allergic.'

'Well if I know . . . knew . . . David, he didn't commit suicide. So either he mistook it for something else, or someone slipped it to him.'

'My thoughts exactly. And given the improbability of a chap with that sort of allergy keeping penicillin around the place, I regret to say that I am drawn to the latter possibility.'

'Oh, Patrick. If it weren't Charlie and Lydia's boy, I'd say that you didn't regret it at all.'

'Well, it is rather challenging to think why anyone should want to kill David. I suppose it still hasn't sunk into my thick skull that he's dead. Still, you're right. I shouldn't sound so pleased to have my hands on the possibility of a murder. I shall practise concealing my excitement from others who know and love me less than you do.'

Virginia asked me what David had done between dinner and death.

'I have a few ideas about that, which I shall hope to work on between now and dinner. Let's talk tomorrow. The Master has suggested you might come down for a few days, too. But we can think about it: tomorrow I'll have a better idea of how long I shall be here. Oh and, Jinny, I really *am* sorry about the party.'

*

My 'few ideas' about where David had been were simple enough. David was a member of the Society; there would have been the usual meeting on a Wednesday night. The chances were he was at it and that *that* was why he had dined early at the Pitt Club. In the scenario I had imagined he had spent the time between dinner and his return to his rooms at a meeting. I had now to get hold of a few of the current members of the Apostles and ask them what had happened. I had been ahead of the police in getting to Caufield; they would get to him soon enough. But they might well never find out about the Society . . . unless I decided they had to. And I hoped very much that it wasn't going to prove necessary.

One call, to Hugh Penhaligon at Corpus, established that David had been at the meeting, that the paper had been on the 'paradox of the surprise exam' (which Hugh promised to explain to me sometime) and that the six members present had not left until after eleven. 'Isn't that odd?' Hugh said. 'Only last week David mentioned his pencillin allergy at the meeting and Hugo McAlister gave us a massively erudite disquisition on allergies. God, how we shall all miss him.'

We agreed to meet later that evening, and Hugh thought he could round up some, perhaps even all, of the others.

It was late afternoon. By the time I got Paul Fenton's call just before dinner I had all the materials for inventing a hundred versions of the final hours of David Glen Tannock.

# 3

At dinner I sat next to the Master. He was keen that I should unburden myself of what I knew, and had invited David's tutor (who turned out to be neither Adkins nor Parker, as Fenton had suggested, but a young philosopher named Peter Tredwell) to sit opposite me, on the Master's left, facing the body of the hall.

I was struck immediately by Tredwell. For one thing, he was the first person I had spoken to about the death who displayed any depth of feeling. Even the boy's father had managed to control his feelings when he spoke to me that morning, minutes after hearing of the boy's death. I supposed Charlie was still too shocked to have taken the whole thing fully on board. But Tredwell's regular features were ashen; he had evidently been weeping; and it was obviously going to be hard to get coherent responses out of him about his late charge. Because he faced the hall, it was plain that the undergraduates could see he was in something of a state, even in the candle-light. This sort of thing would be round the college like a Chinese whisper, glossed, amplified, misreported, as it passed from mouth to ear. Perhaps, I thought, this image of the distraught philosophy don would provoke some member of the college to useful speculation.

Tredwell ate little, turning over the jugged hare absently as he listened to my report, occasionally sweeping his chestnut hair back out of his eyes, exposing to the candle-light his serious, regular features, with a look of such pain that I wondered as I spoke whether I ought to go on.

The Master's response to the whole business was, as I expected, that of a bureaucrat on whose patch something unseemly had occurred and who planned to tidy the matter up as swiftly and quietly as was possible. Dominic seemed to have taken it for granted that we were dealing with a murder and raised a questioning eyebrow when I suggested that we could not yet rule out an accident.

Tredwell's reaction was quite different. 'D'you mean he didn't kill himself?' The scepticism seemed quite genuine: and, of course, I wondered at once whether Tredwell's distress was the result of a conviction that David's death was a suicide, brought on by something Tredwell knew about and had not, in his view, done enough to mitigate.

'Jumping to conclusions is the only mental exercise some people ever take' was the favourite formula of old 'Bunty' Hunter, the master who had taught Dominic and me classics in the sixth form, and, though a poor joke, it had become an axiom of mine to engage in a healthier range of mental exertions. And since (as Bunty would also have said) there is no time like the present, I thought it was about time to ask Tredwell for his own views. 'I gather you think it likely that Glen Tannock killed himself for some reason,' I began, pouring a little water from the jug between us into first his and then my glass in order to have a suitable reason not to challenge him with my gaze.

Tredwell spoke quietly, glancing infrequently at me and grasping the table firmly. His voice broke once or twice; and each time it did so, he raised his right hand to his mouth – his left still securely anchored to the table – and cleared his throat before going on. 'I'd rather not tell you *everything* I know, since I promised David that I would keep . . . certain confidences. But I do think he believed he had a motive for suicide, and I regret that I hadn't had more success in persuading him that it was a quite unreasonable one.'

'But you knew David well enough. I must say I find the idea of his contemplating suicide at all rather surprising, but doesn't it seem especially out of character to kill himself *this* way? He must have known that the allergic reaction would be rather awful. After all, it was pretty ghastly the one time he took it before – he nearly died then. Why choose to die painfully, when there are a hundred ways to kill yourself quickly? And wouldn't he have worried about the shock to his bedder when she found him like that in the morning?'

Tredwell thought about it for a moment. What I had said seemed to gave him some relief. 'He *was* a very thoughtful young man. But surely when you're thinking about suicide, you don't normally worry about that sort of thing?'

'A lot depends on what you think his motive for suicide was. And the fact that he spent a normal evening and that nobody, at least until after dinner, thought he was in an unusual state, suggests that he wasn't especially distressed. There are only two serious possibilities: either he had calmly planned to take his own life – in which case he would surely have thought about the consequences for others; or it was a sudden decision. And if it was a sudden decision, why did he, of all people, happen to have some penicillin handy?'

'I don't know,' Tredwell said. 'But it seems to me terribly unlikely that someone would have wanted to kill him. After all, whoever did it, would have had to have known him well enough to know about the allergy. And . . .' there was that little break again, and the hand raised to cover the cough that followed it, 'I don't see how anyone who knew David could have disliked him.'

Peter Tredwell apparently laboured under the common misapprehension that murderers must dislike their victims. In his current state, it did not seem apposite to observe that in murder – as in much of the other business of mankind – feelings of liking and loathing are seldom as important as what our transatlantic cousins call 'the bottom line'.

The meal was coming to an end and the Master, who had been listening to our conversation attentively, looked up briefly to check that we had all finished eating. 'Let's continue upstairs,' he said, rising from his place. The other Fellows rose at his example – and the undergraduates rose, too (more noisily, I thought, than tradition demanded) and watched us follow him out in a column, chatting in twos and threes as we climbed the stairs to the gallery overlooking the hall. There we cast our robes over the balustrade, and walked through into the combination room.

The Master gathered Tredwell and me and the Senior Tutor about him – thus breaching the convention that one seek new companions over dessert – and settled down with a glass of port. I poured myself a cup of coffee.

Tredwell was silent now. Finch, the Senior Tutor, had gathered a large whisky and soda and it was plain that he had had more than his share of the claret over dinner. He reached for the snuff-box, sniffed loudly, cleared his throat noisily and addressed me in stentorian tones from his position across the table. That was the way with Finch.

'Well, Patrick, what's the answer?'

The room fell quiet, and the Fellows at the other tables looked across towards us.

'I'm afraid, Alan, I don't know.'

'I mean, why should the boy kill himself? He's your cousin, isn't he? Did you know him well?'

'Well enough, I think, to suppose that he probably didn't kill himself. Not even by accident.'

Unlike Dominic Wratting, most of the Fellows – save those, at our end of the table at dinner, who had picked up snatches of the conversation – had obviously not considered the possibility that someone else had killed him. Surprise showed on most of their faces. 'But if anyone knows anything that might suggest otherwise,' I finished, 'perhaps you would mention it to me.'

There were no takers.

I looked around the table. There was Dick Bunting, an historian who specialized in the history of the secret services, a man with whom I had had many happy conversations about my work breaking codes at Bletchley during the War; Basil Smallpiece, an engineer with a prodigious memory for the form of race-horses; John Dunning, a young biochemist; Peter Mason, a mathematician who had worked in group theory, but now devoted his time to improving mathematics teaching in schools; Dominic, Finch, and Tredwell. A decent bunch of highly intelligent men, brought together by the accidents of fellowship elections over the last thirty years. David's murder was a terrible intrusion on the regularity of their lives here. Nobody had been killed in the college in their lifetimes thus far, probably no one would be again.

The clock on the mantelshelf chimed the quarter hour: it was a quarter past nine.

'Dominic, I'm afraid I can't stay too long – I've promised to go over to meet a friend at Corpus at about half-past nine. But I wonder,' I added, turning to Tredwell, 'if I could have a few words with you privately, Dr Tredwell, before I go?'

Tredwell seemed eager to talk to me alone. We rose together, collected our gowns as we walked down the stairs, and moved in silence past the dining hall and out into the Old Court.

'Will you walk me over to Corpus?' I asked. He nodded quickly.

It was a cool, clear summer's night, and the feel of the college overwhelmed me with an absurd sense of nostalgia. I was reminded of how much it had meant to me that David had chosen to come here, too, and that I had wanted him to know this feeling. It struck me then fully for perhaps the first time after a busy day of knowing David was dead and trying to find out why, that I was going to miss him dreadfully, and that his death was for me a sadder thing than I had yet acknowledged. All this rushing about had been a way of protecting myself from that realization. Soon, I would be grieving too.

But to let these feelings take over now would distract me

from the task at hand; and the chance of working it out was bound to grow less with every hour. I had to keep control.

'Tredwell . . .' I began.

'Peter . . . do please call me Peter.' The tremor in his voice suggested that our thoughts had been running along the same lines.

'Peter, I know you must keep David's confidences to the extent that you think right. But they may be crucial to understanding what happened; and if you wish to protect his memory, it might be better to tell me than to tell the police.'

We had reached the porter's lodge and as he passed through the shaft of light from its door, it looked as though it was going to be hard for him to decide to tell me what he knew.

'I've known David all his life,' I continued. 'I was very fond of him and I believe he was fond of me. If he had known he was to die, I think he would have felt that you should at least tell me enough to allow me to understand why you thought he could have killed himself. And, of course, I shall tell no one more than is absolutely necessary.'

I paused; and still he said nothing. 'Look,' I said, 'you don't have to decide now. Why not sleep on it? I suppose I may find the answer without your having to tell me anything.'

Tredwell stopped and turned to me. 'Sir Patrick, you have a reputation in the college as a decent man. What I know might shock some of my more conventionally-minded fellows; and, frankly, it won't be easy for me to tell you. You say you won't tell anyone more than is necessary. What would you say if I told you that you must tell no one anything I tell you, without my consent? If you will give me your word, I'll go back to my rooms and write down what you want to know.'

'Peter, I'm a lawyer, an officer of the courts. I'm bound by law and by my professional obligations to reveal information that is germane to a criminal investigation.'

'Oh, there's no question of law-breaking.'

'But if he had a motive for suicide, the police and the coroner have a legal right to know it: unless it is plain that he was killed by someone else.'

Tredwell's gaze would not meet mine. As he spoke he looked nervously about him. Yet his tone was quite definite and the tremor had gone from his voice. 'I'm sorry but all I can tell you, then, is this: two nights ago I heard David Glen Tannock say he wanted to die.' And with that he turned and walked back down the Senate House passage towards Clare.

I confess I was mildly piqued by the fact that Peter Tredwell thought I would believe this fanciful concoction. Nothing in David's character or the circumstances of his death gave any grounds for suspecting suicide. Tredwell plainly wanted me to think otherwise and this little fantasy was the result. But I resolved that until I found out why he was lying, I would practise my favourite spiritual exercise: granting someone the benefit of the doubt.

Still, this was the first piece of really useful information I had gathered: for some reason, Tredwell had something to hide. Sometime soon I had better find out what it was. Perhaps, I thought, Hugh would have some ideas.

# 4

Hugh Penhaligon was now the senior active member of the Society. There were other older dons who came from time to time, but of those that still attended regularly, Hugh had been in the Society by far the longest. Meetings occurred most often in his rooms and had done so now for several years. Hugh had been elected when a young research Fellow of King's in the early fifties, as he was beginning his work on the origins of English individualism. So far as I could gather from the papers I had occasionally heard him give to the Society over the decades, he thought he had succeeded in pushing these origins back earlier and earlier; and those few who still think individualism a phenomenon of the seventeeth century and the birth of capitalism are regularly subjected in the *TLS* to his withering scorn. Hugh, apparently, thought this was several centuries too late.

But like many dons whose reviewing style is acerbic, Hugh had always struck me as a very genial fellow. Now in his mid-fifties, his high forehead shining over the gold pince-nez he affected, he retained the good looks that had broken many a heart when he was a younger man. Hugh Penhaligon looked like a man in the prime of life.

After three years at King's, he had become a member of the teaching faculty in history and been elected to a Fellowship at Corpus, where he had remained ever since; now he was happily involved in the life of the college, and relished, in particular, the irony that he was the first crusading atheist to have been appointed dean. His account of the matter almost always ended with words to the effect that while there were surely deans before him who did not actually believe, they had remained 'in their musty theological closets about it'.

Hugh stayed with us from time to time in London, when he was up pursuing what he called, rather litotically, his 'musical hobbies'. He had a strange mixture of musical interests: editing Purcell's keyboard music, which he played exquisitely on the clavichord in the corner of his rooms, and conducting the 'Consorte of Aunciente Musicke', which he had started as an undergraduate, on the one hand, while composing richly romantic orchestral works in an English tradition that harked back to Elgar, on the other.

'I'm afraid no one actually wants to *listen* to my stuff,' he told us once before a concert at the Queen Elizabeth Hall (a concert that was attended, as it turned out, by an audience that almost filled the enormous space!). 'It doesn't fit with the current vogue for the dry.'

'Well, *we* like it,' Virginia had said truthfully, 'but as for dryness; may I recommend a tome by a certain Dr Penhaligon on labour mobility in fourteenth-century Norfolk?'

Hugh laughed, of course – and not out of politeness; he took great pleasure in Virginia's gentle mocking.

I found Hugh waiting under the great arch of the Corpus porter's lodge. 'Patrick, marvellous,' he said. 'I thought I'd come down and meet you myself; Warren, our Senior Porter, is on duty and he's famously nasty to visitors who pass through at this sort of time. Can't have him insulting a leading barrister – especially if he's also one of our most loyal Angels.'

We sauntered diagonally across the lawns of the main court and each stooped as we stepped through the arch into the tiny court where his rooms were. I looked across, up at the window of his college sitting-room, to see a pale face staring down at us. Hugh glanced at me, to see if I had noticed.

'Ah that, my dear, is James Hogg; the youngest of the present breed. Clever boy, interested in mathematical economics, if you please, but civilized enough to see that not everyone need share his enthusiasm for the recursive function theory. Whatever that is, exactly. At any rate, he certainly has a way with numbers.' The facetiousness of this description struck me as mildly out of place, until Hugh paused and added less briskly, 'I believe he was rather fond of David – as indeed we all were – but he is taking it especially badly.' As he spoke these words, the light from an open window caught his face, and the softening in his voice was reflected for a moment in his eyes. I could see that Hugh's chatter was masking a desperate sadness. When he started again, it was in the same brittle tone he had begun with. 'Otherwise, there's Vera Oblomov – yes, really, Oblomov . . . ah, but I think she had already left the phenomenal world when you last attended a meeting. She is a rising star at King's – a late starter, but the finest blooms come at the end of the summer. Vera is a philosopher of a rather rigorous bent, and she plays an amazingly fine game of chess. I gather the main thing the Russians were worried about when she defected was that they were losing the world's finest grand mistress – if that's the expression. And yet, you know, she won't play in competition any more. A bit of a moralist, our Vera. Of course, like all those Russian *émigrés*, Vera is fanatically anti-Red, which suits me very well. And last, but by no means least . . .' Hugh paused here as if gathering strength to mount the steep flight of stairs to his rooms, 'Charlie.'

'Charlie' was Charles Phipps, a member of the Society who had been elected in the years when my son, Sebastian, was an undergraduate. He had been a particular friend of Sebastian's – they had both been typically mischievous medical students – and he had often stayed with us in the vacations. A few years back, Sebastian had been his best man; a year ago he had had a baby whom they had thoughtfully named for me, and Sebastian was the boy's godfather. From time to time in the colour magazines, people suggested that Charlie's work on brain chemistry had put him in line for a Nobel Prize; and he was still only in his early thirties. Because he was one of the stars of the Cambridge physiology department he was constantly being pestered to take a college Fellowship. But he always turned the suggestion down. He contended it would keep him away from his wife – and, now, his son – and that his work did that too much already.

It was Charlie who strode across the room to grasp my hand – looking splendidly full of vim – when I followed Hugh into the clutter of his chambers.

'Sir Patrick. Very good to see you – sorry it had to be in such dismal circumstances. How's Sebastian? Haven't seen him in a couple of months. I'm afraid a baby rather ruins your social life.' Charlie's eyes always had marvellous laugh-lines; he had what my mother would have called a 'twinkle' about him.

'Sebastian's very well, thank you, so far as I know. His practice keeps him rather busy – headlines to the contrary notwithstanding, a few people are still having children in England. How *are* Claudia and young Paddy? I'm sure domestic bliss is a fine compensation for a lost social life.'

'You're right. It's marvellous, couldn't be better. They're both in tip-top shape. Your namesake has a pretty spectacular pair of lungs on him. You must pop in to see us while you're here.' Charlie beamed at me and turned to Hugh, inviting him to continue the introductions.

'Vera, you remember Sir Patrick Scott,' said Hugh. We each bowed slightly in acknowledgement. 'And this is James Hogg.'

James Hogg's face was as pale in the warm light of Hugh's room as it had seemed through the leaded glass of the window. His dark hair was cut short, save at the front, where it fell over his face. His eyes were extremely striking – they were a strong, Celtic blue. Between the dark blue of his eyes and the dark brown of his hair, his fair skin seemed especially pallid.

'How do you do, Mr Hogg.'

'Hello,' he said, his eyes scanning me diffidently and returning to the coffee cup in his hand. 'I gather you're trying to find out what happened to David.'

'That's the general idea.'

'But before we start,' Hugh interrupted, 'we should settle him down with a little comforting drink. What will you have, Patrick?'

I accepted a cup of the coffee and a small scotch.

'Well,' Charlie said, apparently addressing no one in particular, 'what can we do about David's death?'

Hugh looked about ceremoniously and the room took on an unaccustomed silence. The evening's real business was about to begin.

'The question for discussion at this meeting of the Society,' Hugh began, in the time-honoured style of meetings of the Apostles, 'is: Who killed David, Lord Glen Tannock? And, though I am at the hearth rug, I regret that I have very little light to throw on the matter. As our late brother, Ramsey, might have said: it seems there is nothing to discuss.'

The practice in the early years of the Society had been for the members to gather after dinner in their evening dress, and for the speaker to address them standing on the hearth rug in front – at least in winter – of a roaring fire. Once the paper had been read, members responded in turn, in a stylized routine that discouraged real discussion.

The business of actually standing to address one's Brother Apostles had been abandoned sometime in the late twenties or early thirties – about the time that Frank Ramsey had given the paper 'Is there anything to discuss?', a paper whose fame derived largely from the fact that it was one of the few papers given at a meeting of the Society that had ever been published.

Dinner jackets had disappeared sometime after the War; and the style of the meeting had changed (commendably, in my view) with the times, so that now the paper was read by a seated member and usually interrupted long before it was finished by animated interventions.

Hugh, who had not, of course, been a member in the more formal days, nevertheless often parodied the old style in this way; and there was, no doubt, no harm in it, in the ordinary run of things. But I could see that James Hogg was having a hard time restraining himself from breaking in. It was clear that he felt that Hugh needed reminding that we were trying to understand the death of someone who had been, for him at least, a very close friend.

Since Hugh was looking at me, I gestured vaguely in James's direction – indicating to Hugh, I hoped, that he was upsetting James – and interrupted sharply.

'Hugh, I think it might help if I got a sense of what happened at the meeting. Anything unusual? Did David do or say anything odd? Did he leave in a normal frame of mind?' As I spoke, Hugh glanced over at James: and as their eyes met, it occurred to me that their relationship might fit the pattern of one of the Society's other old traditions.

Vera Oblomov clucked quietly like a babushka, but when she spoke it was with the carefully-formed diction of someone whose mastery of a second language is complete. 'We should begin, Sir Patrick, with the fact that we are not a complete party. There was one other person at the meeting on Wednesday evening.'

'And that was . . .?'

'Sir Oliver Hetherington.'

'Really? And what was he doing here?'

'Oliver,' Hugh's genial tone suggested that he was either oblivious of or accepted the rebuke implicit in the tone with which I had interrupted him a few moments earlier, 'as you know, is one of our most devoted Angels. And whenever he is back in England, and not serving as her Majesty's Ambassador Plenipotentiary in some absurd foreign land, he makes it a point to come up and see how we are doing. As it happens, however, this time he was up to talk to Alan Blumberg at Trinity about the Russians. I understand, *entre nous*, that he has been offered Moscow.'

'Blumberg?' Charlie Phipps asked. 'D'you mean that left-wing professor of modern Soviet history?'

'No, dear boy, Oliver Hetherington.'

'Ah,' said Charlie, smiling, 'and I thought he only listened to my report of the Moscow Congress of Neurosciences out of politeness.'

'Oliver, like most diplomats, rarely does anything merely out of politeness,' Hugh said.

'So, tell me what happened,' I prompted. 'Anything at all that anyone can remember. I should like to be able to imagine it all.'

They had gathered in Hugh's rooms the night before at about half-past eight. Hugh had been there from about eight fifteen, having slipped out early from one of Corpus's long, delicious dinners to prepare for the meeting. He had made coffee and then settled down with a glass of port to wait. David had arrived first, followed by James Hogg and Vera Oblomov, who had met outside the gates of Great Court at Trinity, where she had been dining, and walked over together. Charlie arrived a little after half-past eight and apologized: he had an experiment running in his lab – one that he had described in his paper the week before – and he had to be there to supervise the administration of some drugs to a chimpanzee.

'Where were you all sitting?' I asked.

'I sat there.' James pointed to the armchair.

'Charlie and I were on the sofa,' Vera said, 'and Hugh sat over there by the window.'

At about a quarter to nine Vera had begun her paper on the surprise-exam paradox, only to be interrupted a minute later by Oliver Hetherington's gentle knocking on the door. Introductions had taken a further few minutes – Vera and James had not met Sir Oliver before – and they had then proceeded with the paper.

'It is very simply explained,' Vera told me. 'I am a teacher. I tell my class on Monday that I will give a surprise exam this week. I promise it will be a surprise in the following precise sense: no one will know on the evening before the exam that it is going to happen the next morning. A clever student raises her hand. "But, teacher, that isn't possible." "Why?" I ask. "Well," the student says. "If you give the exam on Friday it will not be a surprise: that is the last class day of the week. So we know you can't give it on Friday. If we get to Wednesday evening, we shall know, therefore, that the exam will be on Thursday. So we know you can't give it on Thursday either." And so she proceeds backwards, up the week, proving that I cannot give a surprise exam. But on Thursday I do give the exam: and no knew that I would. So, despite her apparently rigorous reasoning, she was wrong.'

It seemed a suitably Apostolic puzzle. But as she explained it, my attention was divided unequally between her words and her appearance, the latter eventually capturing the flag. Vera Oblomov was an extraordinary-looking woman. Her straight black hair was cut severely, and her button-nose perched comfortably in the middle of an almost perfectly circular face. It was not a beautiful face, but it was an oddly pleasant one.

On the few occasions I had met her, I had formed the impression that she dressed without regard for fashion; but nor did she ever quite manage to dress conventionally. I had remarked something of the sort to Hugh the second time I met her. And Hugh, who was attentive to such things, had said, 'If she wears a severe wool skirt' – as she did this evening – 'you can guarantee that it will be complemented by some incongruously cheery item of dress' – in this case, a lacy, purple confection. Hugh claimed to have seen her once wearing a pair of ancient gardening trousers and a rather formal riding jacket, the outfit completed by a scarlet waistcoat and battered tennis-shoes. As I marvelled over Dr Oblomov's notions of proper dress, James Hogg addressed me.

'You may think it's a trivial problem,' he said seriously. 'But there's an apparently sound finite induction involved: we have a set of days, and it is true that if you know that the exam won't come on any day after day *n*, you know it won't come on day *n* either; and that ought to allow you to infer that you know that it won't come on any day. But it does. In some ways it poses the same sort of threat to finite induction as the Sorites paradox; though, of course, there doesn't seem to be any question of the issue having to do with vagueness.' I had forgotten how easily one slips into the Apostolic assumption of general omniscience.

Oliver Hetherington had listened to the discussion the night before in a slightly preoccupied manner, too courteous – 'and I suspect,' Charlie said, 'too vain' – to admit that he found the paradox uninteresting; David had chipped in with the odd remark, including, according to Vera, a rather clever suggestion about probabilities; and Charlie had 'felt stimulated by the activity of so many able minds'. But most of the discussion had involved Vera and James. 'I regret to say that I,' said Hugh, 'mostly made facetious remarks about schoolteachers.'

At about eleven, Hugh had suggested it was time to 'roll up the hearth rug', and they had recorded the discussion in the minutes in the characteristically laconic style adopted in the twenties. Hugh showed me the entry; by some of the signatures a little note was scrawled.

*Question:* Could Vera's student be surprised?

| *Ayes* | *Noes* |
| --- | --- |
| V. Oblomov | James Hogg (Not if Vera kept her word.) |
| Charles Phipps | Glen Tannock (What a ghastly question for the day before Tripos!) |
| Hugh Penhaligon (Tell that to Dr Johnson.) | |

Oliver Hetherington

After recording the minutes – since this was to be the last meeting of the term – a certain amount of time had been taken up with discussing summer plans and saying farewells. Then Oliver Hetherington and David had left together – 'It turned out', Charlie said, 'that Oliver knew David's father from their days together in some hush-hush outfit in the fifties' – and they were followed not long after by Charlie and Vera.

'And when did *you* leave, James?' I asked.

Before James could reply, Hugh said: 'Oh, James and I talked on into the wee hours. Chanticleer was clearly chanting by the time he left.' James did not elaborate on Hugh's response.

It was getting late by the time I had pieced together what they knew of the previous evening, and Charles, James and Vera left at about eleven. James gave Hugh another piercing look as he said good-night.

Now that the others had left, Hugh and I had a brief conversation about David. 'He was a very bright boy, you know: reminded me rather of Quentin at that age. An historian, but with very wide interests. Take that stuff about probability he chipped in with last night; Vera meant it when she said it was clever. She's very severe in her judgements about such matters. Of course, he talked a lot to that wonderfully handsome tutor of his at Clare, who's a probability buff of some sort. But David was very honest: if he'd got the idea from someone else, he'd have said so.'

Hugh's remarks reminded me that I needed to know more

about Tredwell. I wondered if he could tell me something that would make sense of his odd lie. 'Do you know anything much about the tutor? Peter Tredwell, his name is. He seemed very shaken up about the whole thing.'

'Not much. David used to talk about him often. But he's not someone I've heard much about otherwise. He lives in college – so I suppose that makes him available to chaps who like to talk to grown-ups. But David really only reported their conversations. Never said much to me about him personally. Why do you ask?'

'No special reason,' I said, 'just curious. Well, now I really must be off; Jinny will be wondering why I haven't phoned.'

But as I reached the door, a further thought occurred to me. I paused for a moment, wondering how to put my question.

'It's not any of my business, of course, but will James Hogg be returning to these rooms after I leave?'

'You are right, dear boy, it is not any of your business: but, yes. Wicked as I am, though, you would be putting the wrong interpretation on matters if you inferred that we would be practising what our Brother Godfrey refers to, I believe, as the lower sodomy. No, the fact is that James stayed last night because he needed consolation in matters of the heart: and he is returning tonight because those matters involved David.'

It was hardly a new idea to me that two members of the Society should enjoy an emotional attachment of a certain intensity. I remembered a remark of Murdoch O'Shaughnessy's at one of the annual dinners in the early seventies. We had been discussing the admission of women and one of the older codgers had objected that the presence of women might be distracting. Dry-as-dust old Murdoch had observed matter-of-factly that it seemed to him there had been periods in the Society when the presence of young men might have been thought distracting. That year the admission of women was left to the active members: that year, the first woman was admitted.

But I had vaguely supposed that the admission of women would have discouraged homoerotic attachments; that the admission of women was bound to reduce the chances of the Society's ever returning to the days of Strachey and Keynes, when Brotherly love was both a theoretical and a practical focus of Apostolic life. Though I knew Hugh Penhaligon was – as my aunt Mary quaintly expressed the matter – 'so', in mixed company he could hardly flirt with the younger members as outrageously as I had seen some of my seniors flirt with him.

'Yes, I am afraid young Jamie was smitten with young David – and this feeling was not, so far as anyone knew, reciprocated. James had taken it, if you will, "like a man", assuming that his lordship was of a different persuasion, until he discovered on Tuesday that this was not the case. That's why he was so upset last night; and, since I am frank in the expression of my own tastes, James had felt that I would be sympathetic . . . perhaps even, shall we say, wise in the queer ways of the heart.'

'How did James discover this?'

'David told him.'

My puzzled look evoked from Hugh a ripple of mirth. 'My dear Patrick, don't look so shocked. David was a friend of Jamie's: he respected his seriousness and his intelligence. He told Jamie because he wanted Jamie's advice. It had not occurred to him that James was similarly disposed; and James, poor fool, was too embarrassed to say.'

'Are you sure of all this?' I asked. It would not have been helpful to explain that my surprise was not at the fact that David had told James Hogg; that the surprise was that David had something of the sort to tell. I suppose you never expect these things in your own family.

'Of course.'

'Why did David need advice?'

Before Hugh could answer, there was a knock on the door. When he opened it, James stood there; and when he saw me, he blushed. 'Oh, I'm frightfully sorry, I thought Sir Patrick would have . . . I mean . . .'

'Come in and don't be silly,' Hugh said. 'Patrick and I were just discussing David's little Tuesday afternoon bombshell – and, your preconceptions notwithstanding, not every ageing Englishman is either a queer or a queer-basher.'

'Not to worry,' I said blandly. 'I shall have to be leaving at any rate: my wife will be expecting me to phone soon and I must get back to my rooms. Can I ask you one more question, though, before I go?'

I waited for James to nod.

'How did David seem to feel about his feelings?' I asked. James looked slightly perplexed. 'I mean, did he seem worried about it; worried, say, about what the family would think?'

'Oh . . . that. No. Not so far as I could tell. What he was worried about was that he fancied his tutor; he was worried whether he – the tutor, I mean – would get into trouble if David persuaded him to . . . I told him to talk to Hugh; and he probably would have on Wednesday night, if Sir Oliver hadn't insisted on taking him off.'

'I see: but he seemed . . . at ease with himself? I mean, for example, he didn't talk of letting down the family, of suicide, that sort of thing . . .'

For the first time since we had met, James laughed. 'No. Not at all. Why do you ask?'

'Just a thought. I wouldn't have expected him to feel that way, either. I must be off then. You've both been most helpful. And James, Hugh's right: some of us old fossils really don't hold with queer-bashing. So that when the police come to ask you about last night, you tell them only as much of the truth as you think relevant: you needn't worry about my spilling the beans. And now, Hugh, I really will go finally.'

'Let me walk you out – it must be after midnight and we close the gates at midnight here. You stay here, James; I shan't be long.'

Hugh and I walked together down into the court; Hugh let me out of the side gate into Benet Street with his key. 'One question, Hugh: which of our Brethren were present last week, when the allergy came up?'

'Well, I think I mentioned Hugo McAlister when we talked earlier; but he only came because he knows Charlie's work from the physiology department. He's no longer active, really; one of our local Angels. Then there was Godfrey – who had a cold that kept him at Heston on Wednesday. He's been coming again recently. Oh, and Dale Bishop. A new Brother, an American.'

'Well, I suppose I ought to get in touch with them, too.'

As I shook his hand in parting, Hugh said: 'Patrick: David wouldn't have killed himself, of that I am sure. I'm not good at showing these things, but I feel his loss deeply, so do ask for my help if you need it. I couldn't bear to see the bastard who killed him get away.' I said nothing; but for probably the first time in my life I saw Hugh's striking face looking old and sad.

'And so, my dear,' he said, brightening, 'you will have to be our avenging Angel.' The brittle mask of Hugh's good humour dropped back into place.

# 5

By the time I had reached Memorial Court the main gates were locked. I walked round to the side road that runs up to Thirkill Court and descended the steps to the left of the gate, steps that lead down to the bicycle-stands in the basement and into the bottom of U staircase. Clare's Memorial Court is accessible twenty-four hours a day by this route: the closing of the gates is something of a charade. This was the route David would almost certainly have taken when he came back the night before. I was now three floors below the attic rooms in which he had died.

As I paused at the base of the stairs that led up to U13 and the scene of death, a figure in a dressing-gown stepped out of the bathroom to the right in the entryway, her long hair glistening wet.

She took a step backwards in surprise and then seemed to recognize me. 'Gosh. You startled me. Don't often see old . . . older people here at this time of night. Aren't you the person who's investigating David Glen Tannock's death?'

'Not really. That's mostly up to the police. I'm just seeing if I can help. Patrick Scott,' I said, rather formally, extending my hand.

'Joanna Ritter.'

'But since you ask . . . I don't suppose you noticed anything odd last night?'

'The police wanted to know about that. But I can't think of anything. I mean, I heard various people going up and down the stairs as I was falling asleep – I had my last exam today, so I went to bed quite early, elevenish – and I must have been asleep before half-past eleven. Of course, it was rather quiet last night here – Dr Finch lives in Mem. Court and his bedroom looks into Thirkill and we'd all been told not to disturb him. So that was odd – no music, I mean.'

'Did you know Lord Glen Tannock?'

'Well, of course everybody on the staircase bumped into everybody else occasionally; but his real friends seemed to be mostly in other colleges . . . King's, I think, a lot of them.' She plunged on breathlessly. 'He and Michael Mallory-Browne on the second floor often went in and out together, though. They both rowed for the second eight. And naturally we did things for each other. You know, shopping, that sort of thing. Actually, I delivered him a new thing of powdered milk and some biscuits after dinner on Wednesday night.' My look of mild puzzlement at this unsolicited intelligence produced an explanatory gloss. 'He mentioned he'd run out, and I happened to be going to the supermarket . . .' Joanna Ritter stopped talking. She had obviously realized that something she'd said had caught my attention – I suppose I was looking more thoughtful than the topic warranted – but she couldn't imagine what it was.

'This will seem a rather strange question, I suppose; but was the milk,' I paused, wondering if she would think me just a dotty old man, 'was it in a glass jar or a tin?' I remembered seeing only a glass jar on the gyp-room shelf; if someone had changed the tin for a jar, it might have been because they had used the milk powder to deliver the penicillin.

'A tin. But he always emptied a bit into a glass jar and kept the rest in the tin in a cupboard in the gyp-room.' She spoke more and more slowly, finally coming to a complete halt. I sensed a hint of panic; and I realized that an elderly stranger in the night, obsessed with the details of his young cousin's habits in respect of milk powder, might well be moderately disturbing.

She looked at me slightly helplessly, and finally mumbled, 'I'm sorry. I wish I knew more.' I thought that, on the whole, the best thing to do was move on.

'Not to worry, that's all very useful. I expect you remember Sherlock Holmes's observing that sometimes it's the things that don't happen that matter. The dog that didn't bark, that sort of thing.' We looked at each other uneasily and I realized that my remark must have seemed rather inane. 'Well, I mustn't keep you. Thank you, Miss Ritter; and good-night.'

'Good-night, Mr Scott.' That's the trouble with titles. Why should anyone know about them? And yet, when they don't, you feel you ought to put them right. Naturally, I resisted the urge.

As I walked through Thirkill, it struck me that Joanna Ritter might have had a little bit of a crush on David. Buying the milk he had mentioned he'd run out of was an eloquent gesture. Had there been perhaps a hint of pathos in her remark about his real friends being elsewhere?

When I got back to the Fellows' guest-room, I rang through to the porter's lodge and asked for an outside line.

Virginia was obviously wide awake when she answered the phone.

'Jinny darling. How was the launch?'

'All the usual suspects. What I want to hear about is what you've been up to. What have you found out?'

I told her how I had spent the day – it seemed astonishing, as I recounted it, how much I had done. It was also disturbing how little I had really found out. When I finished reporting my Apostolic evening, Virginia said, 'Oh dear, how will Charlie and Lydia take it that David was queer?'

'Well, I'm not sure that we'll have to tell them that, but frankly I don't think that they'd have held it against him. I know Charlie plays the old-fashioned curmudgeon sometimes, but he's not really all that stuffy.'

'What do you suppose the tutor fellow – Tredwell was it? – what do you suppose he thinks would have made David want to die?'

I had not mentioned to Virginia my doubts about Tredwell's tale. Now was obviously the time.

'*That* seems to me a most interesting question, too. Frankly, I didn't believe a word of it. But I shall just have to try and persuade him to tell me the truth. There is one possibility that occurred to me. Suppose Tredwell and David had been having some sort of affair; he might decide that the police would think that made him a suspect. And then he might want to encourage us to think that David killed himself, just to keep the boys in blue off his back.'

'Not, if I may say so, the nicest metaphor in the circumstances. But look, if Tredwell's a clever fellow, he'll want you to work out a motive for suicide for yourself – one that you believe in. D'you suppose he might expect you to think that David would kill himself because he was queer? Perhaps he thinks you're of the "I thought chaps like that shot themselves" persuasion.' Virginia chuckled. 'You do come on as rather a conventional type, don't you, darling? And if he's a young don, surrounded with all those truly stuffy Cambridge types, he might think you were one of them.'

'It's a possibility,' I said, hoping I had kept the surge of irritation at Virginia's teasing out of my voice. 'But there's tomorrow to look into that. Are you going to come up for the weekend as Dominic suggested? Julia runs a decent table, and I could move from these Fellows' guest-rooms into the lodge, if you did.'

Virginia said she would come up on Saturday morning.

'Why don't you bring the car, darling?' I said. 'Then we shall be independent, if we want to move above . . . Gosh, I'd completely forgotten to ask: how did Sebastian take the news of David's death?'

'Sebastian was his usual philosophical self. But I think he was only holding back because he didn't want me to go all weepy on him. Deep down, I'm afraid, he was terribly, terribly upset.'

'I don't suppose he'll want to, but you might tell him where I am and drop the hint that I would like to have a chat. Our Dr Scott isn't one for heart-to-hearts with his ageing papa.'

'Maybe it's because his papa isn't one for heart-to-heart chats with Dr Scott,' Virginia said severely.

It was an old argument. 'I don't really think now is the time, Jinny.'

Virginia was silent for a moment and then set off in a new direction; but I knew it was only a temporary reprieve.

As we were winding down the conversation she suddenly interrupted my good-nights.

'Patrick, what about Oliver Hetherington? I mean, mustn't you talk to him soon? He may have been the last person to see

David alive.' She paused. 'Well, at any rate, the second-to-last,' she added bleakly.

'It's on my list. I'll telephone Blumberg at Trinity in the morning and ask if he's still about. I don't suppose the police have yet discovered what David was doing between dinner and bed: they hadn't got in touch with Hugh or any of the people at the meeting. I say, look; there's one thing you could do before coming down. Go and have a chat with Charlie and Lydia – they were going to come down to the London house this afternoon; tell him that I'm working things out and that it might be better if he didn't come up to Cambridge. I don't much want to have to talk to them until I know how much of the story I'm going to have to tell them.'

'All right, darling. Good-night.' There was a click and the line went dead.

I awoke rather later than usual the next morning. My watch said half-past nine; too late for breakfast in college. But before I went out to seek sustenance, I thought I should try and catch Oliver Hetherington. I rang through to Trinity and asked for Professor Blumberg's rooms. There was no answer, and a short conversation with the college office revealed that Blumberg lived with his family on Millington Road and that he rarely came in to college in the mornings.

The secretary seemed quite happy to discuss all aspects of Blumberg's life with me, so I wondered aloud whether he had anyone staying with him. 'He's not got anyone *staying* with him, exactly. But there's some ambassador staying in the Master's lodge and he seems to be seeing a lot of him. They were in to dinner last night and they're booked in again tomorrow night. And tonight Professor Blumberg and the ambassador are going to a dinner-party at the lodge.'

'Well you've been most helpful,' I said. 'I wonder if you could now put me through to the Master's lodge.'

'Of course, Sir Patrick.'

After a bit of fumbling and various electrical noises, I heard the phone ringing. After it had rung half a dozen times somebody picked up the receiver.

'Hallo.'

'Ah, hallo. I wonder if you could tell the Master that Sir Patrick Scott would like to have a word with him.'

'Patrick, it's Oliver, Oliver Hetherington. I'm afraid the Darwins have gone off to some college do, and I'm alone in the lodge here. Can I pass on a message?'

'No, no, Oliver; actually it was you that I was hoping to catch. How are you, old boy? Hugh tells me that you are about to be sent off behind the Iron Curtain.'

'Wonderfully indiscreet, old Hugh, isn't he? But I suppose we can trust Brother Apostles to keep secrets, eh? Yes, HMG has decided that it's my turn to sit by the Kremlin and be bugged. Actually, I was up consulting with Alan Blumberg; astonishing how much he knows. Amazing chap. Frightfully up to date. He has all this information about the Soviet economy in a great bank of tapes somewhere and a terminal in his rooms in college. He just types in his code and a password and he can look for hours at wheat yields from the Ukraine and steel production in Novosibirsk. I've been wondering whether some of the people we have hidden away in our basements in Whitehall shouldn't have a line into his files.'

'Yes, Hugh told me that you were up to see Blumberg.' There didn't seem an easy way to come round to the topic of David's death. I cleared my throat. 'Look, I don't know if you've seen the papers yet this morning, but if you haven't I'm afraid that I have some rather bad news.'

'Really, Patrick? What's the crisis?'

'David Glen Tannock, Charlie's boy, died yesterday morning – too late for the papers yesterday, I think. I imagine there will be some sort of note in *The Times* today.'

Oliver paused for a moment before he spoke again.

'Good Lord. But I saw him only the night before. He walked me back here after the meeting of the Society. God. How awful. Such a nice boy; and Charlie and Lydia must be devastated.' He paused for a moment – obviously Oliver was looking for a tactful circumlocution – and then, apparently having failed, asked bluntly, 'What killed him?'

Despite what he said, his surprise did not seem altogether genuine. But Oliver, I thought, was a diplomat. Covering one's feelings was his stock in trade.

'I'm afraid it looks as though it's a matter of *who* killed him.

He died of a severe penicillin allergy, which he knew he had. Someone must have given it to him. Of course, there's an outside chance it was suicide . . .'

'Absolutely out of the question. The boy was tired when he left me, but extremely cheerful and all gung-ho about a history exam he was to do the next day.'

'What did you talk about?'

'Oh, we talked about his father, mostly. I told him that Charles had been extremely influential as a young man in British Intelligence after the War; about how brave he had been, working the other side of the Berlin Wall. Most of it stuff that came out when our unlamented Brother Philby and his chums went over to the other side. I mentioned we had been members of the Society at the same time and told him a little about the others. He asked about Gregory Ransome. Of course, I didn't know Ransome as well as I might have, since he died not long after I was elected. But he was a sort of mythical figure when I was active in the Society. David seemed to be doing a little research for a short biographical essay on Ransome. He said he might read it to the Society in the autumn.'

Gregory Ransome had been one of the young stars of the Society in the thirties. A brilliant mathematician, he had made important contributions to economic theory – 'some elegant stuff about taxation,' Keynes was reputed to have remarked laconically at his funeral – and to the philosophical and technical foundations of probability theory. Society mythology had it that when he died he had been working on a theorem that was later proved by his friend Godfrey Stanley – a theorem that had established Stanley's reputation. Ransome had died, tragically, in a skiing accident in the late thirties, while he was spending an Easter vacation with Stanley in the French Alps. I had once heard Stanley – who was now a Fellow of Trinity and had attended Society meetings over a longer period than anyone this century – try and explain the significance of his theorem to the group when I was an undergraduate; it was central, so he said, to the branch of modern mathematics called 'algebraic topology'.

'I must make sure to see if David left any notes about Ransome. It would be nice to publish some sort of piece in a memorial volume. Anything else you remember?'

'No, I think that's about it . . . Oh, we laughed a little about the fact that Hugh had recruited for MI6 and had mostly sent us rather good-looking boys he had trained to despise Marxism. But nothing, so far as I can see, that would have upset him. Are you playing the detective again, Patrick?'

'Well, I thought I'd have a go. Actually, Charlie asked me; and Dominic Wratting, who's the Master here, seemed rather keen on it, too. But I'm not having much luck, so far.'

We chatted a little longer, and Oliver kept returning to the awfulness of David's death. He told me he was to be in town for another few days – 'probably until after the weekend' – and I said I would try to arrange to see him with Virginia.

'Oh, before you go, Oliver, there's one thing I didn't ask you. Did you happen to notice the time that David left you?'

'Funny you should ask; David kept looking at his watch while we were standing by the Trinity gates. When the clock chimed at a quarter to midnight, he said he must be off. Of course, it didn't strike me as especially odd, as he had exams in the morning. But I suppose he did seem mildly more agitated about the time than I should have expected. He really didn't seem to think the exam would be any trouble.'

Once I had spoken to Oliver, I walked out of Memorial Court and across the road.

I had settled on having coffee and a bun at the Copper Kettle on King's Parade and was making my way purposefully through Old Court, when Peter Tredwell hailed me from the open window of his rooms above the college library.

'I say, Sir Patrick. Hold on.'

A minute later, he was down in the court and we stood together at the intersection of the cobbled pathways that divide the court into four rectangles of grass. A night's rest had obviously calmed him; and without the reddened eyes, it struck me for the first time that he was indeed, as Hugh had said, an extremely handsome man. We greeted each other.

'Look,' he said. 'I'm sorry I took that rather unfortunate tone with you last night. The fact is, I was dreadfully shocked by Lord Glen Tannock's death. I'm sure he would have wanted you to know what he told me; and I'll leave it to your judgement to decide what to pass on.'

The suspicions I had voiced to Virginia seemed somehow inappropriate to Tredwell's new mood; and I felt inclined to make things easier for him.

'I think you should know that I have found out at least one thing about David that you might not have chosen to tell me.'

Tredwell looked startled. 'Oh, really?' he mumbled.

'Yes. I gather that he had decided that he was . . .' in the circumstances the right words seemed to be 'what we now are invited to call "gay".'

'Well, then I don't have to break any confidences. How did you find out?'

'I talked to some friends of his,' I replied vaguely. 'But do you think that would have been a reason for him to take his life?'

Tredwell reddened. '*I* don't. But *he* did.'

I asked Tredwell to join me for a cup of coffee at the Copper Kettle. I suspected that his story wasn't something to face on an empty stomach.

# 6

We left the college, and as we walked in silence I had time to think about what I was to say. Tredwell was about to try to mislead me. I wanted to know why.

We collected coffee and my bun – Tredwell said he had already had breakfast – and I guided him to an empty booth in a corner, where no one would be likely to hear us. I didn't want Tredwell to worry about being overheard.

'Well, Tredwell . . . Peter . . . let's hear your *récit*, shall we?'

'I'll just tell you what I know,' he said. I doubted it.

According to Tredwell, David had come to his rooms last Tuesday evening and asked to use the telephone. Tredwell had shown him into his study and returned to his sitting-room. He had heard little of the conversation – 'I was not eavesdropping' – but he had heard David raise his voice at one point and say, 'I think I should kill myself.' Tredwell had asked him whom he had been talking to, and he had said that it was a friend in London. David looked upset; but when Tredwell asked him why, he would say only that his friend was in difficulties.

That at least was the gist of it. He hardly met my eye as he related his story, and did so with much stammering and nervous repetition. Had the story been written down, it might have carried some authority. But lying is a performing art; and Tredwell was not doing well at it.

Even that was significant, though. In my experience, a poor liar is usually preparing the ground for admitting he's lying. If you don't believe him, he wants his attempts to seem more pathetic than devious; if he's found out, he wants you to doubt that he ever seriously tried to fool you.

But, oddly, I had come rather to pity Tredwell, and so I tried to give him an out. 'Are you sure that is what he said? Or that he meant it? I mean, could he have been repeating somebody's else's words? Or could he have said, "If that happened, I should kill myself", as it were hypothetically?'

Tredwell's response was quick . . . too quick, too definite; we were not to consider these other possibilities. 'No. I'm sure that he meant it the way I took it.'

For the moment, I decided to play along. I asked the question someone who did believe him would logically have asked next. 'Didn't you think you should stop him from leaving in that frame of mind?'

'I tried. I told him to stay for a drink. Asked him if he was all right. He was uncharacteristically quiet . . . unresponsive. I told him he had a bright future; I even brought the subject round to his sexuality and told him that in these days it was really not so much of a burden to be gay. I told him . . . I told him that I could give my own personal testimony to that. He seemed to accept what I said. But he said very little himself, and I wasn't sure I had persuaded him.'

'So the burden of his homosexuality became too much to bear and, tormented by unnatural desires, he chose death.'

Tredwell nodded gravely.

'Rather old-fashioned of him, don't you think? Still, it's quite a gripping story in a quaint way, I suppose.'

Tredwell shrugged and looked uneasily about him.

Quite suddenly, I felt my patience evaporate. 'Look here, Peter. It's quite ridiculous of you to expect me to believe any of this rubbish. David didn't kill himself, not by design. If he was gay, he was perfectly happy to be so. At his age, he would have been experimenting, he would have been forming his first adult relationships, and, yes, boys his age often have turbulent emotional lives. But that penny-dreadful melodrama you've concocted dishonours the memory of someone who meant a great deal to me.'

Tredwell was clearly stung by my words and I was glad of it, even relieved. He spoke now with his head turned half away from me, quickly and clearly, wanting, so it seemed, to be over with it. He had decided, I thought, that he did not much like me. In the circumstances, that was not something I cared about much.

What Tredwell told me was essentially quite simple. The story about the telephone conversation in which David spoke of killing himself was indeed a fabrication. What had happened on the Tuesday evening, he said, was something rather different. David had come to him to say that he was in love with him. Tredwell had for some time suspected something of the kind. 'David was quite grown-up about it. He told me he understood that if we had an affair I would be risking a good deal; and he told me that he knew I would probably think that he merely had a "crush". But I had already decided what I would say if this happened. So I told him that I was fond of him, too. That it was possible for two gay men to be close friends without sex. And that I hoped he would accept that. Then I embraced him.'

They had talked a good deal longer – 'probably until one or two in the morning' – and Tredwell had given him a Fellows' pass key (with strict instructions not to let anyone see him using it) so he could let himself out through the gates to the avenue over to Memorial Court. They had agreed to talk again on Thursday evening. 'I told him that since he had the key, he could come and see me after that, if he wanted.'

'And did he?' I asked.

'No.' Tredwell bit his lip and screwed up his eyes. 'I wish he had . . . none of this might have happened.'

'Why didn't you tell me this at the start?'

'Isn't that obvious? How was I to know whether you wouldn't assume that we had had an affair and that that gave me a possible motive for murder? You know: *cherchez l'homme.*' He snorted ironically. 'I had no reason to think you would be sympathetic.'

'Unfortunately, when we spoke last night I had no reason to indicate that I would be sympathetic: I didn't know that you and David shared . . .' I stopped, embarrassed, and he dared me to finish. I declined the challenge; I had had enough of this conversation. Still, there was one more question I had to ask. 'But why try and make me think that David had killed himself?'

'No murder, no motive to seek; no motive to seek, no suspicions raised. I thought if you were convinced it was a suicide, you would pack your bags and go home.'

'Don't you want to find David's killer – if, indeed, there was one?'

Tredwell sighed deeply and his face assumed an attitude of despair. 'Of course, I do,' he said slowly. 'Whoever killed him deprived me of the only man I ever loved.'

If he was lying now, it was an awfully convincing performance. Still, if you're going to tell a lie, it's wise to make sure the punchline is a stunner. And sitting there in the little coffee shop listening to a Fellow of my college announcing that he had been in love with my young cousin struck me as fairly stunning. It isn't always relaxing to find you have guessed right. For a moment I said nothing.

And then I saw that if I didn't do something, he was going to weep. 'Look,' I said briskly. 'Let me now share a confidence with you. As you know, David *was* an Apostle; so am I. And there are two other people – "gay" people – who were at that meeting who were very fond of him and are grieving also. I think it might help if I put you in touch with them.'

'So all the gay boys can cry together?' he said.

'Dr Tredwell,' I said, 'I don't think that's very fair.'

'We have not got off to a very good start. That's a pity. David thought the world of you and his judgement was good.'

As he finished speaking, I wondered whether in paying me this compliment, he had not been reminding me that David had loved and respected him also; and that I who loved David after my own fashion should judge him in that light.

He looked at his watch and got up to go. 'It's after half-past ten, I must go. Thanks for the coffee . . . and, for what it's worth, I'm sorry I tried to deceive you. It was foolish. David once told me that you could sniff out a lie at a hundred yards. Odd that, isn't it. It's almost as if he knew something like this was going to happen.'

I sat for a while after he left wondering what to believe. I only wish David's boast had been right. Tredwell had told me two stories, now. The latest was plausible enough – and he had not had much time to invent it. After all, he hadn't known until we sat down to coffee that I had discovered that David was homosexual. It seemed frankly unlikely, though, that Tredwell had exercised the restraint he claimed. 'I embraced him,' he had said. It was altogether too coy to be plausible. And I still wasn't sure that I believed his story about why he had wanted me to think David killed himself. Perhaps, I thought, he simply couldn't think of anyone else to put the blame on. And that was beginning to be my problem, too.

I ordered another cup of coffee. I had had a good number of surprises in the last day or so – it was still less than twenty-four hours since I had arrived at the railway station – and they didn't seem to fit together. This was as good a place as any to decide what to do next.

I had still formed very few ideas when I left the Copper Kettle, but as I walked back up King's Parade I suddenly remembered Hippo Buckingham, who had entirely slipped my mind. There remained a good hour before I had to be back in college for lunch, so I strode off at a vigorous pace towards Jesus College.

As I reached the beginning of the terraced row of houses beyond the Pitt Club, the tall, lean, elegantly distinguished figure of Hugo McAlister hailed me from the other side of the street. Hugo was one of those Apostles whom I knew vaguely because we had overlapped in our active periods in the Society. I had always found him something of a cold fish; with his grand manner, and his astonishing formality of dress, he reminded me of nothing so much as a diplomat of the Old School.

'Patrick, old boy, I didn't know you were in town. The dinner isn't till next week.'

'I'm afraid I'm up on rather nasty business, Hugo. You know my cousin David Glen Tannock, I believe.'

'Certainly. I was in his rooms last week to listen to a brilliant paper that Charlie Phipps gave on his recent work.'

'Well, I'm afraid David died yesterday.'

McAlister was silent for an odd moment before he said: 'Oh, I say, I am most awfully sorry. One of those ghastly May Week accidents, was it?'

'No, I'm afraid he was poisoned.'

'Good Lord.'

'With penicillin.'

'How extraordinary. You know he mentioned his allergy last week. And I'm afraid I rather ran on about allergies. How frightful. Anything I can do?'

'I don't think so, Hugo, but thanks for asking.' I paused. 'Unless . . . There wasn't anything odd about last week's meeting was there?'

'Odd? No, not that I can think of.'

'Ah, well.'

We stood for a moment in embarrassed silence. 'Well, I suppose I may see you next week?' Hugo said; and I nodded distractedly. 'Though, of course, we shall all understand if you don't come.' He paused again. 'How frightful for the Ivors. I really must drop Charlie a note. God. These tragedies do rather knock you for six.'

I nodded again. There seemed nothing to say. We each went our separate ways.

I am always surprised, when I see Jesus, exactly how hideous it is. I walked with a sense of foreboding down the claustrophobic pathway to the main gate, with its high walls and the general gloom cast by the main building, and stepped into the porter's lodge.

'I don't suppose you could tell me where I could find Jeremy Buckingham?'

The porter glanced up from his paper. 'Well, sir, I think I *can* help you with that. Mr Buckingham was in here not two minutes ago and, though I shouldn't say so, I'd say he wasn't lookin' at all well. In fact, I would go so far as to say that he looked deathly. Family, are you?'

'Er . . . no, but I am the uncle of a very good friend of his who has, unfortunately, died rather recently.'

The porter peered at me for a moment. 'Ah yes, I should have seen it, of course. Sir Patrick Smith, isn't it? You was in the papers. It's that dead Viscount, isn't it? Done in with penicillin. I just read about it in the *Evening News*, here. Shockin' thing. Saw him come in here with Mr Buckingham a few times. What a cruel twist of fate. Ah well, dust to dust . . . now, why didn't I think of that when I saw Mr Buckingham just now? Well, of course, I 'adn't seen his picture then. I mean I was still readin' about it, wasn't I? Condolences. Should have given my condolences.' He paused in his monologue and noticed me again.

'Look, sir. I think you'll find him in his room. P6. Here, let me show you. I can apologize for not condolin' with him earlier. Oh dearie me. What a thing to 'appen.'

In a flash he had locked the lodge and was dragging me along to the new building of Jesus that backs on to Jesus Green, chattering all the way.

Hippo Buckingham's rooms were not exactly tidy. There were books and glasses strewn about the place and half-empty cups of coffee filled with cigarette ends. In the few minutes since he had passed through the lodge, he had stripped off, and was standing with a towel about his waist, when he opened the door. The porter condoled busily for a minute or two and then attempted to explain roughly who I was. 'Sir Patrick Smith,' he said. 'Your friend Lord Glen Whatsit's uncle come to see you.'

'Thank you so much, Mr Barker. How do you do, Sir Patrick; please come in.'

Hippo Buckingham was a good few inches shorter than me in his bare feet; I guessed he was about five foot eight. His current state of undress made it obvious that he was rather overweight. He looked as though, like me, he ate too well and drank too much. His sandy hair and pale, almost invisible eyebrows, along with his slightly bloated look, gave him a mildly porcine air.

He cleared an armchair of clothes and a tennis-racket for me, apologizing all the while for the mess. 'I'm afraid I'm in the middle of Tripos and what with one thing and another a terrible mess has built up, which my bedder refuses – quite rightly – to have anything to do with.' He seemed suddenly to notice that he was rather underdressed. 'I've just been for a run to work off some of my nerves. I was going to have a bath.'

Standing among the debris, Hippo Buckingham looked tremendously helpless. He was embarrassed by the mess, distressed by David's death, and probably worried about how he was going to do in his exams. He was also practically naked. Naturally, neither of us felt at all comfortable.

'Look,' I said, refusing the offer of the chair, 'this is obviously terribly inconvenient and I didn't mean to barge in like this . . . it's just that the porter didn't give me time to suggest that we meet later.'

Hippo Buckingham spoke quietly, uncertainly. 'David talked about you quite often. I'm sure it's a terrible imposition, but I don't think I could face going out just at the moment.' I made a move to go.

'No, don't go,' he said. His tone was almost pleading.

I was now standing beside Hippo's desk and as he spoke I glanced down. There on a pile of papers was a cheque for two hundred and fifty pounds drawn on an account at Coutts. I glanced back up – it hardly seemed any of my business – but my eyes were drawn down again by the fact that I thought I recognized the handwriting. There, quite unmistakably, was David's signature: Glen Tannock. And the date was yesterday's.

Distracted as I was by the discovery, it was a moment before I could think how to respond to Hippo's remark.

'Quite understand, old boy.' I'm afraid I rather mumbled it. 'It's a terrible shock. And I gather you were very good friends.'

'Yes, I suppose we were. We spent a lot of time together.'

We chatted idly for a quarter of an hour, without discussing David's last meal. That would have to wait for later. I practised my avuncular style (perhaps I would ask Hugh for tips on talking to unattractive young men in bath towels). Hippo seemed to calm down somewhat as we talked. As I was still standing, it was natural to take a step towards the door during a momentary pause in the conversation. 'I'm afraid I ought to rush off to lunch at my college. Will you be all right? Is there someone I could telephone for you? A friend in college I could fetch? A tutor?'

'No, no,' he said hurriedly . . . obviously especially appalled by the last suggestion. 'I'm all right now. Perhaps I could meet you later on this afternoon somewhere?'

The suggestion was diffident; but I accepted it eagerly, asking him for ideas about a mid-afternoon meeting place.

'I'm afraid I've got exams till five.' His voice firmed. 'How about over a drink at the Pitt Club later? I'll have to get used to going in there without David.'

'Splendid, I'll meet you there at six. Perhaps I could give you dinner afterwards – why don't you think about a restaurant during your spare moments in the exam room.'

Hippo laughed and I smiled and somehow that broke the strain.

'Thanks a lot, Sir Patrick.'

It seemed better not to ask him to explain what I had done for him.

Twenty minutes later I was eating a rather awful salad in the small Fellows' dining hall, and waiting to see which of the Fellows would break the ice and ask me how my investigations were going, when Jenkins, the butler, sidled up behind me. 'There's a policeman looking for you, sir, outside. Inspector Fanshaw, his name is. He says he'd like a word. Urgently. It seems, sir, that another person has . . . passed away.'

# 7

Inspector Fanshaw did not beat about the bush. 'A Dr Charles Phipps has just been found dead in his lab, sir.' I felt the blood drain from my face. I was stunned, and I must have looked it. 'I believe you knew him.'

First David, now Charlie; two of the most aureate of the golden boys I knew. I remembered Charlie as a young man, playing cricket in the village with Sebastian and some of our neighbours, laughing as he struck out boldly and ball after ball flew to the boundary. I remembered how sweetly he flirted with Virginia, courteous, teasing, a young man flattering an older woman, his best friend's mother; I remembered his wedding – he and Sebastian, his best man, standing by the altar, and the radiant smiles (Charlie's nervous, Sebastian's reassuring) as Claudia walked down the aisle.

And Claudia. Whenever anyone uses the word 'gamine', I think of Claudia. Fine-boned, slight; and yet so lively and strong: exactly like a starving street urchin. I always say I married Virginia for her legs, which is, in a manner of speaking, true. It was her legs I saw first, coming down the stairs at the Admiralty where she worked in a planning group as a Wren, and it was love at first sight. But Charlie said he had married Claudia for her eyes; enormous hazel eyes, which seemed especially gigantic in so tiny a person. How would she take it? How to console her?

Fanshaw reached out to support me by the elbow. 'Are you all right, sir?' The concern in his voice drew me back from those memories. I flinched and tried to focus my attention.

'I'm sorry, Inspector. It's rather a blow. He was my son's best friend.' It's odd how one speaks in clichés at moments of crisis. It is easier, I suppose, than trying to explain.

'I'm sorry, sir. I didn't know. His wife told me that he had been to see Dr . . .' He checked his notes. 'Dr Penhaligon at Corpus Christi last night, and *he* told us that you had been there, too. I just wanted to ask if you might know anything about what he did when he left. My people didn't mention that you were so . . .' He searched for a word and settled, finally, on 'close.'

'It's all right, Inspector. I shall be all right in a moment. I wonder if we could go and sit down upstairs for a minute?'

We walked up the stairs to the combination room and I wondered as we climbed how I should tell Sebastian and Jinny. Two dear friends in so many days. I collected a cup of coffee for the Inspector, and he told me what they had found.

'Dr Phipps was found late this morning dead in his laboratory – at about eleven. His laboratory assistant claims to have gone out for a break at about ten thirty . . . leaving him alive, of course. And, from a first impression, since his body was still warm, he certainly hadn't been dead long by the time we got there at about half-past eleven. We haven't, of course, had time to do the autopsy, yet. But according to McAlister, the Professor of Physiology, Dr Phipps was working with some very dangerous chemicals.' He consulted his notes again. 'Neurotoxins. Fast-acting poisons that kill the brain in seconds. It would have been very quick.' Somehow that wasn't as reassuring as it was obviously meant to be; but I was grateful to the man for trying.

'So it was an accident, you think?'

Fanshaw looked puzzled. 'Why not?'

'No reason, except that Charlie was a very thorough, careful worker, with a wife and a young child. He knew – better, perhaps then anybody – how dangerous that stuff was.'

'Well, unless the forensics show reasons for suspicion, I think we shall have to put this down to an accident.'

That's not possible, I thought. For the first time since I arrived in Cambridge I felt a moment of panic: whatever Fanshaw said it seemed utterly incredible that the deaths were accidental. If I had had any remaining doubts, they were gone now. Fanshaw's composure simply underlined the dangers.

'I don't suppose you know anything about where Dr Phipps was going when he left your meeting last night?' Fanshaw said.

'I'm afraid, Inspector, that I can't tell you anything much about Charlie's movement last night. Why do you ask?'

'Well, according to his wife, he got back around one in the morning; but Dr Penhaligon has him leaving Corpus at eleven. And it's only a five or ten minute walk back to his house in Portugal Place. Now Mrs Phipps was used to his getting in late because he often had to do things in the lab at odd hours – as a matter of fact, she said he didn't get in till long after midnight the night before – and so she didn't think to ask him this morning what he had been doing. But a Mr Prince, a research student, was working in the neighbouring laboratory all night and says Phipps wasn't there.'

'Well, if it turns out there *is* something fishy about the death, it would be nice to know what Charlie was doing between eleven and one this morning.'

'That's right,' Fanshaw said. 'I've already got my chaps checking on where everybody was at that time.'

We sat in silence for a half a minute, sipping coffee. I realized that with the shock of Charlie's death I had forgotten to ask about David. 'Oh, Inspector. About the other matter – Lord Glen Tannock. Anything new?'

Fanshaw seemed at first to know a good deal less than I did. He knew about dinner at the Pitt Club and he had interviewed Caufield. He was due to interview Hippo Buckingham late next morning, having agreed with the boy's tutor that the day of his last final was not one on which to subject him to further pressure.

Fanshaw had also met Tredwell, when he returned from our meeting at the Copper Kettle, and Tredwell had simply told him that David was an exceptional student and a great loss. In the circumstances and for the moment, that seemed good enough.

That much said, he stopped and shifted nervously in his seat. 'Sir Patrick, I don't want you to think that there's any question of your . . . er . . . good faith and all; but Dr Penhaligon mentioned that everyone who was in his rooms last night, except you, had been there the night before: and the night before, Lord Glen Tannock was there too. Isn't that a bit strange? I mean, two evening meetings, each followed by what looks at first sight like an accidental death. And such an odd collection of people, if you don't mind my saying so. Different colleges, different occupations, different ages.'

I inferred that Hugh and the others had decided not to tell the Inspector that Oliver Hetherington had been there also. I took it that they didn't wish to embarrass a man who was about to be made ambassador to Moscow. It would hardly look very good to find that Sir Oliver Hetherington had been the last person to see David alive. Until I had spoken to them it seemed best to leave Inspector Fanshaw in the dark about that,too.

'Didn't Dr Penhaligon explain that they were a discussion club?'

'Yes sir, he did.' He was back with his notebook. 'The Cambridge Conversation Society.'

'Conversazione,' I corrected. 'It's the Italian pronunciation.' Hugh had used the old official name of the club; hoping, I suppose, that Fanshaw wouldn't make the connection. Fanshaw looked at his notebook and nodded.

'And you, sir, are a member also?'

'Was,' I said. 'But old boys sometimes come back to enjoy the sparkle of brilliant intellectual exchange.'

Fanshaw looked at me oddly – and I realized that in trying to put him off the scent, I had struck the wrong tone; the good Inspector was justifiably suspicious.

I had to make a decision. If I took Fanshaw into my confidence, there was a chance he would understand why the name of the Apostles might best be left out of it. If I didn't, and he went around enquiring about the Cambridge Conversazione Society, somebody would make the connection for him. There didn't seem to be much choice.

'Inspector,' I began, 'I am going to have to take you into my confidence.'

It took me more than half an hour to tell him about the Apostles. The Society began in the 1820s, I told him, as a group of young men who met regularly for friendly discussions of various issues of the day. Lord Tennyson, Queen Victoria's favourite poet, and his friend, Hallam, in whose memory he wrote 'In Memoriam', Queen Victoria's favourite poem, were members, as were many lesser nineteeth-century literary figures. By the turn of the century, it had fallen into desuetude, but was resurrected in the early part of the century as the intellectual centre of the Bloomsbury group. From the Society, Keynes set out to revolutionize economics, Bertrand Russell to rewrite the foundations of logic, Strachey to write *Eminent Victorians*, a new kind of biography.

By the thirties, the Society, though its membership was supposed to be secret, was widely believed to be the natural home of the 'brightest and best' of the university's bright young things. And, at a time when the Spanish Civil War and the inaction of the Western powers in the face of the rise of Fascism were drawing many of them to the left, Philby and Burgess and Blunt were members of the Society at the same time as Victor Rothschild and Dick White; and all of them went on to work together in British Intelligence in World War Two. In the serious business of the War, which the Russians entered, finally, on our side, the left-wing antecedents of many of these bright upper- and upper-middle-class young men were forgotten: and it was only with the defection of Burgess and Philby along with Maclean in the fifties – and the later revelations that Blunt,

Keeper of the Queen's Pictures had, for a while, been a Russian spy, also – that the intelligence establishment realized how much of a mistake this had been. It hardly mattered that the Society had also contributed some of the most outstanding of the country's secret servants; that Dick White went on to head British intelligence. In the minds of the press, 'Apostles' meant 'spies', and every story about the Apostles was a chance to rehash the story of the 'Fourth Man' – the 'mole' some fanatics believed was still hidden in the intelligence services, the man who had tipped off the others.

I didn't have to explain to Fanshaw, then, why many of us would rather the name didn't get into the press again. 'The deaths could hardly have anything to do with the others. Lord Rothschild, Sir Dick White, Lord Annan . . .' I reeled off a list of establishment names. '. . . It would just be an embarrassment and the press would have a field day. I'm afraid the very word "Apostle" is an excuse for journalistic sensationalism.' Since, in my experience, the police don't have much time for sensational journalism – they are too often the victims of it themselves – I hoped he would go along with this.

I told him, too, everything about David's last meeting, save that Oliver Hetherington had been there. If it had to come out later, I could plead forgetfulness in a time of shock. That wouldn't be very plausible if they found out that I had talked to him that morning. But no one in the college office at Trinity could prove that I had got through. And so long as I got to Oliver first, he would surely back up my story if necessary.

'I think we shall find, Inspector, that I will do better following up any leads that involve the Society: as you see, their secretiveness is not unjustified. And I shall certainly keep you informed of any relevant information. After all,' I finished, 'David was my favourite cousin.'

Fanshaw pondered the proposal. He was being offered a frankly irregular deal by a well-known barrister – a Queen's Counsel, no less – with a reputation as a sleuth. He knew, from years in the Cambridgeshire Constabulary, that the university had ways of keeping its secrets; and that I had a beter chance than he of fathoming its mysteries. He also knew that I wanted David's killer.

He sighed and tore a page out of his notebook and wrote a

telephone number on it. 'That's my home number. Any time, night or day, you can call me. If I'm not there, my wife will tell you how to get hold of me. And, off the record, sir, I hope this never comes out.'

I wondered what Tredwell would think of me if he knew what I was doing: keeping secrets from a perfectly decent policeman who was doing me the favour of breaking the rules. I consoled myself with the thought that I was not interfering, so far as I knew, with the detection of David's murderer, that I had a better chance of finding him – or her – on my own. If it came to it, I would have to get the permission of the others to tell all.

And as I consoled myself with this last thought, I remembered the annual dinner.

# 8

This year, as every year, at the end of the summer term, Apostles and Angels would convene for an annual dinner. It was this dinner that Hugo had mentioned to me when we met on the street; this year he would be presiding. Sometimes as many as thirty, sometimes as few as a dozen, we gather in one of the smaller college dining-rooms for a splendid meal.

After dinner, someone takes to the hearth rug. Some members regard the dinner as the occasion for another amusing after-dinner speech, one of the many they will hear in a year of dinners at livery companies and Inns of Court and gatherings of old boys of one kind or another. They sip their brandy in a mildly resentful torpor, while those of us whose memories of the Society are of youthful discussions of the 'good and the true and the beautiful' try to recapture the intellectual intensity of our earlier lives.

I had agreed at the last dinner that I would take to the hearth rug this year: in a few days – next Tuesday, to be exact – I would have to live up to that promise.

I suspected that I had been invited to speak as a concession to the amusing-after-dinner-speech school of thought, because I have a reputation as something of a wit at the bar. But I had wanted to talk about changes in the law of trusts, which seemed to me to raise interesting ethical issues. I had been working on the paper when Charlie Ivor had called to tell me that David was dead. In case I got cold feet, I had also polished up a jolly post-prandial romp that had gone down rather well at the Middle Temple Christmas Feast.

Now, it seemed, there was a way out of my dilemma. For if any group was entitled to discuss and decide how much should be made public, the annual meeting was it. It was the largest gathering of the Society, a gathering which had discussed such contentious issues as the admission of women and the opening of the Ark (as our archives are called) to researchers; and Angels, especially the older ones, liked nothing more than a heated discussion of the virtues of the secret Apostolic life. If this gathering of the great and the good agreed that even a pair of murders was no reason to expose the Society to the world, I, at least, should be inclined to go along with them. And, of course, in the unlikely event that they judged that on the whole we should admit that David and Charles had been Apostles, each of whom died after a meeting of the Society, who would I be to gainsay them?

Of course, in telling Inspector Fanshaw who the current members were, in telling him that I was – though I did not use the term – an Angel, I had breached the time-honoured code. The words of Malinson, our no-doubt notional founder, Bishop of Gibraltar in the 1850s (words quoted in the letter that is read at the induction of every member), resounded in my memory: anyone who broke the code would be expelled to the 'Outer Darkness', doomed forever to the 'phenomenal world', 'utterly cast out'. Somehow, with a murderer at large, it all seemed more than usually ridiculous. But some of our seniors took it very seriously.

I made a resolution: if, by the time of the annual dinner, we did not know who killed David, then I would begin by repeating the question Hugh had put last night in jest: Who killed David, Lord Glen Tannock?

And if it weren't necessary, if the case could be solved

without Angelic intervention, I would probably be in a mood for my jolly after-dinner romp.

Once I had resolved to put the question to the Society, it was time for what PR types call 'damage control'. I made a few telephone calls. Hugh, who was back in his rooms after lunch, accepted my decision and the limited amount I had told Fanshaw and agreed to pass the message on to James Hogg, so that we could all tell the same story.

Hugh said, 'You probably don't want to make a habit of this, but why don't we all – those of us that are left among the living – gather for a short meeting in my rooms after dinner. Oh yes; what about asking the other currently active members of the Society, Godfrey Stanley and Dale Bishop? Godfrey has only started coming again recently – after years as a pretty remote Angel – and Dale Bishop's only been to one meeting so far. I don't think there's any point in asking Hugo McAlister. He's always tremendously busy and, as I said, he only came to hear Charlie.'

'Yes, no need to ask Hugo, I've already seen him. I don't think he knows anything that'll help.'

'But the other two were both at the meeting last week, in David's rooms, when Charlie gave his last talk . . . Oh Lord, it really was his last talk, wasn't it? He even mentioned how toxic the stuff was he was working with. You don't think somebody's after *us*, do you?'

He waited for a moment and prompted, when I said nothing, 'Well, Patrick, what do you think?' He had spoken as if in jest, but there was nothing casual about his interest. The apprehension I had felt earlier was reinforced by Hugh's echoing disquiet.

'I think we should all be very careful.' In the circumstances I knew that was understating the risks. 'You're right, of course, it's a real possibility. We'd better get to everyone as fast as we can.'

'Shall I ask Godfrey and Bishop, then?'

'Yes, it might help. Godfrey is awfully sharp still; he might have some ideas. And I'd like to talk to him anyway since David was apparently doing some digging in the archives about Gregory Ransome.'

'Yes, I know. He mentioned it at last week's meeting. Godfrey was going to help him out over the summer, I think. And he planned to put him in touch with Oliver, too. David, you see, was going to do a little biographical piece. A work of piety. Ah well . . .' His voice trailed off. 'You know, Patrick, this is all very depressing.'

I didn't know how to respond, how to cheer him up. It was difficult enough keeping myself from despair.

I told him that we should probably meet at about ten, since I didn't want to rush my talk with Hippo. 'I'll telephone Vera Oblomov,' I said, 'if you will organize the others. And Hugh . . . do tell them to be careful.' I rang off.

Vera Oblomov, in her office in the Faculty of Philosophy at Sidgwick Avenue, listened to my warnings and my proposal that we all meet again and observed laconically, 'I am sure you know best, Sir Patrick.'

I said, 'Hugh has invited us all for a drink at about ten p.m.'

She agreed to come, adding with apparent seriousness, 'Let us hope that we shall not have to meet tomorrow night with one less member.' It really didn't seem at all funny: and I thought I detected a whiff of apprehension in her gallows humour.

When I suggested that it might also be best for us all to keep silence on the matter of David's sexuality, she agreed to that also. As she put it, 'It is hardly Mr Fanshaw's business with whom David chose to make luff. After all,' she added, 'it will only give the press another chance to behave with their characteristically indescribable lack of judgement.'

It was harder to get hold of Oliver Hetherington. A telephone call to the lodge at Trinity produced a genial Lady Darwin who hadn't 'the foggiest where anyone is, Sir Patrick,' but suggested that I might ask Alan Blumberg. The phone at the Blumberg house rang a dozen or so times before I gave up. Still, I decided, finding Oliver wasn't so urgent; after all, if the others said nothing, how could Fanshaw know he had anything to do with it?

My last call was to Virginia. Phoning the others had given me time to gather strength. I knew she would take it badly; I knew, too, that she would manage.

'My darling, I'm afraid that something awful has happened.'

'Oh, Patrick, are you all right?'

'Yes, yes. *I'm* quite all right. But something horrible has happened to Charlie.'

I heard her sharp intake of breath. 'Is he . . . dead?'

'Yes.'

'How?'

'Poisoned with some chemical he was researching. I'm going to see if I can find Claudia as soon as we finish talking.'

She said nothing for a while and I knew she was trying not to weep. 'I know, darling,' I said, 'it's awful. Do you want to come up this evening? Shall I come down to London?'

'No, Patrick. Don't be silly, you must stay where you are; and I can't come up until I've been to see Sebastian.' Her voice was thickening. She paused, recovered control. 'I think I would rather tell him in person . . . and I ought to speak to Charlie's mother, she's all on her own now, it'll be an awful blow. Perhaps Sebastian could have her to stay for a few days?' And so, as usual, Virginia managed her own emotions by worrying about other people's. 'You'd better go and see Claudia at once. And for God's sake, Patrick, take care.'

I hadn't had to tell her that until we knew why David and Charlie had died, we must all assume that every member of the Society was in mortal danger.

# 9

When I arrived at Claudia's at about four she had stopped crying. 'Come in, Patrick,' she said quietly, leading me back along the hallway into the kitchen. She sat down at the kitchen table, rocking the pram in which Paddy was sleeping. For a while we were silent. When she looked up at me, I went over to her and placed a hand on her shoulder and she rose, put her arms around my neck and convulsed in sobs. 'It's all right, Claudia. Let it out,' I said.

After a while she disengaged herself. 'Let me make you some tea.' Her voice was flat.

I nodded. There was already a single cup of tea on the table. It was somehow conspicuously solitary. I had assumed that Fanshaw would have left a police constable to watch over her. 'Police?' I asked. Claudia gestured vaguely at the ceiling and I assumed she meant that there was someone upstairs.

'Has she been here all day?' I asked.

'Yes.'

Once the tea was made, we sat in silence for a few minutes. Then she started talking about Charlie and Sebastian, and how Virginia and I had meant so much to Charlie. I said nothing, making encouraging noises occasionally; listening to her, wondering what she was going to do.

'We'd seen so little of each other in the last few days. Somehow that makes it worse. Last night he came in when I was asleep; and when we got up in the morning we had breakfast – we're not very talkative at breakfast – and then he had to be off to the lab. It was the same the night before.'

'Working, I suppose,' I interjected quietly.

'Not last night, according to the police. But he gets all hyped up sometimes . . .' She stopped. 'I shall have to get used to saying "got", won't I? . . . No, I'm all right.' She drew a paper handkerchief from a box on the table and wiped her eyes. 'He got all hyped up and used to go walking if he had to think a problem through. Sometimes he walked out to Grantchester Meadows and lay by the river. Sometimes he walked up and down along the Backs. It helped him think. It helped him work things out. He was very clever, wasn't he?' she asked suddenly, turning to look me once more directly in the face.

'Everybody said so.'

'He told me that you were an Apostle, too. That I mustn't tell anybody. Did you ever hear him give a paper?'

'Several times. He was always very clear. He made me regret, sometimes, that I hadn't been a scientist, too.'

She smiled. 'That's a lovely little lie, Sir Patrick. I shall cherish it. He gave a paper last week, you know?'

'I know.'

She sat, small and lost, once more gently rocking the pram. 'I wonder if Paddy will remember him,' she said. We let the silence hang in the air.

After a while I spoke again quietly. 'Virginia sent you her love. She's gone to see Sebastian, to tell him. And she's going to get in touch with Charlie's mother. Is there anything else we can do?'

'If I think of anything, I'll tell you.'

'Virginia's coming to Cambridge tomorrow. We were going to stay at the lodge at Clare. Would you like it if we stayed here?'

'Oh, would you, Patrick?' She brightened. 'I'd just rather not be alone.'

'And tonight?'

'Tonight' – she seemed calmer now – 'tonight, I *would* like to be alone . . . with Paddy; just for one night.'

When I left Claudia, it was about five in the afternoon. As I stepped out into the emptiness of Portugal Place, I felt that I too needed a little quiet time alone to absorb the day's events. I made my way to the Backs, then through the back gate of Trinity, down the avenue, between lawns and tennis courts, to the river. I paused on the bridge, looking up the river to Clare one way, down to the Bridge of Sighs the other; and passed on to sit on a bench in front of the Wren library.

I spent a quarter of an hour in that beautiful spot as the afternoon turned into a bright summer evening. At a quarter to six I walked through the back of Trinity and into Great Court, moving as swiftly as I could, so that I should get to the Pitt Club for my appointment with Hippo Buckingham by six. But as I reached the centre of Great Court, Oliver Hetherington – tall and thin, with a great mop of greying hair – called to me from a window on the ground floor of the Master's lodge.

I looked at my watch – I had about eight minutes till I was due at the club – and strode towards him. 'Where are you off to in such a frightful hurry?' Oliver asked, smiling affably and shaking my hand through the open window. 'Haven't you a moment to come in and meet the Darwins?'

'I should love to, Oliver, but I promised to meet someone at six o'clock and I'm going to be late if I stop. But I expect Lady Darwin told you I was trying to get in touch with you earlier and I do need to talk to you soon – a rather delicate situation has developed, you see. Charles Phipps died this morning and the police want to know why he was meeting with us the evening before; and so they're on to the Apostolic connection. Hugh and the others decided it was best to try and keep you out of this, and so far we've kept it quiet that you left the meeting the night before with David. But the thing is, I think we have to conclude that Charles and David were killed; and that means we should all take the greatest care. Have you a bodyguard with you?'

'Good Lord, no. We don't normally have protection when we're at home. But thanks for the warning.' Oliver seemed oddly sanguine. But he was ever the diplomat. If the tale I told worried him, he simply wouldn't let it show.

The clock on the Great Gate struck six. I had to leave. I didn't want Hippo to think I wasn't coming and run off. 'Look, could you meet us in Hugh's rooms later, at about ten?'

'Very decent of you all; of course, I'll come. May be a bit late, though. The Darwins have a dinner party for me.'

'We'll wait. And now I must run.'

I arrived at the Pitt Club at ten minutes past six. Hippo was already drinking at the bar.

'I'm sorry I'm a little late,' I began. 'I got held up by an old friend. Doesn't do not to be punctual.'

Hippo waved my apologies aside shyly and offered me a drink.

'On a warm summer evening,' I pronounced, 'nothing quite beats a gin and tonic.'

I'd had little time to think about what I was to say to Hippo and hadn't spent much time thinking about the cheque on his desk either. It was probably an entirely private matter, nothing to do with David's death. Still, if he tried to cash it now, the police would ask him about it; I might as well get there first. But there was plenty of time for that.

'How were your finals?' I asked. Chit-chat, I thought, start with chit-chat. It was difficult keeping the tone relaxed: but it wouldn't help to let Hippo know that I feared David's death was the act of a double murderer.

'Fine, thanks. I'm going to be running our Somerset farm, so it doesn't matter much, anyway. But my mother will be pleased if I get a second.'

'Well, keep your fingers crossed.' Hippo thrust the crossed

fingers of his right hand rather close to my nose and I realized he had been drinking before I arrived. 'You have lots to celebrate,' I said. 'Now, come on, where have you decided we shall have dinner?'

He looked at me oddly for a moment. 'Lots to celebrate, eh? Bloody David's gone and bloody died and I have lots to celebrate.'

'I'm sorry, I wasn't thinking.' I paused for a moment and clapped a hand on his shoulder. 'But life has to go on, Hippo . . . Jeremy.'

He smiled wanly at that. 'No. It *is* Hippo.'

'So where shall we eat? David used to take me to a place just up in the Kite; Italian, Camillo's or some such.'

'Tarquino's. It's rather pricey.'

'Price no object – where else can a barrister spend his ill-gotten gains, if he can't grow fat on expensive Italian cooking?'

It was agreed. And so, after another hour of chatting in the Pitt Club, with Hippo introducing me to some of his friends, we walked out up to the Market Square. I had persuaded Hippo to hold back on the alcohol by dint of agreeing to let Bill, at the bar, concoct a dozen or so strange *alkoholfrei* drinks for us to sample. By the time we left the club we were both stone cold sober.

Tarquino's is an excellent restaurant, too expensive now for most undergraduates. We sat downstairs in a quiet corner and, after agreeing that we would both have calves' liver done in what promised to be a rather rich sauce, preceded in my case by an avocado and in Hippo's a mixed plate of antipasto, I consulted with Hippo about wines. It wouldn't do to reveal my anxieties by declining to eat; and a good meal would help Hippo relax.

'I gather from Mr Caufield that you and David had rather a taste for decent wines; I don't think that this wine list will compete with the best of the club's wines, so why don't we be adventurous and try one of these rough Italian potions?'

'Mr Caufield ought not to discuss members' habits,' Hippo said in a tone that somehow mixed the grand and the resentful.

'Oh, I don't think he meant anything by it. I simply asked

him what David had had for dinner on Wednesday night and he mentioned the wines. Were you two celebrating?'

'No. Well, sort of.' A waiter arrived and we ordered. When he left Hippo lowered his voice and adopted a more confidential tone. 'Look, Sir Patrick. This is all frightfully embarrassing. But the fact is, David took me out to a grand dinner because I told him I was rather short of money. He was like that. Rather generous . . . tremendously generous in fact. To his friends, I mean . . . well, I suppose, mostly to me.'

'Hippo,' I said, 'I know it's not always easy to stay within a budget and keep up with the other chaps at the club.'

'Not easy,' Hippo snorted. 'On my allowance, it's practically impossible. My father has no idea . . .' He stopped.

'Can I ask you a rather personal question?'

Hippo glanced around the room and reddened slightly. 'What about?'

'About the cheque on your desk.'

'Oh, that. I wondered if you'd noticed it. David gave it to me on Wednesday night. The fact is, David's on the committee and had gathered from Caufield that I hadn't paid last term's bill. Well, if you haven't paid last term's bill by May Week, you can't use the club and your name is, you know, posted. I had to get a cheque in by Thursday morning, and I'd only got the courage up to accept David's offer of a loan that afternoon, when we'd arranged to have dinner.'

As Hippo spoke I tried to decide what it was that he had expected me to ask, that had caused him to redden. I wondered whether, despite David protestations of love for Tredwell, he had actually been sleeping with Hippo. It should, I suppose, have struck me before. But the fact was that Hippo in his towel had seemed rather unappealing even to my disinterested eye, and until now, frankly, the idea that David should have found him desirable had simply not crossed my mind. Could David have been to bed with Hippo before going back to his rooms after the meeting? Even as I asked myself the question, it struck me as rather unlikely.

'Good. That's a fine straightforward explanation. Did David give you any other money?'

Hippo blushed again. 'Yes, once.'

'Look, old boy, I'm only asking these questions because you'll probably have to answer them to the police sooner or later. You see, when someone is killed . . .'

Hippo interrupted. 'Killed? The paper only said he'd taken penicillin.'

'You haven't read today's paper, then?'

He shook his head. 'I just read last night's *Cambridge Evening News*.'

'Well, the police think that he may have been given it by someone. It hardly seems likely that he would have taken it deliberately.'

Hippo seemed to think that I had a point. 'So you think that they might suspect someone he'd been paying money to. Why? Wouldn't it be more suspicious if I'd been paying money to him? Blackmail, that sort of thing. Why should the blackmailer kill his victim?'

'That's true, of course: but suppose someone had been blackmailing David and he had finally decided to go to the police. They might kill him then.'

As the food arrived, Hippo fell quiet, wondering – I imagined – how his interview the next day with the police would turn out. Over the meal we chatted about life in college and his plans for farming and the memories of Cambridge he would take with him. As I listened to him he grew more relaxed. I returned to David's cheque.

'By the way, when did David give you that cheque?'

Once again he reddened; and this time he looked frankly shifty.

'I'm sorry to return to that embarrassing question, but any evidence I can get as to David's actions on Wednesday may help nail his murderer.'

'It's not the cheque that's embarrassing. It's when I got it.'

'When did you last see David?'

'At about midnight.'

All this sexual intrigue was rather embarrassing for me, too, of course. But I had now to ask the question I had been pondering earlier. Hippo would obviously not want to discuss it with David's elderly relations unless I made it plain that I had some idea of David's tastes.

'Hippo, I know – though the police don't yet – that David was gay. If you and he were . . .'

Hippo Buckingham roared. 'Don't be revolting!'

'But if you and he met for any other reason, what's so embarrassing?'

'Since you already know that David was queer' (Hippo pronounced the word with extreme distaste) 'it won't do any harm to tell you, I suppose. But it's really not a very pleasant story.'

Pleasant or not, Hippo's story was extremely interesting; and it was told with compete conviction.

After dinner on Wednesday night, David had told Hippo that he had left his cheque book in his rooms and that he didn't have time to go back to his rooms to fetch it, now. They had agreed to meet outside Corpus at eleven, walk over to Thirkill Court and collect the cheque. David and he both had exams the next day, and David had said he would be busy the next evening; if Hippo was to get his cheque in by the deadline and avoid being 'posted', he had to get the money that night.

When David came out of Corpus with Sir Oliver Hetherington, they had had a slight altercation with Warren, the head porter. It seemed that Warren had felt entitled to enquire what they had been doing in the college at that time of night and I could tell from Hippo's account that Oliver had unsuccessfully adopted his grandest Foreign Office tone. I made a mental note that if Warren had seen Oliver, we should have to tell Fanshaw about him soon. Fanshaw was bound to talk to the porter sooner or later; it would be best not to be caught out.

Hippo had seen all this, but had been too embarrassed to join David while he was with Oliver. 'I mean, it looks a bit odd, hanging around for a chap in the middle of the night.' David had looked around for a moment and decided that Hippo – who was hidden in the shadows on the other side of the street to escape Warren's infamous wrath – was not there, and had obviously made up his mind to walk Oliver home and look for Hippo later.

And so Hippo had followed along behind Oliver and David, hoping to talk to David alone later. He saw them talking in front of the gates of Trinity, and when Oliver disappeared he rushed up to David.

'Where *have* you been?' David had said. 'I looked for you outside Corpus.' Hippo had pretended that he had arrived late and they had then walked back down Trinity Street and through Trinity Lane over the bridge towards Memorial Court. David seemed to be in a bit of a hurry and said something about having promised to meet a friend at midnight, so they went briskly to David's room. David wrote out the cheque, refused Hippo's effusive thanks and came back down with him to see him off.

Hippo had gone back by the same route, and stopped about half-way down the narrow road between the Clare Fellows' Gardens and Trinity's tennis courts because he heard someone moving in the Clare Fellows' Gardens. Curious, he had peered through the bushes and seen someone standing alone by the samll fish pond.

'Whoever it was,' Hippo said, 'was smoking a cigarette and pacing up and down. The moon was quite bright but I didn't really see his face. I was just about to move off, when somebody else joined him: and I recognized him as David. He must have climbed around the gates at the end of the avenue and run down to the garden to meet his chum.' Hippo's tone, now, was rather unpleasant.

'I suspect he didn't have to climb round the gates – he had a key.'

'Oh, yes, of course.' Hippo looked across at me. 'That makes sense, the other person must have been one of the Clare Fellows.' He breathed in deeply and fastened his eyes on the wall above my head. 'I'd better get the worst part over with. I suppose it was rather off to go on watching, but I didn't think there'd be much harm in it. But then David and this other fellow started, you know . . .'

'Kissing?' I ventured.

'That's all I stayed to see. I was disgusted, appalled really. David was my best friend and I just couldn't think of him doing that sort of thing.'

'So, if David had lived you would have thrown him over?'

'In the circumstances.'

'Why?'

'Well, you know.'

'I don't know, Hippo, really I don't.'

He eyed me suspiciously.

'No,' I laughed a little. 'Some homosexuals do have heterosexual cousins. And besides my wife wouldn't stand for it. But the truth is, Hippo, that you know from first-hand experience that at least one queer was a very nice young man. Something to think about back on the farm.'

It was about nine; and as we waited for the bill I asked Hippo what he was going to tell the police. 'I'm certainly not going to tell them about the episode in the garden. I mean, I owe him at least that.' I did not try to dissuade him. If Fanshaw ever needed the information, he could get it from me.

We walked upstairs and I was rather surprised to see Peter Tredwell sitting with an elegant woman whom I recognized as Hermione Porter, another Fellow of Clare. He had a cigarette hanging off his lower lip, after the manner of a charlady or a French film star, and he was holding a large glass of what looked like unadulterated Campari. He looked oddly ill at ease, and it struck me that Tredwell wasn't the sort to lounge about drinking cocktails. Something – something that had happened since we last met – had obviously upset him a good deal. As we approached, he coughed tipsily and waved the smoke from the cigarette away from his eyes with his left hand while stubbing it out clumsily with his right. Tredwell did not look like an habitual smoker.

I introduced the two of them to Hippo, who gave Tredwell what can only be described as a surly look.

'Well, Sir Patrick,' said Tredwell who, as was now obvious, was more than a little drunk, 'tonight it is I who am dining a lady and you who are entertaining a Ganymede. Ah well, you will find my cause for celebration in a little note that I have placed for you in the Memorial Court lodge. Perhaps,' he added with a hint of mock flirtatiousness, 'my note will bring you to my room later?'

'Peter, I know you're very upset, but you're embarrassing Dr Porter, my guest and me. Of course, I'll read your note. And I'll phone through to your rooms round about midnight; I have something I need to discuss with you, too.'

Peter acknowledged my remark with a generous wave of his

hand, and I was turning to go when Hermione Porter spoke in a cool voice. 'Sir Patrick, I suppose it may have occurred to you that you were patronizing Dr Tredwell dreadfully. That is bad enough. Matters are hardly improved by your patronizing me as well. Peter is upset; I am his friend; I am comforting him. And since, unlike you, I am not homophobic, what I feel is not embarrassment but sympathy.'

*Touché*, I thought. You patronize my chum, I'll patronize you.

I succeeded in disentangling myself from the two young Clare dons, and took Hippo out into the street. Throughout our exchange he had stood there looking hostile and shooting at Peter Tredwell glances of the purest bile.

'So sorry to put you through that,' I said jovially. 'Misunderstanding.'

'That', said Hippo, 'was the man in the garden. I'm sure of it. That man seduced David.'

# 10

When Hippo left me in the Market Place, I had a little less than an hour to kill before the meeting with the Society: time to collect Peter Tredwell's note and phone Virginia. I made my way across the river by the route that Hippo and David had used the night before because I wanted to look through the bushes into the Fellows' Garden and see how much I could see.

It was still a good deal lighter than it would have been just after midnight two nights earlier and as I peered through the bushes I could see one of the apple trees and the bench by the pond. There was no doubt about it. If Peter and David had been together there that night, anyone who walked down the pathway could have seen them.

I reached the porter's lodge, collected the note and returned to my room. As I stepped in, my foot caught a small piece of folded paper, sellotaped together and addressed to 'Patrick Scott'. This was obviously an evening for notes. I turned on the light and settled down on the bed to read my two messages.

The untidy note on the floor was from Miss Ritter. *Mr Scott,* it said,

> *Michael Mallory-Browne heard someone talking to David after midnight on Wednesday. He says he must have left about one in the morning. Hope this helps.*
>
> *Jo Ritter (U3)*

'Tredwell,' I thought. Things didn't look good for young Dr Tredwell. As I opened his blue envelope I wondered what new lies he had concocted.

But all there was in the envelope was a folded sheet. I opened it. It was a xerox copy of a page from *Private Eye,* dated the day before. Tredwell had circled a passage from a section entitled 'University News'. *Fellows of Clare College, Cambridge,* it began,

> *one of the oldest foundations in our second oldest university, will no doubt be interested to hear of the nocturnal activities of one of their number. They will be especially interested because these activities involve a tutorial pupil of the learned Peter Tredwell, Doctor of Philosophy – and the pupil is none less than the young nobleman Viscount Glen Tannock, scion of the house of Ivor. It seems that the Fellows' Gardens of the college has become their nightly trysting place. Dr Tredwell, whose lectures this term included a series on the foundations of probability, no doubt hoped that the sight of an older and a younger man earnestly discussing Uganda by the college pond would strike passers-by on their way up to Trinity Lane as too improbable to be believed. We wonder whether the good Lady Clare, the college's foundress, had any especial fondness for the Socratic method. Our university correspondent has written to suggest that Dr Tredwell should announce a lecture course on* The Symposium *this autumn. We feel certain that many of the university's large band of 'sad' dons would attend.*

It is very difficult not to sympathize with anyone whose name appears in *Private Eye,* and in spite of the information that Joanna Ritter had just provided, I felt a twinge of regret. This was a particularly nasty piece of work.

The conduct of the *Eye* in its search for the sort of scabrous rubbish that even the *News of the World* might draw the line at, is a matter on which I have very strong views. It has not always seemed congenial to me that my own chambers has at least one senior partner who spends much of his time, and, I regret to say, makes too much of his money, defending the rag from the numerous libel actions brought against it by outraged citizens whose private lives they had hoped would not be eyed.

I read the piece again. 'Earnestly discussing Uganda' was, of course, the standard *Private Eye* formula for what policemen are disposed to call 'having relations'. (Virginia has developed this theme – 'He's not an orphan when she's around' in her private lingo means, of course, that 'he has relations when . . .'). Poor Tredwell. The piece had been published the very day David's body was discovered. It could hardly have been less conveniently timed. But that meant that he and David had already met in the moonlight at least a few days, and perhaps even weeks, before. *Private Eye* is hardly a news magazine: its more salacious gossip often appears long after the event. That made at least two problems for the stories I had heard.

One, of course, was what Hippo had told me. According to Hippo, Tredwell had lied about having seen David on the night he died. In the circumstances that was understandable. But the other was why David had had chosen to seek James Hogg's advice on the ethics of an affair with Tredwell after he had already begun it. Perhaps David felt that he had put Tredwell at too great a risk – a suspicion the odious *Private Eye* story all too swiftly confirmed. If he thought *that*, he might have wanted to keep the fact that they were already lovers even from someone as trustworthy as James, while still talking out with him the risks of what he had already begun. And if he really was worried about Tredwell's position, might he not, in one of the heroic gestures of courtly love, have decided to end their relationship?

David could have gone to the garden to tell Tredwell that he would not go on. And if that was true, then the voice in David's rooms could have been Tredwell's . . . and Tredwell would have had the oldest motive in the world for murder.

As he himself had said, *'Cherchez l'homme.'*

*

I sat for a few minutes to digest all that I had learned so that I could summarize it briefly in a telephone conversation with Virginia. I took out a notepad from my suitcase and made a few jottings. I could imagine how the scenario might have run.

David and Tredwell start an affair. But David – who always did look out for the other chap – decides that it is threatening Tredwell's position in the college and comes that evening to their normal meeting place to tell him so. He lets himself into the avenue with the key Tredwell had given him and walks down the avenue to the pond. He and Tredwell embrace as usual and Hippo sees them at it. Shocked by the sudden discovery, Hippo rushes off, assuming that they will soon be *in flagrante delicto*. But David tells Tredwell it has to stop and they go back to his rooms to discuss the matter. Their conversation is heard by Mallory-Browne. Tredwell, distressed beyond endurance by his loss, persuades David to make cocoa for both of them and somehow slips in some powdered penicillin.

I imagined Peter Tredwell persuading David to prepare for bed – 'We can't talk now, David, you have exams tomorrow; put on your pyjamas, I'll make you a cup of cocoa.' I saw him unfolding a piece of paper in the gyp room while David undressed; pouring the white powder into the cup; offering David the murderous brew with the soft smile of murder. Then, aware perhaps of the horrifying speed of the allergic reaction and able to kill David but not to watch him die, he would have hurriedly made a rendezvous for the next day, and left.

If there was a gap in this story, it would have to be why Tredwell had the penicillin with him. But if he had been expecting David's ultimatum – perhaps on the basis of the conversation that really occurred on Tuesday – he might have come prepared. That, of course, would establish premeditation. It was, therefore, a serious issue. Until I was sure about this last matter, I should have to keep any suspicions to myself. Or rather to myself and to Virginia.

There was one other problem with the story – and that was that I couldn't quite bring myself to believe it. Something about it wasn't quite right. Perhaps, I thought, I would be able to find my way through the maze if I talked it all out with Virginia.

*

It is often the case that, as an investigation comes to an end, new pieces arrive and fall into place with increasing speed. So I wasn't much surprised when, just as I was about to pick up the phone to ask the porter to call Virginia, it rang and the porter told me that Inspector Fanshaw was on the line. If I had made progress, so probably had he.

'Sir Patrick?'

'Yes. Good evening, Inspector Fanshaw.'

'I'm afraid that I've got some more rather unfortunate news.'

I regret to say that I did a mental catalogue of my Cambridge friends and wondered whether it wouldn't be safer to leave town.

'All right, Inspector. Who is it?'

'Who?' he said in a puzzled tone. 'Charles Phipps, sir, of course.'

It didn't take him a moment to interpret my sigh of relief. 'Oh, I see, sir. Yes. I shouldn't have put it like that of course. No, it's Dr Phipps's cause of death. We were right about the chemicals. But I don't think it was an accident. You see, we found a cup of Coca Cola on the bench in his lab. And it was full of the stuff. Somebody must have mixed the concoction and left it for him, or given it him, to drink. The boffins say that even if he detected the taste he would probably have taken in enough to kill him with the first sip, even if he spat it out. It would have been absorbed through the mouth. I'm afraid what we've got here is a murder. I don't think he'd have poured four or five hundred quid's worth of chemicals into a cup of Coke by accident.

'As I see it,' Fanshaw went on, 'someone has to have visited him between ten thirty and eleven and poisoned him. We've checked on the cleaning woman and she swears there wasn't any Coke around in the lab when Dr Phipps came in in the morning. So: it has to be someone he knows comes in, knows that he likes the Coke, pours him a cup and somehow slips some of his own poisons into it when he's not looking.'

As he spoke, my mind raced. I had been right all along. There could be no doubt now that someone killed Charlie. But why? Could he have seen Tredwell coming back from David's rooms on one of his midnight rambles along the Backs? If so, why did Tredwell wait a whole day to kill him?

It dawned on me that Tredwell probably knew from David who the Apostles were. Surely David would have told his lover. And if David had told him about the Apostles, why shouldn't he have told him also that Charlie worked with dangerous chemicals? That, after all, was what had stuck in most people's minds after Charlie's last paper. In this scenario, Tredwell would have to have gone straight from coffee with me to Charlie's labs and killed him.

I recalled that Tredwell had asked me to come and see him later that night. Perhaps it was a good thing I had only said I would phone. I should have to be very careful. After all, if any of these speculations were right, Tredwell's next victim might well have to be me.

But of any of this there was no guarantee. To begin with, there was the puzzle about why Tredwell would have been carrying penicillin around in his pocket. And then there was the emotional implausibility of it all: crimes of passion are usually passionate crimes. However convinced I might be, however much I disliked him, I couldn't very well accuse a man of a pair of murders without some more compelling evidence. I would have to wait at least until *I* was sure. Still, I thought to myself, you had better go carefully, Patrick, old boy.

When Fanshaw finished, I had decided firmly to tell him nothing for the nonce. 'Do you think there could be some connection with David's murder, Inspector?'

'It's possible. Similar MO. Two poisonings. Both of them involving some knowledge of the victim – that should help narrow it down. I mean, not everybody knew that Lord Glen Tannock had a penicillin allergy and not everyone knew that Dr Phipps worked with 'orrible poisons.'

'Well, Inspector, perhaps we could meet tomorrow morning to compare notes?'

'How about ten in the Fellows' combination room?'

'That will be fine.' Virginia would not be arriving until eleven at the earliest. 'And now, I must rush. I have agreed to meet with Dr Penhaligon and some friends again tonight for an after-dinner drink.'

'Going to have a bit of a *conversazione*, are you?' Not such a bad chap, Fanshaw.

It was now only a few minutes before ten and I didn't have time to phone Virginia. I hurried out into the Queen's Road.

# 11

As I made my way along the path towards the back entrance to King's I turned and looked back at the little lane that leads up to Thirkill Court. Anyone coming out of it would be plainly visible from a good stretch of the Backs, so long as there was enough light: as much as the street lights on Queen's Road and the moon together gave off this evening. I stopped for a moment and watched as an undergraduate couple walked across the road from the Old Court into the shadows. They were clearly visible until just a few seconds before they reached the entrance.

I realized that in constructing the picture of David's death I had imagined for myself on Thursday evening before dinner, the picture that I must now distrust, I had assumed that there was moonlight. I tried to recall if anybody had mentioned the light. Hugh? Oliver? No. None of the people who had gathered that evening had said anything about the moon.

And then I remembered that Hippo had said that the figure in the garden had been standing in the moonlight with his back to him. I had better check with the others, but for the moment it seemed that there was indeed a moon. It was a good deal later than I had intended when I entered Hugh's rooms.

Vera Oblomov and James Hogg were standing with their backs to the window that looked into the court, each holding a glass of wine. Godfrey Stanley was nearest to me, short and extremely distinguished; and wearing, after the manner of many of the older dons, the gown he had worn to dinner.

Now in his mid-sixties, Godfrey had the look of a man used to the exercise of power. It was a look he had done a great deal to earn . . . and, if the truth be told, to develop. Godfrey's moderate height and stocky build were not obviously the materials of a distinguished appearance. His aquiline nose – which would have done honour to a Roman senator – might have seemed merely out of place, a single aristocratic touch in a commonplace appearance. But Godfrey's moustache, the cut of his hair and his clothing, his gestures, all had been crafted to achieve a particular effect: the impression that he was born to authority. It was, to put it mildly, a misleading impression.

Godfrey had, in fact, been born into a lower middle-class family in Manchester. It was a respectable family, with a deep reverence for education and self-improvement, but his background hardly destined him for greatness. Godfrey had once told me that his father did clerical work of some kind. It was the most I had ever heard him say about his background.

Yet he had early shown an extraordinary mathematical gift. When he came to Cambridge, he had moved, like other grammar-school scholars, from the pedestrian world of northern semi-poverty into the glamorous *demi-monde* of King's in the late twenties; but he came with a reputation as someone who might turn out to be the cleverest mathematician of his generation. He had soon been befriended by the legendary Gregory Ransome – they had been respectively Junior and Senior Wranglers, winners, between them, of the top mathematics honours of their year.

Godfrey and Ransome had starkly contrasting personalities. While Godfrey quickly adopted a series of notorious affectations, Ransome was famous in the Society's mythology as a person completely without pretension, totally unconcerned, in a way that was then still rather unusual, with distinctions of class. His background was quite different from Godfrey's. He came from the heart of the upper middle class, from a public service family that had inherited a Whiggish notion of *noblesse oblige*: his father became Principal Secretary at the Treasury and Head of the Home Civil Service.

Ransome had introduced Godfrey Stanley to the Society – and to the life of his class. And, over the years, Godfrey's real background had quietly disappeared. He affected now the style of a particular breed of old-world don; indeed, rather than aping Ransome's manner, he had translated himself into an early twentieth-century aristocrat.

By taking advantage of the connections his position as a Fellow of Trinity afforded, he had gradually collected a string of public roles. After a few years managing the college's investments in the fifties, he had acquired various directorships; and the careful management of his own income had left him extremely well off. He was a famous connoisseur of eighteenth-century Dutch painting, a collector of Meissen, the possessor of a widely admired cellar. He was on the Board of the Royal Opera and the Public Schools Commission; he was a Trustee of the National Art Fund.

In short, he had settled into the life of an ersatz High Tory; he sat as a lay member of Synod; delivered sermons on 'Christian Management' at St Paul's Cathedral; and generally behaved in a way calculated to irritate the younger left-wing dons in his college.

But the fact was that he was jolly hard to dislike. When I first described him to Virginia, after he had summoned me to work with him at Bletchley during the War, she had said, 'Sounds awfully stuffy to me.' But when she finally met him, she turned on me the moment we left the dinner-party and said crossly, 'You didn't tell me he was such a charmer.'

Godfrey had married his wife, Catharine, rather late in life; and, as befitted his self-conception, she was the daughter of an Earl. I had never really got to know her, however; for a few years after he married her, in the early sixties, Lady Catharine Stanley had died in a riding accident. Godfrey, people said, had never quite recovered from the blow.

He sold their house in Herschel Road and moved into college, retiring each weekend to their country house in Suffolk – often with a distinguished house-party of people from the City, and a judicious sprinkling of famous actresses and rather less well-known peers. He ceased the constant barrage of Senate *non-placets* – as motions disapproving a proposal from the council are called – with which he had resisted every important change in the university since the War and seemed to have given up fighting the unrelenting tide of 'socialist barbarities'. He continued to be amusing and grand, but the spark had somehow gone out of him.

Yet despite the tragedy of Catharine's death, despite the sadness that seemed now always to accompany him, Godfrey had a real generosity of spirit underneath his affectations. I had watched him from time to time gently urging on one of his protégés; often a bright working-class boy, someone thrown, like himself, by the accident of genius into a social world for which he was ill prepared. In his dealings with these young men – or with Mrs Porteous, his over-protective housekeeper – Godfrey displayed an endearing touch of what the Good Book calls 'loving-kindness'.

And all the time, over all those years, he quietly went about his mathematics. He never did anything that achieved the importance of his earliest work in topology. But then, as Godfrey had observed at many a meeting, 'mathematical achievement is, like beauty, a thing of youth.' I wondered how much he cared that his intellectual reputation stood on the rather flimsy foundations of a couple of papers published nearly forty years ago.

When I greeted him it was with genuine warmth.

'Godfrey, how marvellous to see you,' I said. 'You *do* look well.'

'That, my dear Patrick, is the sort of fib that people of our age ought to give up. But it *is* marvellous. You must come and stay for the weekend again, soon.' He coughed a little. 'A little cold on the chest, I fear. Kept me home on Wednesday night.' He held a brandy snifter, swirling the brandy occasionally as he talked. Now he took a sip. 'But Patrick, my dear boy, these are not the happiest circumstances in which to meet.'

The only person in the room I did not know now thrust a firm hand in my direction and announced himself: 'Dale Bishop Junior,' he said. 'Good to know you, sir.' An American, as one might expect from both name and manner.

Hugh took it upon himself to explain Mr Bishop. 'This, Patrick, is our latest recruit. Charlie's paper was actually his first meeting and he was busy in London on Wednesday so he missed Vera's magnificent performance.'

'And what do you do, Mr Bishop?'

'Well, sir,' be began, turning his wine glass nervously by its stem, 'I'm a graduate student in English. I guess I do literary history. The natural sublime . . . eighteenth century . . . the influence of Boileau's translation of Longinus.'

I didn't have much of a notion of what he was talking about either. But I nodded a few times and mumbled, 'Ah, Longinus.'

'My dear Patrick, it's no use pretending you have the faintest idea why Longinus matters to eighteenth-century aesthetics.' Hugh was not one to miss an opportunity to tease me gently with a display of erudition. 'The boy has simply shattered settled opinion on the eighteenth-century sublime and aesthetic theories quite generally. He has got us all re-reading Burke and Baillie, rewriting the origins of romanticism. It's very tiring having to keep up with the changes in the intellectual landscape that Dale has forced on us.' He paused, glancing about to see that we were all settled comfortably. 'Well, now that we all know who we are – I explained you to Dale earlier, Patrick – we should get down to business. What do we know?'

I wanted them to help me work through the evidence. The best way to do that was to tell them as quickly as possible the things I was sure of and see if we could fill in the blanks.

'Let's start with David. We all know that somebody spiked his cocoa with penicillin and that he drank it and died sometime between midnight and two in the morning. All I've managed to find out is some of what he did between the end of the meeting of the Society and drinking that cocoa. Here's what we have. David left here at about eleven on Wednesday night with Oliver Hetherington, who'll be along later . . . By the way, I take it he was his normal self when he left?'

'Absolutely. A little tired, perhaps; slightly less ruddy than his usual healthy colouring. But that was all,' Hugh said.

'I don't think we should draw any conclusions from his colouring,' Vera said staunchly. 'He often looked slightly washed out; I'm afraid he sometimes burned his candle at both ends. When he left the meeting he seemed quite cheerful to me.'

'I see. Well, he'd agreed to meet his friend, Jeremy Buckingham, outside Corpus at eleven. David was going to give him a cheque he had promised, lend him some money. Because he found the business embarrassing, Buckingham was hovering in the shadows opposite Corpus to avoid the wrath of Warren . . .' As I glanced around the others I noticed that Dale Bishop was taking notes. 'Buckingham didn't want to approach David, so he stayed hidden. Warren had some sort of row with Oliver and David – we'll have to find out about that later, but it means, of course, that we can't go on shielding Oliver . . . . Fanshaw will find out soon.'

'Who's Fanshaw?' Dale asked.

'The police Inspector investigating the death . . . deaths.

Anyway, David and Oliver walk along KP, followed at a judicious distance by Hippo. They say good-night – by now it's probably a quarter to midnight – and at this point Hippo approaches and he and David walk back to Clare.'

'What route?' said Vera.

'Between Trinity Hall and Trinity down past the Clare Fellows' Garden. They go on to David's room, the cheque is signed and handed over and they come back down. Hippo . . . I'm sorry, that's Buckingham's nickname . . . walks back the way they came but stops to look into the garden because he sees a man standing by the pool.'

'Who was that?' Vera asked.

'I'm coming to that. Let's just say that at the time he doesn't recognize him. He isn't there long before David arrives, too. His tutor had given him a key to the avenue, so he hasn't had to climb the gate.' I didn't know how to put the next point tactfully, so I hummed and hawed for a moment over my notes.

Hugh came to the rescue. 'At this point, we have slipped into a novel by Mistress Barbara Cartland. The man takes David in his strong passionate grasp, that sort of thing.'

I smiled at Hugh. 'Thank you . . . yes, that's right.'

Godfrey and Dale both looked mildly surprised and Godfrey observed, 'Quite the coy boy, our David. I shouldn't have guessed that he was queer . . . begging your pardon, Hugh.'

'After twenty-odd years, I am used to your nasty verbal tics.' Godfrey and Hugh smiled pleasantly at each other, knowing that neither of them meant any harm by it. 'But I think you will find that James would rather you said that David was gay.'

James blushed and looked uncomfortable and I had the distinct sense that Dale Bishop was about to make a dash for the door. I gather some of our transatlantic cousins are less relaxed about these things.

'When you chaps have finished,' I continued, 'I shall be able to get to the end of this. Though, actually, those are almost all the facts I'm certain of about David. I should only add that a friend of David's heard him talking to someone in his rooms after midnight. So we know that David returned from the garden.' I paused for a moment and looked over the notes again. 'Oh' – I thought I might as well save the best bit for last – 'Hippo Buckingham identified David's tutor as the man in the garden when he and I bumped into Peter Tredwell this evening. Tredwell, by the way, has denied having seen David at all that evening . . .'

'Do you believe him?' Godfrey asked.

'I'm afraid not. He has already told me a sufficient number of lies about various other matters. But I don't have any evidence that he went back to David's rooms.'

'He seems the most likely candidate, though, doesn't he?' Godfrey spoke again. 'On the other hand, we all met in David's rooms last week. And we all know that anyone could have entered the college through the basement and walked past the bicycles up to the top floor. It's all circumstantial. I'm sure that a competent barrister, let alone one as able as your good self, Patrick, could get him off. For one thing, he hasn't a motive. Unless, like Brother Penhaligon's hero, Mr Wilde, we believe that "each man kills the thing he loves", which would make some of us' – he looked again at Hugh – 'mass murderers.'

'What about the penicillin?' James asked quietly from the floor.

'So far we have no evidence that anybody had easy access to the stuff; so that's not going to help. Come to that, it wouldn't have been *difficult* for anyone to get their hands on some,' I added.

'Couldn't Jeremy Buckingham have doubled back and done it?' It was James again.

'It's consistent with the evidence, I suppose. But we don't have any reason to think that he had any penicillin either.' Still, James was right. None of us had thought it through properly.

It was time to try.

We sat in silence for a while and the clock struck a quarter to eleven. Once more Godfrey seemed to have the clearest grasp.

'There are two problems in supposing that Mr Buckingham is our murderer. First, if he had been intending to double back, why did he set off towards the centre of town? Why not wait on the Backs? Why not give David the cocoa while getting the cheque?'

'Because he couldn't get David to drink the cocoa then, since David was rushing to his appointment with Tredwell, I suppose.' Vera was speaking slowly, carefully, as if thinking out loud.

'Good.' That was Godfrey. 'Second problem. He has no motive either.'

We were stuck.

Dale Bishop pondered his notes for a while and then suggested that, since motive seemed to be the problem, we might usefully ask ourselves what anyone might have to gain from David's death.

'For example. The tutor. Why would he kill Dave, if they were an item? Wouldn't it be more likely that Dave was doing something that threatened somebody? Might even be somebody with nothing to do with the university.'

'Why would David be a threat to anyone?' Vera asked.

'Because he knew something that somebody didn't want let out.' Godfrey spoke in the tone of one remarking something too obvious to merit even the slightest degree of doubt.

James murmured, 'Of course,' in the tone of one who has heard something that is not obvious at all.

'What David knew.' Hugh was not smiling. 'What David knew.'

'We have neglected something entirely. Whoever killed David knew about the penicillin allergy. We have also neglected the possibility – the probability, in fact – that David's killer killed Charlie. And if he – or she – did, then he or she knew that Charlie worked with dangerous chemicals. Did Buckingham or Tredwell know these things?' Vera asked me this question in the tone of a teacher addressing a dim student.

'Buckingham knew about the penicillin. But I don't think he knew anything about Charlie . . . though, frankly, I didn't think to ask.'

'But he must have known. He was reading natural sciences; and he did physiology. He must have been to Charlie's lectures.' James Hogg looked puzzled as he spoke. 'I only met Hippo a few times with David at the Pitt. But he didn't seem to me the kind of person . . .'

'Does Tredwell? Does anyone seem that kind of person?' Godfrey sounded rather severe as he addressed the boy. I was about to offer James some kind of solace, but he looked unperturbed; and I reflected that he would have been used to Godfrey's manner in discussions at the Society. For Godfrey an Apostle was an Apostle. No holds were barred; and despite his stuffy image in the 'phenomenal' world, he would never have been worried by an undergraduate Brother who addressed him in the same tone. An Apostle was an Apostle; Godfrey might have been an aristocrat out there in the Outer Darkness, but here, in Hugh's rooms, was a democracy of the elect. It pleased me that young James Hogg had grasped this so immediately.

'In my experience, James,' I said, 'almost anyone can be that kind of person if circumstances conspire to make murder seem to be a way out.'

Godfrey once more took control. 'We know, then, that Mr Buckingham had the opportunity and the knowledge. We cannot establish a motive. But,' he looked at Vera, 'if the good lady will permit me, I should like to return to the line of thought from which she led us. David Glen Tannock was a very clever young man. He was, as I saw in his work on our late and much-lamented Brother Ransome, a careful scholar, a servant of Clio.

'As you know, I had been helping David with his work, disentangling Gregory's *Nachlass*. I myself went through all the papers after he died, just before the War. It was a way of repaying him his many kindnesses to me. And I needed to occupy myself with something after the sudden, tragic loss. But there was nothing of mathematical interest in the papers and I suggested to Margery Ransome,' he directed the explanation at the younger members, 'his widow, that they could be destroyed. She kept them, quite rightly, for her own sentimental reasons and David had persuaded Margery to let him go through them again. Naturally, my mathematical judgement was confirmed. The only unpublished mathematical material he found was the work that I had rightly judged to be of no value. Gregory had published his best work, the paper we had worked on together on a conjecture of Fréchet's, and his beginnings at the work that led to my own discovery of the theorem that bears our name. At the same time, David had discovered many fascinating titbits about Gregory's life. But nothing, nothing at least that he had mentioned to me, was in the least bit troubling. And, in any case, we can hardly imagine Margery Ransome . . . who has arthritis and is, alas, not so young as she was . . . we can hardly imagine her trotting down the Queen's Road to Clare and murdering the dear boy.'

Godfrey shook his head. 'I wonder, Hugh, if I might have a

little water.' Hugh disappeared out to the gyp room and Godfrey gave a quite audible sigh. 'I shall miss my discussions of those days with David. I had been expecting him to telephone and arrange to see me again this week, once his examinations were over. Ah well.'

'What could he have found in those papers that would provide a motive for murder?' Vera said. 'It could hardly be a mathematical theorem.'

'Even if David had found something of mathematical interest, I don't suppose he'd have recognized it,' James said carefully. He had obviously been pondering Godfrey's remarks. 'I tried to explain some fairly straightforward group-theoretic ideas to him once and he just didn't seem to get the hang of it. If he'd found anything that looked like a piece of maths he'd have asked one of us about it. Probably you, Godfrey . . . or Vera; he certainly never mentioned anything of the sort to me.'

Godfrey nodded in agreement. 'I am sure you are right, James; and, as I say, he mentioned nothing to me either.'

'Nor to me,' Vera said. 'But it's most unlikely that the secret he uncovered has anything to do with mathematics anyway. Surely it is much more likely that it had to do with . . .' She paused a moment for thought. 'Well, for example, some sort of scandal.'

'Quite right, Vera. But I think you are being a little unkind about David's mathematical aptitude, James,' Godfrey continued. 'It is true that he wasn't any sort of mathematician; but you have rather high standards, James. You know, Patrick,' he said, turning to me, 'James here had a little paper on monster groups accepted by a quite reputable journal, the other day. In fact, frankly, as I've told him, he is wasting his time in economics; you should do the thing properly and take the maths Tripos. The only interesting mathematical economics has not the slightest economic interest; and the mathematics that economists actually use is quite trivial.'

Hugh returned with a glass of water, interrupting Godfrey's celebration of his own discipline. James smiled and declined with a shake of his head to take up the implicit challenge to defend his choice. It was plainly a disagreement they had had before.

Hugh looked around the room. 'Would anybody else like

something more sustaining to drink? Oh dear, Patrick, I never gave you anything. What shall it be?'

'To tell you the truth, I hadn't noticed, Hugh. But a little of the claret that Vera and James and . . . Dale are drinking would do the trick.' Dale smiled; he evidently appreciated my effort to remember his name.

'You know,' Dale said, 'if Dave was digging through the papers in the Ark for stuff to do with the thirties, then there could have been something else that he found. I mean, something to do with the spying business, say. Couldn't that be it?'

'It's a possibility,' I said. 'But who would have known that he was doing this work?'

'Any of us; Oliver, of course, Margery Ransome and anyone she mentioned it to. Hugo McAlister, since it came up in passing at last week's meeting . . . and anyone any of us or David mentioned it to – including Tredwell – as well.' Hugh stopped. 'That's enough people to be getting on with.'

There was a footstep on the stair, and we all turned towards the door. 'My God,' Hugh said, 'it takes a pretty engrossing conversation to allow one to forget Oliver for over an hour.' He rushed to the door and opened it – and there was Inspector Fanshaw.

Naturally, we all stood up.

# 12

'Good evening, sir,' Fanshaw addressed Hugh when the latter opened the door. 'I wonder if I could come in and have a word?'

'Of course, dear chap, do come in. I shan't insist on a search warrant.'

Fanshaw wisely ignored Hugh's remark and spoke next to me. 'I'm very sorry to trouble you, Sir Patrick.'

'Not at all, Inspector Fanshaw. Let me introduce you. Let me see, you know our host, Dr Penhaligon, of course. And I believe you have talked to Dr Oblomov and Mr Hogg.' Fanshaw nodded at each of them courteously. 'This is Professor Stanley; and that is Mr Bishop.'

Bishop strode across and wrung the Inspector's hand. 'Dale Bishop Junior, sir. Good to meet you.' Fanshaw withdrew his hand slowly, eyeing Bishop with an appraising glance.

'Professor Stanley and Mr Bishop are members of the Society who were not present on Wednesday night; but, of course, they knew Lord Glen Tannock and Dr Phipps and they are naturally concerned to do all in their power to help find the murderer,' I said.

'Before we go on,' Vera interrupted, 'we should surely tell the Inspector that we have discovered that we all forgot to mention one person who was at the meeting on Wednesday, who is not here.'

'And who might that be, madam?'

'Sir Oliver Hetherington.' It was a wise move on Vera's part. I thanked her inwardly for it.

'Would that be a Cambridge person, madam?'

'No, he is a member of our club' (Godfrey winced) 'who was visiting for a few days. He works at the Foreign Office.'

'Might I ask where he is now?'

'Dining with Sir Richard and Lady Darwin at Trinity. He should be along soon. As a matter of fact, we thought you were he.' Vera had obviously been unhappy about keeping Oliver's presence from the police. Now she relaxed a little, honour satisfied, and sat back down on the window seat.

'Perhaps we should all settle down,' said Hugh, disappearing into an inner room and returning with an upright chair from his study. 'There we are, Inspector. We are all ears.'

'It's a rather delicate matter, sir. But I thought that since you gentlemen . . . and Dr Oblomov . . . were friendly with Lord Glen Tannock, you might be able to answer a question for me.'

'Yes.' Godfrey had obviously decided that he was to be our spokesman. Given the number of things I did not want to tell Inspector Fanshaw, that suited me very well.

'Well, the fact is, sir, that an article in a certain publication has been drawn to our attention. The article in question implies that Lord Glen Tannock was . . .' Fanshaw had obviously been dreading the moment.

'Don't distress yourself, Inspector,' Godfrey said with a genial condescension. 'We have been having the same difficulty. I myself used the word "queer" earlier; Dr Penhaligon informs me that the most up-to-date usage is "gay". But since we are scholars, perhaps we should settle on the word "homosexual".'

It seemed to be my turn to speak. I was sorting through the issues in my mind, trying to decide how best to approach the question, when James Hogg spoke up: 'That's right.'

'Is your evidence of a direct character?' The stilted question, with its police-court overtones, elicited from Hugh a guffaw.

'Good Lord, no. James and David didn't sleep together. But David told James; and, since I have James's confidence, *he* then told me.'

'Well, the fact is, sir, that it has been suggested that he was having relations with' – Fanshaw paused as if to prepare us for a shattering revelation – 'a Fellow of his college.'

'Dr Tredwell, his tutor,' I said. 'Yes, I think that may be right.' The Inspector raised his eyebrows in my direction. 'My evidence is not of a direct character either, Inspector. But I had dinner tonight with David's friend, Jeremy Buckingham. I believe you are to see him tomorrow. And he reported having seen Dr Tredwell and Lord Glen Tannock embrace.'

'Did he tell the paper?'

'*Private Eye*? No. That story was published yesterday morning; it must have gone to press before Mr Buckingham saw the two of them together.'

'Well, when was that, sir?'

'On Wednesday at about midnight.' The Inspector mimed a sense of betrayal. 'I know, Inspector. I was intending to telephone you when I left here with the information. I wanted to confirm as much as I could before I talked to you. And that turned out to be a good thing. Because, so far as we have been able to determine, there is no evidence at all that Dr Tredwell had a motive for murder.'

Fanshaw said nothing. 'Well . . . we've got grounds for arrest,' he said uncertainly.,

I thought for a moment. I still believed I could do better if I could talk to Tredwell before Fanshaw did. I wondered if I could persuade him. 'I wonder, Inspector, if I could have a word with you privately?'

*

We stepped outside Hugh's rooms and I closed both the inner and the outer doors. 'Inspector,' I began. 'You suggested earlier that David's murder and Charlie's might be connected. But we have nothing at all to connect Dr Tredwell with Dr Phipps. And I think I may have a chance of getting to the bottom of the matter.'

I explained my earlier meeting with Tredwell and the envelope with the xerox copy of the *Private Eye* article. 'I wondered how you knew about that,' he said.

'Tredwell is expecting me to phone him when I get back. I may be able to get him to talk. If you arrest him now, he'll say nothing and be out on bail by midday tomorrow. And we simply don't have the evidence to convict him. Why not give it a few more hours? He's hardly going to run off. And you can put a man to watch him; I agree we want to make sure that no one is in any danger tonight.'

As I awaited his response, we heard footsteps on the cobbles at the bottom of the staircase. A moment later, Oliver's head appeared. 'Sorry I'm so late,' he said briskly. 'But I've got some fascinating information.' Obviously, he couldn't see Fanshaw, who was standing in the shadowy doorway of the darkened gyp room.

'Oliver, glad you came. This is Inspector Fanshaw.'

He bounded up the steps towards us and shook Fanshaw's hand. 'Oliver Hetherington, Inspector. How do you do?'

'I was trying to persuade the Inspector not to arrest Peter Tredwell for David's murder tonight.'

'Who's Peter Tredwell?'

'David's tutor.'

'Why on earth should he have done it?' Oliver asked.

'It's a long story,' I said.

'Well it's a jolly good thing you *didn't* arrest him.'

'Why?' Fanshaw and I chimed in together.

'That's my fascinating titbit. Is Vera Oblomov in there?'

'Yes, why?'

'Well. Inspector, what I'm about to say is classified . . . top secret. I had Sir Patrick cleared to hear it; but you're governed by the Official Secrets Act anyway, and I've asked them to send a courier up tomorrow to inform the Chief Constable. And a chap called Peterson from Special Branch will be arriving sometime in the next few hours to help you, Inspector.

'You see, Patrick, there was one thing I didn't tell you about my conversation with David. I said we'd discussed Charlie's doings, but I didn't tell you why. I didn't know it would be relevant and, as I say, I had to get it cleared.'

Oliver leaned towards us and talked in a low whisper. 'You remember, Patrick, that I told you that David's father, Charlie . . . that's the Earl of Ivor, Inspector . . . Charlie and I had been involved in some hush-hush operations behind the Iron Curtain after the War?'

'Yes,' I said softly. 'We all knew that he'd been doing something of the kind – a lot of it came out when Philby did his bunk . . . Lord Ivor was a member of the Society when he was a younger man, Inspector. Naturally, when the spy-revelations came out, all of us fell under suspicion for a period.'

'Well, when Hugh mentioned Vera Oblomov on Tuesday, as he was going through the names of the people who'd be at the meeting, her name rang a vague bell. I couldn't think what it was until just after dinner . . . on Wednesday. And then I put through a call to London . . . that was why I arrived so late for the meeting. I'd brought a scrambler with me, because, since I'm about to go to Moscow, there are various bits of business that I have to attend to that are best kept from the general ear. Well, it turned out I was right. You remember I said that I'd told David that Charlie had been very brave. The details don't matter much. But there was a bit of a fiasco on the Sino-Soviet border and in the mess Charlie ended up having to kill a Russian soldier. It was all very embarrassing, but for various reasons the Russians were as keen to keep it quiet as we were. I was the case officer at this end and so I reviewed all the files, when we got Charlie back.'

Oliver paused, swallowed and continued in his hoarse whisper. 'The Russian Charlie killed was called Oblomov.'

'Really, Oliver,' I objected. 'That could be a coincidence. In fact, if she were some sort of Russian agent, wouldn't she have changed her name?' I was trying to imagine how a plain-speaking woman like Vera Oblomov would manage the subterfuges of life as secret agent. On the other hand, I thought, her persona would provide marvellous cover. Who would suspect?

Fantasies of this sort were rudely disturbed by Oliver's vigorous shaking of his head. I had obviously got the wrong end of the stick. 'It could have been a coincidence, of course. But I thought I should check. Vera Oblomov came over to our side in the early sixties . . . long after I'd moved into the regular diplomatic corps, so naturally I wasn't told. But it didn't take long to get our people to answer my question.' Oliver paused. He delivered his final sentence with relish. 'That woman in there is the daughter of the man that Charlie Ivor killed.'

I must admit that my first thought was a vision of Vera Oblomov busy in Hugh's room poisoning the sherry. But, at least thus far, it simply didn't ring true. At any rate, she had as yet no reason to think she was suspected. I listened raptly with Fanshaw as Oliver told his story.

Oliver wasn't a paranoiac. So even once he had discovered who Vera Oblomov was, he hadn't assumed that there was anything amiss. But he *had* insisted on walking back with David on the night he died because he wanted to find out whether Vera had been making enquiries about Charlie Ivor. If Vera had somehow come to realize that David was the son of her father's killer, she might, after all, have taken an interest. David's response to Oliver's discreet enquiries was that he had mentioned to Vera that his father had been in Russia a few times. 'It seemed a natural thing to say to a Russian,' David had said, 'but, of course, I didn't say much about what he was doing there. Actually, it's never been awfully clear to *me*.'

So far as Oliver had been able to gather, David himself was genuinely vague about his father's doings. Oliver had told David that he and Charlie Ivor had worked together, in case David was keeping something back out of deference to a paternal injunction. But David had merely looked interested at the information and added little.

In any event, the fact that David hadn't admitted his father was in intelligence didn't have much significance. The general outlines of Charlie Ivor's career were public knowledge. Anyone who read about Philby – and what would be more natural than for a Russian defector who had become an Apostle? – could have known. David admitted eventually as they talked that as a matter of fact she had rather pestered him about his father recently . . . but he'd assumed it was snobbism of a perfectly familiar kind and simply either told her what he knew or evaded her questions.

But what David said had been enough to put Oliver on his guard.

'Very natural, Sir Oliver, in the circumstances,' Fanshaw said.

It was now clear that Tredwell was no longer the best suspect. He had the opportunity and the knowledge of David's allergy but no obvious motive. Vera Oblomov, like all the other members of the Society, knew of the allergy, too; and now she had a motive, or at least something that looked awfully like one. If she couldn't kill the man who killed her father, she could at least pay him back in kind. A son for a father. But if she had a motive, there was no evidence at all that she had been to David's rooms on Wednesday night; there was so far nothing solid to connect her to David's death.

'What am I going to tell the assembled company in there?' I asked, gesturing with my thumb over my shoulder.

Oliver replied stoutly, 'Tell them that you've persuaded Inspector Fanshaw to leave the tutor for a while. You'd better go on for a bit as if you're still looking for information about him. I'll come in with you. If somebody saw me coming earlier and I pretended to arrive now it would be rather suspicious. We don't want Dr Oblomov to suspect we might be on to her. The Inspector might as well leave now. Oh, and if I were you, Inspector, I'd have someone wait for Peterson at the railway station. And perhaps you can get someone to keep an eye on Oblomov when she leaves here.' Oliver was taking charge.

Fanshaw had said little throughout Oliver's explanation. He looked as though he felt that matters had got rather beyond his control. 'Very good, sir. I suppose I should just keep following the other leads and leave Dr Oblomov to the Special Branch.' He sighed. Oliver and I bade him farewell and he trudged downstairs.

We looked at each other in the semi-darkness. 'Well, here we go,' Oliver said. And we stepped back into the room.

'I'm sorry it took so long,' I said, 'but I think we've persuaded the Inspector to leave Tredwell for the moment. Oliver was especially persuasive.'

Oliver laughed airily. 'I'm frightfully sorry I'm so awfully late. The Darwins have a rather Iberian conception of the proper timing of dinner. I gather from Patrick's chat with the Inspector that we have an excellent suspect in one Dr Peter Tredwell.'

The others had obviously been talking about Tredwell and Hippo while we were out. 'The consensus is' – this was Godfrey of course – 'that though Mr Buckingham has, as yet, no obvious motive, it might just as well be he or, indeed, almost anyone else. After all, as our Sister Oblomov has so rightly pointed out, though David Glen Tannock took the fatal dose between midnight and two in the morning, the trap could have been baited at almost any time in the last week. Vera, perhaps you would explain.'

As she spoke I looked at her; it was hard to believe that this strange, forthright woman could be concealing the emotional consequences of a pair of murders. She said, 'We were discussing the last meeting we had in David's rooms. James pointed out that he had given us coffee and apologized for not having any fresh milk. He gave us powdered milk, which he kept in the gyp room. I simply observed that if someone had mixed penicillin with the milk powder, it could have been done any time between Wednesday night and the penultimate time that David had cocoa . . . or coffee, or tea.'

'Probably not tea,' I said without much thought. 'It had to be something with sugar. Penicillin's rather bitter. And David didn't like sugar in tea. Still, we should tell Fanshaw to have the milk powder analysed.' I was remembering Joanna Ritter's remarks about the milk powder. Because of her little love-offering, I knew, of course, that Vera was wrong. Vera was, in effect, inviting us to consider the possibility that the murderer had had a much longer time than we had been supposing within which to poison David; and she was thus increasing the pool of candidates. If she *was* guilty, it was an intelligent move; and the time was not yet ripe to disabuse her.

Somewhere near by, the first clock began to chime midnight and was joined by a chorus of others. 'Oh, my God,' said Hugh. 'Is that really the time? Oughtn't you rush back and talk to the murderous Tredwell?'

'I suppose I should. But I wonder if I could just phone Virginia quickly?'

'Of course, Patrick, pop into the study.'

'Good-night, everyone,' I said. 'I don't want you to have to wait for me to come back. If anyone thinks of anything give me a tinkle.' I gave them the college's phone number. 'From tomorrow evening, Virginia and I will be staying with Claudia Phipps; their number's in the book.' It struck me as I said it that in the present state of uncertainty publishing my movements wasn't necessarily the wisest move.

As I reached the telephone I remembered something and hurried back. 'James, I wonder if you could do me an enormous favour. I'm afraid I rather suggested to Hippo that it was all right for him not to mention the scene in the garden. He obviously disapproved deeply, but he's loyal enough. If he tries to keep it from Fanshaw now, the good Inspector will naturally be suspicious. Would you pop into Jesus on your way home – well, it's hardly on your way, I suppose; but would you pop in and tell Hippo to tell all? I expect you know how to get into Jesus after the gates are closed.'

'Actually, I'm not sure I do.'

'Don't be silly, James,' Hugh said. 'It's perfectly well known. There's a gate by the cottages at this end of Jesus Green that's always been quite easy to climb. Hang about till the others have left and I'll take you myself.'

James's obvious relief at Hugh's offer reminded me that, so far as James knew, Hippo was still a candidate for the part of the missing murderer. With all the excitement of Oliver's revelations I had forgotten, for a moment, the chord of danger struck by Fanshaw's announcement as I left Memorial Court a few hours earlier that Charlie had almost certainly been poisoned. Virginia's words came back to me: 'For God's sake, Patrick, take care.'

'Virginia. It's me. I'm sorry I've left it so late. It's been a rather hectic day. Oliver Hetherington has been doing some sleuthing of his own, of a kind I don't think I should talk about over the telephone. So I'll fill you in tomorrow. How did Sebastian take the news of Charlie's death?'

'He didn't say much. I'm afraid he's taken it very badly.'

I told Virginia that Claudia was expecting us to stay and that

I would mention it to Dominic and his wife and apologize and that I would see her in the morning about eleven at Claudia's and explain all.

'Patrick, darling; don't do anything silly.' This remark irritated me rather more than it should have. It took me a second or two to realize what it meant: Virginia was now seriously worried for my safety.

When I came out of the study, Oliver was still there. 'I thought I'd walk back with you,' he said.

He and I, James and Hugh, walked out together. Today had been the last day of exams and there were carousing undergraduates wandering all the streets around the Market Place. We walked in a huddled group, four sombre figures in a crowd of festive spirits.

'Nice to see Godfrey Stanley,' Oliver said. 'David mentioned he had arranged to see him on Thursday. They have obviously been beavering away together about Ransome.'

'Godfrey did say one rather odd thing,' James interrupted. 'While you were out of the room, he asked me whether I thought Hippo would have known that penicillin would make cocoa bitter? I suppose he asked me because I'd said that Hippo did physiology.'

'What's odd about that?'

'When Charlie gave his paper last week about his neurotoxins and how dangerous they were, he mentioned they didn't affect everybody to the same extent. That was when David mentioned his penicillin allergy. "Even ordinary medicines affect people very differently," he said. "Penicillin would kill me."'

'Yes,' said Hugh. 'So?'

'Well, Godfrey said he didn't hold with these newfangled drugs and that he'd never let his doctor give him antibiotics. But if he's never tasted penicillin, how does he know that it's bitter?'

'Now, really, James, wait a minute,' I said. 'I mentioned that penicillin was bitter earlier on in the evening, when I said that David couldn't have taken it in tea.'

'Besides,' Hugh added, 'Godfrey wasn't in Cambridge that evening, anyway; that's why he wasn't at the meeting. He'd gone to the country to nurse his cough.'

'Simple enough to check with his housekeeper,' Oliver said easily.

'I suppose all this looking for clues is going to my head,' said James. 'I mean, I even found myself wondering whether Dale Bishop Junior wasn't rather shifty?' James looked at each of us in turn. 'All that taking of notes.'

'He did that at the meeting last week,' said Hugh. 'It's a terrible American habit.'

I remembered how, in the past, when I'd been trying to puzzle out a crime there often came a point when everything seemed suspicious. 'Don't worry, James, I often find myself suspecting the most unlikely people,' I said laughing.

When we reached the Senate House, Oliver volunteered to accompany me back to Clare. 'I'll let myself into Trinity the back way. The Darwins have given me a key.' James and Hugh said good-night and continued on their way to Jesus Green.

'You noticed, I suppose, that Vera was the person who pointed out that the stuff could have been planted at almost any time. It's as if she wanted to widen the pool.' Oliver had remarked exactly what I had.

'Perhaps. But, as it happens, she was wrong.' I explained about Joanna Ritter. 'Still, we can't draw too many conclusions from the fact that she suggested it; after all, it was a perfectly sensible thought and we did gather together to see if we could examine all the possibilities.'

'But she ignored the fact that if the same person killed Charlie, then it was probably because he saw something after David died. And that means it was probably something he saw on Wednesday night.'

Oliver's remark reminded me that I had not had a chance to find out where everybody was during the crucial ten or fifteen minutes before Charlie's death; and, as my mind turned once more to Charlie, a thought occurred to me.

'Why Wednesday? Why not last night? I was puzzled myself this afternoon by the gap between David's murder and Charlie's. If Charlie saw something last night, though, that would explain it. Claudia said he didn't come in until two in the morning.'

'It's certainly a possibility. Perhaps you ought to make the point to Inspector Fanshaw,' Oliver said. 'What can we do to unsettle Vera Oblomov?'

'I don't know. I think I shall ask her to have lunch with Virginia and me on Sunday and see if we can't get her talking about her family. Maybe something will come out. But unless we find evidence that she was in David's rooms or Charlie's lab, we may not be able to prove anything at all. She's obviously a very bright woman. I don't think she would confess if she didn't think we had enough evidence to catch her.'

'Well, it's still early days. Fanshaw might still turn up a witness who saw someone coming in to or out of David's rooms or Charlie's lab at the right moment.'

'You're right, of course. Once people read about it in the newspapers, they may remember having seen something slightly odd. After all, quite a lot of undergraduates had finished their exams by Wednesday evening. There would have been lots of people about. When must you leave Cambridge?'

'Well, if it turns out there are grounds for suspecting Dr Oblomov, the Office will expect me to stay and see it out. But at all events I'll be here at least until Sunday night.'

When we reached the front of Memorial Court, Oliver took out a packet of cigarettes. 'You don't, do you?' he said, adding wryly, 'Elizabeth has been trying to get me to stop.'

The strong smell of the Gauloise reminded me of Hippo's story of Tredwell's smoking in the garden. It gave me an idea. 'Actually, Oliver, could I take a couple of those cigarettes?'

'Of course, old boy.' He winked conspiratorially. 'Jinny too, eh? Why don't you take the packet? You won't be able to buy any at this time of night.'

'Thanks. Thanks very much. You know, Oliver, when I arrived at Hugh's rooms this evening I was pretty sure that Tredwell was our murderer. Now it seems possible that Vera Oblomov or Hippo, or some other person or persons unknown, might be involved. We even had James being suspicious of Godfrey. Things are really getting very messy.'

Oliver grunted. 'Well, perhaps you can at least get clearer about Tredwell. It would be nice to be able to rule him more clearly in . . . or out.'

We said good-night. It was time to phone Peter Tredwell. Perhaps, finally, I thought, he would tell me the truth.

# 13

I made my way up to the gyp room beside David's rooms. I wanted to taste the cocoa powder and the powdered milk, if the forensic people had not taken them away. I switched on the light and scanned the room. The cocoa powder was still there. So was the glass jar of powdered milk that I had seen on Thursday. I opened it and dipped my finger into the powder, raising it to my mouth to taste. It tasted normal, but it might be worth checking for traces. The cocoa powder tasted intensely bitter, of course, but there were no traces of any white granules. You wouldn't be able to conceal white penicillin in the fine dark brown powder, at least, not if someone was looking for it. Still, someone could easily have washed the glass jar out and put in new powder. Or, of course, they could have put the penicillin directly into the cup.

I opened the cupboards. There was the tin that Joanna Ritter had bought, and from which David would have filled the jar. *Its* contents, too, tasted normal. There was an open packet of biscuits. Everything looked normal, harmless.

There was music playing quietly in the room opposite David's. I knocked on the door. After a few moments, there were sounds of movement and a young man stepped out, wrapped in a blanket, and looked at me enquiringly.

'I'm frightfully sorry,' I said. 'I assumed you must be up . . . the music.'

'No problem. I was wide awake, lying in bed, that's all.'

'I'm a cousin of David Glen Tannock's,' I said, 'and I wondered if you had used any of the powdered milk in the gyp room?' He looked at me strangely. 'You see,' I added, 'I think it may have contained the penicillin that killed him.'

'Oh,' he said, obviously only half convinced. 'I haven't heard much about that. I've been away for a few days. Only got back last night. But there was still stuff there when I went to bed; I used some. David and I shared milk and stuff . . . Horrible thing. Poor chap. He was a very nice person, your cousin. Friendly.'

'Did it taste odd – bitter, I mean?'

'Not specially. But I wouldn't have noticed. I take three or four spoonfuls of sugar in a mug of coffee.'

'Oh well, then. Sorry to disturb you. Good-night.'

Another dead end.

I had delayed calling Tredwell for long enough. It was nearly half-past twelve. I rushed across to my rooms, looked his extension up in the college directory, and dialled the number.

The voice that answered the phone was Hermione Porter's. 'Ah, good, we've been expecting you. We'll be across in five minutes.'

For a moment I felt a little afraid. It didn't seem very likely that Tredwell had engaged Dr Porter as an accomplice. On the other hand, there was still reason to suppose he might have killed one, perhaps two people in so many days. I wondered vaguely whether I oughtn't to telephone Hugh – ask him to come over and keep guard; and I then remembered that he was probably still out with James Hogg.

Then I thought of the porter. If I was with him when they arrived, then they would know he had seen them. I stepped out of the room into the court. There were lights on in many of the undergraduates' rooms and somebody's footsteps crunched on the gravel behind me. I spun round nervously, but it was only Joanna Ritter, coming out of the staircase next door. She'll do, I thought.

'Hallo, Sir Patrick. I'm frightfully sorry I got it wrong before. Somebody told me this evening you had a title. You must have thought me awfully stupid.'

'Not at all, not at all. Why on earth should you know? After all, I expect I called you "Miss Ritter", without checking you weren't the daughter of a Duke.'

She giggled. 'Well, anyway, I apologise.' She was obviously planning to leave, but I needed her to stay until the others came.

'Your note was very helpful. I passed the message on to the police,' I lied, making a note to put that right in the morning.

'Oh, Michael's already told them,' she said.

I deleted the mental note. 'I'm afraid it's still not at all clear exactly what happened that evening.'

'Well, I asked everybody on the staircase, after you spoke to me. Paul Cross, who lives opposite David's room, was away. And a lot of the others were at a party in King's until one or two in the morning. We weren't supposed to make any noise here, you see. I'm afraid that's not much help.' Her voice trailed off.

'Did you ever see David row?' I asked, to keep her there.

'No,' she said. 'But I saw him dancing last week at a party in the JCR. As a matter of fact, I nearly asked him to dance with me. He was very good at it . . . Lots of the girls rather fancied him, actually . . .' Including, I suspect, you, I thought.

My visitors finally arrived. I saw them across the court. Tredwell, obviously still a little tipsy, supported on Hermione Porter's arm.

'You may not believe it,' I said, 'but I am having a little gathering in my room, now, just like some of the others.' I gestured to the lighted rooms around the court. 'Do you know Dr Porter and Dr Tredwell? Let me introduce you.'

Before she could answer, they arrived.

'May I present Miss Ritter?'

'Good Lord, Sir Patrick, I'm her French literature supervisor,' said Hermione Porter. 'What's up, Jo? How did the exams go?'

'All right, I suppose. The Balzac questions were harder than I expected.'

'I'm sure you did very well.' The fierce Dr Porter spoke the perfunctory words with real warmth.

The three of us entered the Fellows' guest-room. Tredwell flopped down on the bed, and Hermione Porter settled tidily next to him. She was, I thought, an extremely handsome woman. But there was something of a challenge in the austerity of her appearance; her long, dark hair, unadorned; her face with only a hint of make-up; the dark polo-neck shirt under the linen jacket, over her dark blue jeans. I'm not just a pretty face, her look said. I thought: in Cambridge, even at Clare a couple of years after the admission of women, the challenge would probably need to be offered daily. It was a reflection that made her earlier sharp remark somewhat less piquing.

'Let the games commence,' Tredwell said, his eyes half-closed.

'Pull yourself together, Peter.' Hermione was obviously cross with him. 'This is very serious. Now, Sir Patrick, you've seen that piece in *Private Eye*. It's a disaster. I mean, Lord Glen Tannock was over twenty-one, so it wasn't strictly illegal, I suppose, but he was Peter's tutorial pupil. And now that he's dead, the police are bound to suspect Peter, just because he's gay.

'I'm sorry I snapped at you earlier,' she continued. 'Peter tells me that I was wrong to. But you've got to help him persuade the police that he couldn't possibly have done it.'

'Why do you think that?'

She paused for a moment, before deciding to indulge me by taking the question seriously. 'It's completely out of character.'

I restrained myself from comment.

'And anyway, Peter didn't even see David Glen Tannock on Wednesday.'

'I'm afraid that's not true.' I spoke with more conviction than I felt.

Peter looked up at me sharply. 'What the hell do you mean?'

'Somebody saw you in the gardens with David at around midnight.'

'But they couldn't have. I wasn't there. David had exams the next day. He needed to sleep. In fact, I didn't want him to go to his Apostles' meeting. Hermione and I went to a late flick in the Market Place. We weren't back till about half-past twelve. Then we had a glass of brandy and went to bed.'

'David didn't necessarily take the penicillin until as late as half-past one,' I pointed out mildly. 'Peter still had time.'

Hermione Porter stood up and stepped towards me, her face crimson with outrage. 'You're the most blindly prejudiced bastard I've ever met. Why the hell should he have killed David? He loved the boy. And your cousin loved him. Passionately. It was not the wisest choice in the world. It wouldn't have done either of them any good if it had come out. But think about it. What possible motive could he have had? Would you have made your accusation if David had been having an affair with me? This isn't a game, you know. His bloody career's on the line.' She paused. I said nothing. 'Go on, answer me. Tell me what his sodding motive was.'

I didn't know what to say. She was prejudiced by loyalty, but I doubted she was blinded by it; she knew Tredwell. And she was right. Not only did I know of no conceivable motive, I also knew, which she didn't, that there was at least one other person with a strong motive.

'But . . .' I stopped. I resisted my first impulse to fight back, to point to Peter Tredwell's lies and to Hippo Buckingham's accusations. Hippo could have been lying. If Peter hadn't been in the Fellows' Garden, the only alternative seemed to be the absurd possibility that David had been having affairs with two Fellows of the college. So Hippo would have to be suspect too. But *why* would he lie? That would bear thinking about.

'All right. I'm sorry. I have no reason to think that Peter wanted to kill David. But you must understand, there's evidence that the police will want explained. I have just two questions, both of which Fanshaw will ask you tomorrow.'

'Go ahead. Shoot.'

'Where did you go yesterday morning after we had coffee?'

'What has that got to do with anything?'

'Answer the question, Peter,' Hermione said. 'The man's trying to help you. Presumably.'

Peter shrugged. 'I walked back to college and bumped into Alan Finch, who wanted to talk about what we should do to set up a prize in David's memory if the Ivors gave us any money.'

'Would Finch have noticed the time?'

'Yes. He had a meeting at eleven fifteen. We talked in the college offices. There were lots of people about.'

I could get Fanshaw to check on this, but *I* believed it. If it hadn't been true it would have been a very stupid lie. And it meant that Charlie had not been killed by Tredwell.

'Now will you tell me what this is about?' Peter's bloodshot eyes focused on me.

'Another Apostle was killed this morning.'

The two of them looked surprised at the same time for the first time of the evening.

'Now, my second question. Do you know the young man I had dinner with?'

'No,' Tredwell said, 'but I'd seen him before with David.'

'He claims to have seen you that night, with David, in the Fellows' Garden.'

'Why would he say that?' Tredwell seemed genuinely perplexed.

I recalled that Hippo had also said that the man was smoking; and that Tredwell had looked distinctly uncomfortable smoking earlier. It was the sort of convincing detail that a clever liar would introduce. But maybe Hippo's lie had been too clever.

I took the packet of cigarettes I had borrowed from Oliver out of my pocket and offered them first to Hermione Porter and then to Tredwell.

'We don't smoke,' he said firmly.

'I'm so sorry,' I said. 'I thought you were smoking earlier in the bar.'

'Just the strain. Haven't been so drunk for a long time and I couldn't resist the temptation. Nasty habit, really. I stopped at the beginning of the term.'

'Have you seen Hippo Buckingham at all since then?'

'No.' He paused. Now he seemed entirely sober. 'Look, I don't see what . . .'

I interrupted. 'Buckingham said you were smoking in the garden. Apparently, he was lying. Presumably he put in the detail about your smoking because he'd seen you smoke.'

Peter chuckled humourlessly. 'Nasty little trick, Sir Patrick,' he said. 'Still, at least you now know the little bastard was lying.'

Hermione, who didn't seem to have been listening for a while, suddenly exclaimed, '*Private Eye*' in a loud voice. 'Of course. When did he tell you this, that boy you were with?'

'This evening.'

'Well, there you are. He must have read the piece about David and Peter in that filthy rag and simply told you he'd seen what they reported.'

'Suppose I buy that. Why would he do it?'

'How the hell should I know?'

I turned to Tredwell. 'Look, Peter, you've got to tell me the truth this time.'

'I told you the truth last time.'

'Not the whole truth. You didn't tell me that you met regularly with David in the Fellows' Gardens.'

'Not regularly, damn you. Twice. Last week. It's such a beautiful spot. And once the gates are closed it's so private. None of the Fellows ever goes there at night. Except Hermione and me. The blossom smells wonderful, you can hear the odd splash from the river. It's the most romantic spot in the world. And, daft as it may seem to you, I was passionately in love with David. When we sat together on the bench under the apple trees, or walked along between the yews . . . I've never been so happy . . .' He stopped and began quietly to cry. If Hermione hadn't been there, it would have been the most embarrassing moment of my life.

She placed a hand on his. 'It's all right, Peter darling. You cry. You have every right.'

I may not be able to sniff out a lie at a hundred yards, but sometimes truthfulness shines through. When Peter Tredwell and Hermione Porter left, I sat down to write a short note on the college notepaper that lay on the desk.

*Saturday 1 a.m.*

*Dear Peter,*
*I'm afraid I've treated you very badly. Please accept my unreserved apologies. You are very lucky to have Hermione Porter as a friend. I hope very much that you will both forgive me.*

*I loved David, too. I am only sorry that he did not live to introduce you to me and to my wife. I shall make the strongest representations to the police on your behalf. And if they fail, it would be an honour to act for you.*

*Patrick Scott*

I suppose it was rather a grovelling note, really. Peter Tredwell had hardly acted wisely, and I had been misled by the evidence. But he was not a killer.

Every time I have an hypothesis about a murder, I imagine it, flesh it out in my mind. That is my method, the only one I know. But then, if I'm not careful, I mistake the image for reality. I had made the mistake before. After listening to Hippo, I had imagined Tredwell and David in the garden, the lovers' quarrel, the return to the room, the mixing of the poisoned cup. I had imagined most intensely exactly the moments for which I had no evidence.

I suppose I think I am, on the whole, a decently liberal-minded chap. And it grieved me to have to admit that I would probably not have been so stupid, if he had been a woman, or David a girl. Hermione Porter had made her point.

I sealed the note in an envelope and walked out with it into the court. I needed a few moments out of the stuffy room to recover. I felt that I had let David down, not trusted his judgement, and I could not yet sleep.

I posted my note through the door of the porter's lodge. Then I made a tour of the court, asking myself over and over again what I had missed. Peter Tredwell did not kill David, but somebody did. And I wanted more than ever to know who it was.

Hippo? Why?

Vera Oblomov? How?

And why was Charlie dead?

Was there, perhaps, no connection between the deaths? Had their conjunction blinded me to things I would have seen if they had not happened together?

Good questions, all of them; but I had no answers.

When I returned to my room, it was half-past one. Tomorrow I had to start again constructing another imaginary scene of murder. I turned in and tried to sleep.

I was awakened about half an hour later, just as I had finally drifted off to sleep, by a gentle tapping on my door. I heard two male voices, talking softly. I got up, dragged on a dressing-gown, and went to the door.

It was Hugh with James Hogg, the latter looking flustered, the former merely tired.

'I know you must be absolutely worn out,' Hugh began, 'but I think it's important. James, tell him what you saw.'

I ushered them into the room and James told me what had happened. They had gone to Jesus, and Hugh had guided

James over the small black gate at the back of the college. James had made his way quickly to Hippo's staircase, and climbed up to his rooms on the first floor.

'They were open. No one seemed to be there.'

Hippo, James assumed, was probably in the bathroom at the end of the corridor. But he stepped into the rooms, calling Hippo's name quietly. The sitting-room was empty and James poked his head into the tiny bedroom, once more calling Hippo's name. Since Hippo was not in the bedroom either, he turned back to wait in the sitting-room, when he noticed one of those small translucent plastic containers that chemists use for pills and tablets. 'With all the talk of penicillin, I'm afraid I just thought I'd better have a look.'

And penicillin, prescribed for J. Buckingham by a Dr Smythe, was what it said it was. James picked up the container and was just putting it down again, when he heard someone coming back. He was about to step back out into the sitting-room, when an unfamiliar male voice said, 'Okay, Hippo, where's my money?'

'I'm afraid I panicked rather.' James looked distinctly uncomfortable.

He had slipped behind the open door of the wardrobe. Whoever it was did no more than poke a head into the room, and then disappeared back into the night.

James waited another five minutes until he heard another person enter. This time it was Hippo.

'He was singing. I recognized his voice.'

Naturally, Hippo had been rather surprised. But James had explained rather bashfully that he had hidden from the earlier visitor and delivered my message. Hippo listened, thanked James and encouraged him to leave.

'Who was your visitor?' James had asked. But Hippo had only mumbled something like, 'Oh, a friend.'

'Well,' Hugh said. 'What do you make of that?'

James's story was undoubtedly accurate: the late-night visitor's line was too melodramatic for anyone to make up. And he was too clever to invent the penicillin prescription which the police could check on quite easily.

I said, 'Since Peter Tredwell has persuaded me that he didn't see David on Wednesday, Hippo's story about seeing Peter was a lie. So: he had the penicillin; he saw David on Wednesday; he lied about David going into the garden with Peter; and he has a cheque for two hundred and fifty pounds from David on his desk.'

'Did he tell you why David gave him the money?' James asked.

'Because he needed to pay a Pitt Club bill if he was to use his account during May Week. That rang true, of course, because it was terribly in David's character. But the late-night visitor presumably means that Hippo was generally short of money.'

'But, Sir Patrick, none of this gives Hippo Buckingham a motive,' James said.

'Still, you must admit, it's all slightly fishy.' Hugh was always one for understatement. 'One reason for coming round at this ungodly hour was to suggest that some of this information might be useful to Fanshaw, when he meets Hippo tomorrow. I thought you might want to phone him early in the morning.'

'I shall have to do that anyway. To tell him to cross Tredwell off the list of suspects.' (Hugh looked questioningly at me, here, but I resisted the temptation to elaborate.) 'But you were right. It's very important. I only wish I knew what it all meant.'

Hugh got up. 'Well let's all sleep on it. Come on, Jamie, walk the old dear home.'

# 14

When I awoke it was nearly a quarter to ten. I remembered that despite our unscheduled meeting with Oliver Hetherington last night, Fanshaw and I had not actually cancelled the appointment we had made the day before for ten in the morning. I wondered if he would come. Another little while asleep would have been just the thing; but I did need to speak to him. I washed and dressed hurriedly and left the guest-room to set out on another day.

Fanshaw had not forgotten. I suppose that he wanted at least to talk to me about my conversation with Peter Tredwell. When I reached Old Court, he was standing at the entrance to the staircase that leads up to the combination room. Somehow, even with Vera Oblomov in play, I suspected it wasn't going to be all that easy to persuade him of Peter's innocence.

As we mounted the stairs, Fanshaw filled me in on the arrival of Inspector Peterson from Special Branch. So far, all they had done was to institute discreet surveillance of Vera Oblomov. On the whole, that didn't seem likely to be very productive, but, for the moment, there didn't seem much else to do.

We settled down in the combination room with a cup of coffee each. I didn't know exactly where to begin. Perhaps a brief summary of the main points would be in order. Addressing Fanshaw, I realized, would be like addressing a jury; and, for the moment, Peter Tredwell was the accused.

'I've discovered two main things since we spoke last night. First, I am almost certain . . . in fact, I am sure . . . that Peter Tredwell did not kill David. And I am sure of it because, second, I am now positive that Jeremy Buckingham, alias Hippo, lied to me last night. He did not see Tredwell in the garden at midnight, as he claimed to me. He couldn't have. Tredwell was watching a film with Dr Porter late that night and did not return to the college until half-past midnight; even then he stayed up drinking with Dr Porter for a little longer. I suppose Mr Buckingham must have read the piece in *Private Eye* and embroidered it to his own ends. Furthermore, Tredwell couldn't have killed Charlie either. He was either with me or with Alan Finch, the Senior Tutor, for all but a few minutes between half-past ten, when Charlie's assistant left him alive, and eleven fifteen, by which time he was dead. It would have taken at least twenty minutes to get from the Copper Kettle to the Downing Site and back to Clare, even running at a good clip. There simply wasn't time. Of course, I haven't had a chance yet to confirm this with Dr Finch; but I don't see why Tredwell would expect to get away with lying about it. At all events, you'll find, I think, that quite a few people saw them together in the college office. Perhaps one of your people could check? Anyway, until we know more about Vera Oblomov,' I finished, 'the real next question is why Mr Buckingham lied.' I paused to let the facts sink in.

After a half-minute's silence, Fanshaw sucked in his breath and said: 'I thought about it all night. I wasn't going to arrest

Tredwell anyway. Why would he kill your cousin? I couldn't see it. I don't hold with that sort of thing, myself, especially with a student, but I don't see why it would lead to murder.'

My relief showed perhaps a little too obviously. 'Good, that's settled, then. If I were you, I'd go and get a statement from Tredwell and Dr Porter – Hermione Porter – who was with him that night. I think now that he'll tell you the truth.'

Fanshaw heaved a heavy sigh. 'So what about Mr Buckingham, then? I'm off to see him when I leave here. Couldn't he just have mistaken Dr Tredwell for someone else?'

'I thought about that. But it is quite inconceivable that David would have been having secret meetings . . . of that sort . . . with *two* Fellows of the college; and only Fellows have keys to the garden.' I paused, organizing the revelations about James's visit to best effect. 'As it happens, I have some more rather troubling intelligence about Hippo Buckingham, anyway.'

I told Fanshaw about the midnight visit to Hippo's rooms in Jesus.

Fanshaw listened intently; the notebook was out again and he was pencilling in the details. When I finished, he asked me, 'One thing, sir. Exactly why did Mr Hogg go to see Mr Buckingham.'

I expect I reddened a little. I had put it out of my mind that the reason James had gone was to stop Hippo telling a lie – or what I then thought was a lie – about the affair in the garden. 'Ah, Inspector. I'm afraid an apology is due.'

Half an hour later we emerged into the bright sunlight. Fanshaw blinked and I shaded my eyes for a moment. I explained to him that I was off to meet my wife at Claudia Phipps's home in Portugal Place. 'You'll find me there tonight, she's asked us to stay. I expect I ought to check in with you to see if either of us has come up with anything.'

Fanshaw nodded.

'And Inspector, I really am most awfully sorry not to have kept you fully in my confidence. It won't happen again.'

I don't suppose he had much reason to believe me. Actually, I wasn't sure that I could keep the promise myself. David's death had led us into a world of secrets, not all of which would be safe in Fanshaw's little black notebook. But the more I saw of him, the more decent he seemed. There wasn't much doubt in my mind that Inspector Fanshaw thought people had a right to their secrets, too.

It was almost time to meet Virginia. As I made my way up Trinity Street, I bumped into Oliver Hetherington, coming out of Trinity Lane.

'Patrick, old chap, I was on my way to buy Virginia's new book.'

'Actually, I was just off to find her. She's due up at any moment. We're to be staying with Claudia Phipps. In fact, if you've a moment, why don't you come along and say hallo? Virginia would love to see you.'

'Good. We probably ought to do a little brainstorming about Vera Oblomov, too. Decide on the next step. But this isn't the place to talk.'

We crossed over to Heffers so that Oliver could buy his copy of *Good Intentions*, then carried on to Portugal Place. There was hardly anyone about. It's not open to motor traffic and it doesn't go anywhere much; so, apart from the occasional local on a bicycle, only the odd tourist, lost or hoping for a back-street adventure, passes through. Oliver stopped me by the church for a moment.

'Have you any thoughts about the Oblomov business?'

'To tell you the truth, Oliver, I've mostly been thinking about the other candidates. Tredwell is now out of the question, I think.'

Oliver raised an eyebrow. 'Really?'

I told him more or less what I had just told Fanshaw. 'I'll give Alan Finch a buzz later to make sure about the times; but I don't see Tredwell lying about it.'

'That leaves Buckingham and Madame Oblomov.' Oliver reflected for a moment. 'Why might Buckingham have done it?'

'That's the question.'

'And if he didn't, then Vera Oblomov probably did, don't you think?'

'After mucking up one possibility so thoroughly, I should be rather cautious about plumping for another. But it does mean that we really must investigate her. If you're free, why don't you get Hugh to take you over for a chat with her? It would be perfectly natural, wouldn't it? You're a close friend of David's father's – if she doesn't know that, you might get some sort of reaction by telling her. And you and Hugh are two senior members of the Society inviting her to help you solve the murder of two of our Brothers.'

Oliver nodded. 'All right, I'll see what I can do. I don't suppose there'll be any difficulty about getting security clearance for Hugh; after all he must have recruited half the current crop of officers at M15. But I suppose I should check, first; they like to be asked. I've been feeling rather useless all morning, so it'll at least make me feel better. Peterson from Special Branch is supposed to have brought up a file on her. I'll try and get it to look at after lunch and see if Hugh can take me over to have tea with her in college. Newnham, is it?'

'It is. By the way, here are your Gauloises.'

'Came in handy, did they?'

'I think so.' I explained my little subterfuge as we walked on down Portugal Place.

Oliver laughed. 'I don't suppose you could just have asked him if he smoked?'

'Reckoned actions speak louder than words. Thanks for the loan.'

When we reached the door of Claudia's house, Claudia was standing in the sitting-room, holding the baby, and looking out into the street. I waved to her and we waited for her to come to the door. She looked as though she hadn't slept much, but she had made herself up so that she no longer looked as pale and vulnerable as she had the day before. She managed a small, swift smile.

I introduced her to Oliver. 'I was so awfully sorry to hear about Charles,' Oliver said. Claudia nodded at him slightly and turned to lead us into the sitting-room.

'Virginia called from a garage in Harston about twenty minutes ago. So she'll be here soon. She said she'd brought lunch for us – that was very sweet of her. You knew Charlie from the Society, I suppose, Sir Oliver?'

'Indeed, I did. We all enjoyed him. I'm afraid that despite the large number of exceptional scientists I've met through the Society, I'm still rather inclined to expect scientists to be philistines. Charlie always reminded me how wrong that was. We shall all miss him.'

Claudia looked as though she was about to burst into tears again; and Oliver, realizing that his remark had upset her, looked terribly guilty.

'No, Sir Oliver. It's really not your fault. I must pull myself together. It helps to know that other people enjoyed Charlie. Somehow the fact that I'm not grieving alone . . .' She stopped for a moment. 'You know what I'd really like?'

Oliver and I looked at her wide-eyed.

'I should like to help you find whoever it was that killed him.' Her voice was small. It was not the spirit of vengeance that spoke; it was something quieter, and yet just as intense, something closer to the spirit of justice.

'I'd say the best way to do that at the moment is to try and think about what he's done recently. I mean, for example, he might have found out something that someone wanted kept quiet,' Oliver said.

'But don't worry about that now,' I added. 'Just tell us what he's been up to.'

'It'll be nice to talk about him. It'll help fix the memories, if you know what I mean.' She sounded uncertain. 'But first, shall we have coffee?'

Over coffee, Claudia told us about the last months of her life with Charlie. His research was going well. He enjoyed his son.

'He wasn't much of a university person, but he loved the Society. I remember he told me when we first met how disappointed he'd been when he came up that there was so little intelligent conversation. Charlie said nobody in college wanted to talk about ideas, and they all thought him a terrible bore for trying to force them to. And then he found the Apostles. It was like the Cambridge he had hoped for . . . better, perhaps.'

Charlie had talked to Claudia about all of the active membership. 'Hugh, he said, was a lovable old queen . . . It was really meant kindly,' she added.

'I know, Claudia. We all say that and we all mean it kindly.'

'Even Hugh thinks he's a lovable old queen,' Oliver said. Claudia smiled more broadly this time.

'David Glen Tannock, he said, was like a story-book prince.

Rich and titled and bright and kind. And then there was Hugo McAlister. Charlie'd been seeing a lot of him recently. Speaking of flattery, I think Charlie was flattered by Hugo's interest in his work. I mean, Hugo's a Nobel Laureate and a grand old man, and there he was asking Charlie all sorts of intricate details about his work and popping in and out of his lab.' She paused for a moment and sighed sadly. A moment later she was caught up with another memory and went on. 'Then there was old Godfrey Stanley who's been so kind. Charlie called him up a while ago and asked for some help with the mathematics of what he was doing and ever since then Godfrey has been egging him on and telling him how clever he is.'

'Godfrey's always been like that. He can be a pompous old thing. But he's always had a soft spot for bright young chaps, especially in the Society. And behind that slightly absurd façade, he's a very kind person.'

'And recently a young American Apostle has been showing great interest in Charlie's work, too. Dale somebody.'

'Ah, our new Brother,' I said.

'Yes. All the best things in Charlie's life seemed to come from your society.'

We chatted on about Charlie, and Claudia brightened as she told us about him. By the time Virginia rang the bell at a quarter to one, Claudia looked almost as if nothing had happened. Almost.

'Oliver, how lovely,' Virginia said, after she had greeted Claudia and me.

'I'm afraid I must rush off now,' Oliver said. 'The Darwins are expecting me to lunch with them, but I did want to see you before I went.'

While Virginia and I walked down to the end of Portugal Place to collect her luggage from the car, she told me about her visit that morning to Charlie and Lydia Ivor. 'I do love them both, Patrick my love, but your family can be very cold fish. I've never seen so many stiff upper lips in my life. I wasn't feeling too solid myself and I could have done with a good cry with Lydia. But she and Charles just listened politely to what I knew about how your investigations were proceeding – of course, I didn't say anything about the sex with the tutor – and asked the odd question. Then they said how very grateful they were to you. Of course, Lydia looked absolutely frightful; never seen her look anything like it. But I did rather wish she'd let go.'

'And that was it?' I asked.

'Well, Caro arrived from Devon just as I was about to set off. She was in a dreadful state and was frightfully cross with Charles and Lydia for being so unruffled. Actually, I think getting angry was good for her. Helped calm her down.'

Lydia had suggested that Virginia go up to talk to Caroline in her room; a proposal seconded by Charles. 'She's always been very fond of you, Jinny,' he said.

'So I had a good weep with Caro and felt much better.' Virginia finished her story. 'That's why I was a little later than I'd intended. Caro's coming to stay with us at Ampney next weekend. She's such a nice girl.'

Virginia slammed the boot and clucked like a satisfied hen. 'Up to the house, then, Paddy boy. But what's your news?'

I began to give her a rough synopsis of what had happened since we had last talked properly the afternoon before. By the time we got back to the house I was recounting my midnight conversation with Peter Tredwell and Hermione Porter. I didn't give an exact report of Hermione Porter's speech, but I gave the gist of it.

Virginia said: 'Quite right, too. The poor man is grieving for David and you're all set to have him locked up for murder. Hermione Porter sounds like an interesting woman.'

'I wrote a note of apology at once, before I went to bed.' I thought I deserved at least a little of her sympathy.

'Oh Patrick, don't look so wronged. I'm sorry. I didn't mean to take their side. You did have lots of evidence, didn't you? Still, I'm glad you wrote the note.' She put down the case she was carrying and gave me a gentle peck on the lips just as Claudia opened the door.

'Just giving your neighbours something to gossip about,' she said to Claudia.

I realized I had been missing Lady Scott a good deal. I gave her another peck.

# 15

Virginia had brought us a magnificent lunch of game pie, a salad and some strawberries and cream, to be washed down with a Gewürztraminer. We ate around a small table in the tiny garden at the back of the house. Claudia ate even less than usual and, despite the quality of the victuals, none of us was able to give them the attention they deserved. We discussed Charlie's mother and what could be done to help her; we talked about Charlie and Sebastian in the old days; and we generally encouraged Claudia to go on talking about her husband. After lunch she seemed a little tired and Virginia packed her off to bed. 'I'm going to take Patrick out for a bit. We'll be back for tea.'

Virginia and I headed off to the Backs, where we found a spot to sit and talk. Half an hour of chat on the grass by the river behind King's brought her up to date. It was a warm day and Virginia looked so very pretty, I thought, in her cotton frock, with strands of her long grey hair falling over her face occasionally as her bun came undone. Virginia's skin is creased, beaten by the wind and the sun from years of sailing, and her once-fair hair is grey. But her looks always came from her bones – the wonderful line of her cheeks – and from those great blue eyes. And those she will have till she dies.

'So, the fact is,' she said, 'there's no real evidence that any of them did it. Take Vera Oblomov – I would have changed my name, I must say, but perhaps she thinks nobody here ever reads that book. I mean, she may have had a motive but there's not a shred of evidence. We don't even know whether she *liked* her father. And killing off Charlie and Lydia's son because Charlie killed her father isn't very grown-up, is it? You don't think she's a crazy, do you? And as for this Hippo person, he's short of money, which isn't a crime, and he's told a rather unpleasant lie. But if he was with David a little before he died he may have felt he ought to implicate someone else just because he was scared of being accused of killing David himself.

And to judge by his reaction to your suggestion that he and David weren't orphans, he probably thinks it's fair enough to accuse a nasty old queer don of anything, including murder. In fact, he might perfectly well have thought that David's tutor did kill him. People who use words like "seduce" rather freely often think that everyone they don't approve of is capable of terrible crimes.'

It was a bleak conclusion, but, as usual, Virginia seemed to have got it right.

'Well, unless something turns up, I'm more or less stuck. What would Bella Sharpe do?' I laughed. Bella Sharpe is the heroine of a string of detective novels that Virginia has written.

'Bella Sharpe has the good fortune to live in a world where I make the rules,' Virginia said. 'And one of my rules is that there's always a clue round the next corner and always a solution at the end of the book. But she's a sensible girl is Bella. So I think at this point she'd go and collect your suitcase from the Fellows' guest-room in Mem. Court.'

'Gosh,' I said. 'That reminds me. I still haven't spoken to the Wrattings about our not staying with them. It's frightfully late; Dominic will think me terribly inconsiderate.'

'No, he won't. I rang them this morning. Julia wants us to come to dinner, if we can. Perhaps we could pop into the lodge after we collect your things and tell them if we're coming. Do you think we can leave Claudia alone?'

'Why don't we ask her? We can telephone her from the guest-room?'

Claudia answered the phone almost immediately.

'I'm having a nice chat with Dale Bishop,' she said. 'Charlie said they were fast becoming great friends. He seems terribly sweet.' She lowered her voice a little. 'Rather shy, actually. But he is being terribly kind.' When we mentioned the Wrattings, Claudia insisted, of course, that we must go to dinner with them.

As we stepped out of the gates of Memorial Court, we bumped into Hugo McAlister.

'I don't think you've met my wife, Virginia, Hugo.'

'Ah, Lady Scott. How do you do. Hugo McAlister.' He looked at me enquiringly.

'Oh,' I said, 'I'm afraid we're still rather in the dark about both of the deaths.'

'Such a tragedy. Young Glen Tannock, of course, I was only beginning to get to know. But Charlie Phipps worked just down the corridor from me: I always thought him very charming. And frightfully clever, of course. Such interesting work. How's his wife?'

'We're staying with her, actually; she's bearing up.'

'Well, it'll be some consolation to have you there. Do call on me, Patrick, if I can be of any help. Glen Tannock was rooting around in some of our *arch*ives wasn't he?' Hugo's inflection was meant to indicate both that it was the Ark he was speaking of and that he assumed that Virginia knew nothing of the Society. 'I'm actually looking after some of the papers at the moment; I've been doing a little historical digging myself. If you have any questions about that sort of thing, you know, you might ask me. Happy to help.'

'Thank you so much, Hugo. I'll bear that in mind.'

'Dear, dear. This is all most tragic.' he sighed, 'Ah well, I must let you be on your way.'

On the way back to Claudia's we walked through Old Court and I popped into the Tutorial Offices to have a word with Alan Finch, leaving Virginia to run across and make arrangements for dinner with Julia Wratting. He confirmed Peter Tredwell's story about their meeting the morning before: there was now no question that Peter Tredwell had killed Charlie. In all the muddle, it was nice to have tidied up one loose end.

By the time we arrived back at the house with my baggage, Dale Bishop had gone. 'But he's going to come and keep me company for the early part of the evening. So now you really mustn't worry about me.'

Virginia and I looked at each other. We had had the same thought. Of course, there wasn't yet any reason to suspect Dale Bishop more than any other Apostle, but it was rather odd of him to appear twice at Claudia's in a day. I motioned to Virginia to keep mum and we went up to our bedroom.

'We can't leave Claudia alone with him,' I said when Virginia had shut the bedroom door.

'On the other hand, we probably shouldn't worry her in her present state.'

'I think I'll ask Fanshaw to lend us a policewoman for the evening. I'm sure he'll understand.'

And, when I phoned him, he did.

We arrived at the door of the Master's lodge at Clare at about a quarter past seven. Julia Wratting had suggested we eat early so we could get back to Claudia. I rang the bell.

Julia opened the door. 'Come along in,' she said. 'I hope you don't mind, but it's just us. Dominic's doing something in college for a few minutes. He won't be long.'

She led us up to the large sitting-room on the first floor. 'I'm afraid there's simply no way to make this place cosy. Dominic and I rattle about like beans in a pod, now that the children have gone. Now, Dominic has instructed me to settle you into a drink.'

We sat in a row, Virginia and Julia with their sherries, I with my gin and tonic, and Julia told us how sorry she was about David. 'He was such a nice boy. And then your friend Charles Phipps has been killed. It's really quite gruesome. Are you any closer to finding out who did it, Patrick?'

I shook my head. 'But I'm sure we will. There are still lots of leads to be checked and Inspector Fanshaw seems tremendously competent. It's just a matter of time.' It occurred to me that this might not be sufficiently reassuring, so I added, 'But one thing we can be sure of, I think, is that the killings aren't random. I'm not sure that anyone outside the circle that David and Charlie belonged to need worry.'

When Dominic arrived, we went down to dinner. Julia seemed quite happy to conduct most of the conversation.

'Did I see you chatting to Hugo McAlister this afternoon, Patrick? I didn't know you knew him.'

'I hardly do, Julia; just the odd meeting over the years.'

'Does he always dress like that?' Virginia asked. 'Not at all donnish, more like a banker, all Savile Row and Jermyn Street.'

'Oh yes, but then he's not just a don, you know, he's a sort of industrialist. He's put everything they own into some sort of biological company, manufacturing bacteria for industry, Margaret says. I think she's rather nervous about it, poor dear. I don't think I'd want to have my future tied up with that sort of thing. Tiny little bugs you can't see. Such a nice couple.' (That was a typical Julia *sequitur*.) 'Margaret and I seem to be on endless committees together of one kind and another. CPRE, that sort of thing.' Julia trailed off into irrelevance.

'Biotechnology', Dominic pronounced, 'is the wave of the future. And few people have Hugo's knowledge and connections. He's also absolutely in the forefront in using computers for biological work. Still, entrepreneurship carries its risks. But he's got a rather substantial financial safety net: he owns some frightfully valuable property in Mayfair, somewhere . . . Yes, Hugo's a very clever chap. He rather dominates any university committees he's on.'

'And that nose of his and those huge beady eyes under huge bushy eyebrows: like an enormous hawk,' Julia said. 'Actually the oddest thing about him is that he still takes a brisk walk along the river or out towards Grantchester every night after dinner. Margaret says he's often out until half-past midnight. Isn't that astonishing? And all dressed up like a banker, as you say, Virginia.'

Dominic plainly did not approve of Julia's style in discussing their friends; so he simply ignored this last remark and asked: 'Charles Phipps was in his department, wasn't he?'

'Indeed he was.'

'He seems to have thought very highly of him. He said so this afternoon,' Virginia added.

'Such a shame,' said Julia, falling quiet. Even her endless stream of small talk was diminished as each conversational topic somehow brought us back to the two murders.

As we chatted desultorily on through the meal, Dominic said nothing about David's death. I suppose he didn't want to discuss it over dinner. But once we had returned upstairs after eating, he asked me to tell him what was happening. I was getting used to telling the story, but I had to keep track of what I should tell to whom. Since I couldn't tell him about Vera Oblomov, and had made no mention of my earlier suspicions about Peter Tredwell, the version that seemed appropriate for Dominic did not take long.

'I'm afraid', Dominic said, 'that some of our undergraduates are mildly hysterical about the murder. I gather there is a good deal of doubling up going on – people sleeping in sleeping-bags in other people's rooms, that kind of thing. A few parents have telephoned the college to ask what we're doing to protect their young. I've tried to sound reassuring. I have asked the Fellows to encourge calm by pointing out that there is absolutely no reason to think that there is a random killer on the loose. And we've asked the porters to keep an extra close eye on strangers about the college. So far everyone they've collared has been a journalist. I'm afraid there's no way to stop them garnering a harvest of ghastly quotes from our young. But really there's not much else we can do.'

'Absolutely,' I said. 'We can be pretty sure, after Charlie Phipps's death, that the college was only the scene of the murder. Whoever did it had a motive – one that had nothing to do with Clare.'

'By the way,' said Dominic, 'the porters have just sent over all of the post from Glen Tannock's pigeon-hole in a large envelope. Perhaps you would care to take it. I am sure his parents will want to go through it. Though . . .' He paused. 'I suppose you know that *Private Eye* has suggested that Peter Tredwell was . . . er . . . involved in some sort of liaison with Glen Tannock.' I nodded. 'Very embarrassing for the Ivors, of course. Anyway, I've just asked Tredwell whether it's true; that's why I was late. He tells me it is, but that the police have ruled him out as a suspect. In the circumstances, I think it may be best just to leave it at that. He has agreed to deny he is homosexual if asked by the press. Since Lord Glen Tannock cannot be asked, the scandal should blow over fairly swiftly.'

'I am sure that's right, Dominic,' I said.

'Anyway, you might think it is wise to go through the boy's mail before you pass it on. You could convey anything relevant to the police. If there were anything of a personal nature, it might be best if his parents didn't see it. It would only upset Lord and Lady Ivor unnecessarily. After all, it hardly matters now. Peter Tredwell assures me, at least, that there is nothing from *him*.'

'I suppose the press will be baying after him like a pack of hounds,' Julia said, adding vaguely, 'I sometimes wonder if the advantages of a free press aren't exaggerated.'

'Still, I don't think it would do the college any good to go after him. For one thing, we'd have to prove it, wouldn't we, if we were going to sack him? I mean, he could drag us in front of an industrial relations tribunal otherwise. Wrongful dismissal. Of course, it would be another matter if he was in any way connected with the death.' Dominic was still thinking as Master.

'I don't actually know what the legal position would be. I'm afraid I leave employment law to other people in the chambers. I could find out if you were interested.'

'That's very kind, Patrick, but I don't think we ought to do that anyway. After all, as Julia pointed out to me this morning, if he was having an affair with your cousin, he must have suffered a good deal already. He's a very clever young man, and we were lucky to get him. He read mathematics at Balliol as an undergraduate and then did research in the philosophy of mathematics with Michael Dummett, who thinks extremely highly of him. I'm surprised he left Oxford; but I think he'd become interested in various issues to do with probability and Hugh Mellor was a bit of pull. I must say I hope this business doesn't drive him off the deep end.'

A telephone rang in the room next door. 'Excuse me,' he said, and he stepped out for a moment. When he returned he was looking extremely concerned.

'I don't know which of you should go, but it's Claudia Phipps and I'm afraid she's hysterical. Something about a note. I suspect it might be best if you went back to her house at once.'

Virginia ran out of the room and I followed.

She was on the telephone soothing Claudia, calming her down, telling her we would be back soon. 'No need to explain now, Claudia. Patrick and I will be back in a few minutes. Will you be all right till then?'

As we left the Wrattings Dominic handed me the envelope of David's mail. 'Quite understand, of course. Do telephone if there's anything I can do. Good-night.'

Virginia and I hurried across the Old Court. 'What was all that about?' I said.

'Claudia's been looking through the mail from the lab. She thinks she's found a note from Charlie's killer.'

# 16

Claudia had calmed down a little by the time we got back to Portugal Place. As she opened the door, she thrust a piece of white bond paper into my hand; behind her, the policewoman Fanshaw had dispatched stood in the corridor looking extremely anxious. Claudia introduced us perfunctorily, and gathered us into the sitting-room. The three of us settled on the sofa.

*Epistula secunda.*
*Charles Phipps.*
*Moriture, te saluto.*

'The second letter. Charles Phipps. Oh, you who are about to die, I greet you. Is that right?' Claudia said.

I nodded. 'It's a reference to what the gladiators or the martyrs . . . I can't remember which . . . said to the emperor when they entered the Colosseum. It's in Suetonius, I think. Of course, they said "*Morituri te salutant*", "Those who are about to die salute you."'

'And the "second letter", I suppose, is meant to suggest the epistles; and thus the Apostles?' Virginia said uncertainly.

'Then, why the second? Did you find another one? I suppose Charlie might have had a message and kept it quiet so as not to worry you. It's sinister, but in the normal course of things you wouldn't take it too seriously.'

Claudia shook her head. 'If he'd been worried about something like this, I would have known something was wrong. Oh God, Patrick, I'm scared.'

'Don't you worry, my dear, whoever it is, we'll find him. Best thing now is to try and think sensibly about what the note tells us.'

'Where did you get it?' Virginia asked gently, and I added, 'And when?'

'This morning. Charlie's research assistant came over with a pile of letters from the office. They'd been gathering in Charlie's pigeon-hole for a while.'

'Well, I suppose we'd better get Fanshaw to come round and collect it. Did you keep the envelope? They'll want to look for fingerprints.'

'I've already phoned Inspector Fanshaw, sir.' The policewoman spoke for the first time. 'He's on his way.'

Claudia collected a waste-paper basket from the kitchen and sorted through it until she found a long white envelope of the same bonded paper as the note. Gingerly, I held the paper and the envelope up to the light.

'You know, I think this was done on a computer. The characters seem to be made up of dots, not like an ordinary typewriter. And the watermark's pretty distinctive. Should give them something to work on.'

As I finished speaking, Virginia leapt suddenly up off the sofa.

'Of course,' she said, 'how stupid. This isn't the second letter to Charles. It's the second letter to the Apostles. David must have got one, too.'

'But why didn't he tell anybody?'

'For the same reason Charlie didn't. Presumably, it arrived after he died.' Virginia rushed out of the room and fetched the large envelope stuffed full of David's mail, which we had deposited in the hall. She opened it swiftly and emptied the contents on the floor in front of us. There in the middle of the rug lay another bonded envelope of the same type.

'Don't touch it,' I said. 'The forensic people will want to check it. For fingerprints, salivary proteins, anything that might identify the person who sent it.'

The policewoman nodded agreement. But Virginia looked at me unbelieving. 'Don't you want to know what it says?'

'I want to know who killed Charles and David.'

In twenty minutes, a police constable arrived. We showed him the envelope on the sitting-room floor and he picked it up off the rug with a pair of tweezers and popped it in a plastic bag. 'Inspector Fanshaw said he'd be along in a little while, and could you ask Sir Oliver Hetherington over to join you.'

By the time Fanshaw turned up, I had got hold of Oliver at the Darwins'. I mentioned the notes to him and he said he would be over in about twenty minutes 'with some riveting information' about Vera Oblomov. It was a quarter past ten.

While we waited, I explained the note to Fanshaw.

'I see,' he said. 'Well, that settles it then. It's someone connected with your Society, isn't it?'

'Or someone who hates it,' Claudia said.

'Or someone who's trying to muddy the waters,' said Virginia.

Fanshaw looked ill at ease. 'There's something I'd like to discuss with you, sir; it's by way of being rather confidential.' I assumed that he either had something to say about Vera Oblomov and didn't wish to talk in front of Claudia and Virginia, who had, so far as he knew, no security clearance, or wanted to say something about Charlie's death that might upset Claudia.

'Of course,' I said. 'Claudia, some of the possibilities that Inspector Fanshaw is following up involve access to top secret papers. He's had me cleared for the information, but he'd be breaching the Official Secrets Act if he passed it on to an unauthorized person.'

'Oh,' said Claudia.

Virginia came to the rescue. 'I'm not cleared, either, so I'd better keep you company. We can at least make ourselves useful brewing tea for the Inspector. Come on, Claudia.'

It turned out that Fanshaw actually wanted to talk about Hippo; apparently discussing these matters in front of the ladies did not fit with his ideas of professional propriety.

'It's all very puzzling, Sir Patrick. It's not just Dr Oblomov. Take that Mr Buckingham. I couldn't get to see him this morning like I planned. Peterson had some things for me to do with Dr Oblomov. So I sent an officer over to tell him I'd see him later. Well, my man came back and said Buckingham was expecting me at four.'

Fanshaw had gone to Hippo's rooms at the appointed hour and confronted him with my report. Hippo had admitted at once that he'd lied to me. 'Said he was sure that Dr Tredwell was the murderer and wanted to put you on to him. As a matter of fact, he seemed to have it in for Dr Tredwell.'

'It's understandable,' I said. 'He was obviously convinced

that Tredwell had corrupted his best friend. But what did he say about the money?'

'That's the puzzle. You see, at first he stuck to his story about the bill at the Pitt Club. Well, I checked with Mr Caufield, the manager there, later, on the off-chance that he would know. And he said that Mr Buckingham hadn't had any difficulty paying his bill. Anyway, to get back to the interview with Mr Buckingham. I mentioned to him the business with the visit in the night, and he said some things I wouldn't like to repeat about James Hogg and how he wished he'd mind his own blanking business. First of all his story was that his visitor was just a friend of his who had lent him some money, like Lord Glen Tannock. Well, then, this chap arrives, and Buckingham says he's the person he owes the money to and he makes him out a cheque . . . for two hundred and eighty pounds.' Fanshaw gave me a meaningful look. On the whole, Hippo had not had much luck timing the arrival of his friends.

'What's the puzzle about that?' I asked.

'Well, he still had Lord Glen Tannock's cheque. In fact, I took it as evidence.'

'So, if he needed two hundred and fifty quid from Lord Glen Tannock, how could he afford to make out a cheque for more than that to this other person? You asked him, I imagine.'

'I did, sir. Well, I put it friendly-like. I said it wasn't a good idea to go bouncing cheques off your friends. And he says he's just got some money today.'

'Where from?'

'That's the problem, sir. At first he wouldn't say. I told him it looked pretty bad in the circumstances and if he wouldn't tell me I might have to arrest him. So, finally, he said he'd made the money on a horse.'

'Well that might explain why he was short of money . . . if he gambled, I mean?

'But I don't believe him, sir. He couldn't tell me which race it was or which horse. Said he'd forgotten. How would you forget a thing like that that happened just an hour or two earlier?'

'And he stuck with that story?'

'Wouldn't budge.'

'I don't understand it.' I thought for a moment whether there was any way of checking on Hippo's movements. 'Did you ask the porters if they'd seen him going in or out today?'

'No, but I can follow the thing up in the morning. What I can't understand is why he would be so concerned to keep the real source of the money secret. I mean he must know that he's risking being charged with murder.' Fanshaw looked about as perplexed as I was. It really was very strange. There was Hippo, someone David had plainly liked enough to lend him a good deal of money, being as shifty as you please in the midst of the investigation of David's death.

'And that isn't the only strange thing that I've found out. I've been checking on the Oblomov woman. She's been behaving very strangely in the last few weeks. It's funny. She seemed so sensible when I talked to her. But the Senior Tutor at King's said she'd been all emotional, recently. Even had to stop teaching one day because she burst into tears. And she wouldn't tell anybody what it was about. Then I asked the porters and they say she's been going in and out of the lodge at all hours asking them if they haven't lost a letter she's expecting . . . Well, Peterson doesn't want her to know we suspect anything, so I can't ask *her* about it. I wondered, maybe . . .'

'I'll do what I can, Inspector. But I think we may find that Sir Oliver Hetherington may be some help. You see, he was going to pay her a visit this afternoon.'

Oliver, whose sense of timing has always been excellent, arrived a few minutes later. And, judging from his grin, he was very pleased with himself.

'Hugh and I went out to Madingley for our chat with Oblomova. She wasn't in college this afternoon, so she asked us out there. Actually the whole thing seemed really quite natural, since Dale Bishop was already there chatting her up. Amiable fellow, but once you get to know him, he's rather inclined to run on. Turned out to be useful, though. Probably distracted Oblomov from the fact that Hugh and I were busy trying to flush her out.

'Anyway, the point is, practically everything she said was a lie. Well, she said her father was dead, which is true. But she was very unwilling to say anything else about her family. And when Hugh mentioned jokingly that the Society's only connection with the Soviet Union was that it had been fashionable in the thirties to plan a retirement there, she asked him what he meant and pretended to know nothing about the Philby thing. Hugh tells me that's ridiculous, because he distinctly remembers it all coming up at a dinner a few years ago when she was present. Anyway, then I asked her about life in Moscow and she relaxed a little. But the point is she's very keen to keep us away from her father's identity and she's terrified that we'll find out she knows that anybody in the Society was involved in intelligence. Towards the end, we talked a bit about David again, and she pretended she didn't know anything about Charlie Ivor. I said something like "Charlie was always a very dashing fellow" and she put on a puzzled face and asked me how Charlie Phipps was related to David.'

Oliver was, no doubt, happy with his story. It seemed churlish to disappoint him. But he was going too fast. 'Let's step back a moment,' I said, 'and see what it might look like from her point of view. She's expecting some important news, perhaps from her family in Russia. It hasn't come. It must be something very troubling, so she's upset. Perhaps she suspects that you have something to do with intelligence and she's worried, as a Russian defector, that the FO is suspicious of her. She might even think you came to the meeting to keep an eye on her. So she's covering up any connection with anything fishy. Seems to me there's no reason to suppose that what she's trying to cover up is murder.'

Oliver was obviously about to respond when the phone rang in the hall. Virginia came in a few seconds later. 'It's for you, Inspector.' When Fanshaw came back he handed me a page from his notebook.

'I copied it down. They spelled it out for me.'

*Epistula prima.*
*David, Viscount Glen Tannock.*
*. . . cum semel occidit brevis lux*
*Nox est perpetua una dormienda.*

'What's it mean?' Fanshaw asked, when he had finished reading.

'"The first letter. David, Viscount Glen Tannock. When once the brief light falls, there is a perpetual night for sleeping." 'It's Catullus.'

'It's madness,' said Oliver. 'That's what it is. What sort of lunatic would want to start wiping out the Society? It makes no sense.' For the first time Oliver sounded distinctly flappable.

'It seems to me that if these notes are genuine, we may have to stop looking for rational motives,' I said. 'On the other hand, as Virginia pointed out earlier, they may be meant to distract us. Still, Inspector, I think that we ought to warn all the active members of the Society. In fact, it might be a good idea to have your people protecting them.' Fanshaw nodded his assent.

Oliver spoke again; and there was an edge of barely suppressed hysteria in his voice. 'If these notes mean what they seem to, somebody may be trying to kill us all.' Even Oliver's carefully constructed diplomatic façade was beginning to fray.

Fanshaw said he would telephone the station and arrange for a policeman to spend the night outside James Hogg's set at Trinity Hall and Hugh's rooms at Corpus.

'Since Dr Oblomov is already under surveillance, there's no need to worry about her.'

'I'm afraid that no matter how hard I try I can't see Dr Oblomov as our murderer,' I said, shaking my head. 'It goes against all my instincts. And I can tell you one thing for sure: she didn't send those notes. I've been racking my brains trying to think what it is that makes me so certain she didn't send them; and I've just realized what it was. The other evening I quoted a passage from Virgil and Vera Oblomov didn't know what it meant. She doesn't know Latin. Now she could have collected those two passages from a dictionary of quotations, I suppose. But she'd have had to have known Latin to know how to change the grammar in the message to Charlie.'

I could see that neither Oliver nor Fanshaw was very impressed by this argument. 'Well, if you still suspect her, you'd better give her an official police guardian too. Otherwise, she may wonder what's going on if any of the others tell her that they are being protected and she thinks she is not.'

'Perhaps', Oliver suggested, 'we should ask everyone not to

mention that they are being guarded, not even to other members of the Society. After all, if one of us were the murderer, that would be a reasonable precaution. We needn't say who we have in mind.'

I said, 'I don't suppose it's reasonable to expect Hugh not to discuss his being guarded with James; and they're the only two, apart from you, Oliver, who were at the meeting. If we tell them not to discuss it, won't they guess we suspect Oblomov?'

'Well, there's still Godfrey and Dale Bishop to suspect; they weren't at David's last meeting but they were at the one before. And they're as much current Apostles as Vera Oblomov.'

'But Godfrey was at Heston and Dale Bishop's too new to the Society to have any obvious motives.' Oliver nodded as I spoke. We turned to Fanshaw.

'All right. It seems it might be best to put an obvious guard on Dr Oblomov, doesn't it?' Fanshaw agreed. He also said he would summon a couple of policemen to Claudia's house, one to replace our policewoman, the other to go back to the Master's lodge at Trinity with Oliver.

While he was making these arrangements, Oliver and I went in to see Virginia and Claudia in the kitchen. Claudia was very tired, and Virginia asked for my support in persuading her to go to bed. 'I'll tell you everything in the morning,' I said to Claudia. 'There's nothing more to be done tonight.' As I followed them out of the kitchen and into the hall, I whispered to Virginia, 'Come back down when you've tucked her in.'

When I got back into the sitting-room, Fanshaw had finished with the phone. 'I've fixed 'em all up except Dr Stanley. Where would I find him?' he asked.

'I suppose Godfrey will either be in college or at home in the country. Perhaps Hugh would know.'

I called Hugh up to explain what was happening and asked him whether Godfrey was likely to be in town.

'I don't know,' Hugh said, 'but I should try the college first. You know, I think it might be a good idea for me to forewarn Dale. I think he's likely to be finding this all rather more enervating than the rest of us. So far he seems to think that our English police procedures are rather amateurish. He's actually rather frightened. And I'm not sure he'll be terribly reassured by having a bobby turn up and announce that he's there to protect him from a mad Apostle-slayer. Of course, he's not on the phone. But he's only in Darwin, I'll wander over and tell him to expect someone; it's only a few minutes away.'

'You're right. It might be a nice gesture to pop over and reassure him. But you haven't any idea about Godfrey?'

''Fraid not.'

'Oliver might know; I'll ask him as soon as I ring off.'

Oliver had been chatting to Fanshaw in the sitting-room, and they had been joined by Virginia. When I asked, he said Godfrey had not been at the Darwins for dinner, so that he was probably at his country place. It was nearly midnight, but in the circumstances it seemed wise to telephone his house and see if he was there.

'It's not far from Weston Colville,' I told Fanshaw, 'a few miles this side of Newmarket.'

But the phone rang about a dozen times and was not answered. So I called the porter's lodge at Trinity and asked for Professor Stanley.

Godfrey sounded as though he had been asleep.

'Godfrey, it's me, Patrick Scott. Sorry to wake you, but it's rather important. Is your door locked?'

'What on earth are you talking about?'

'The thing is, we've just recovered a couple of threatening notes from David and Charlie's mail of the last few days. It looks as though someone may be after the Society. So Fanshaw is going to send over a chap to stand guard . . . keep you company over the next few days, until we find out what's happening.'

'Oh dear.' He sighed deeply. 'Well, at least that explains why we weren't having much luck identifying the killer. I mean, neither Tredwell nor Buckingham is likely to be mad enough to plot something like that. So it must be somebody we haven't thought of.' Godfrey was obviously wide awake now, and his mind was working. 'Look, I had planned to ask you and Virginia out to the country for dinner tomorrow night. Why don't you come and stay overnight? Bring Charlie's widow and the baby with you . . . That way Fanshaw will only have to give us one man.'

I thought for a moment. The trails I had been following in Cambridge had all led nowhere. There was nothing for me to do until I had sorted through the mass of conflicting evidence of the last few days. And Virginia and Godfrey, between them, would probably give me more help than anyone I could think of. Claudia would profit from some time away from the house. And, above all, with a madman apparently on the loose, we would surely be safer out of town. All in all, it seemed an excellent plan.

I accepted.

It was very late by the time we had made all the arrangements. Virginia, Oliver, Fanshaw and I gathered for a cup of tea in the kitchen. I explained to her Godfrey's plan for the next evening and she seemed to think it a good one. A little after half-past midnight, two young constables turned up and Fanshaw introduced us to them.

'Constable Harper will go with you, Sir Oliver; Constable Deacon will stay here and watch this place.' They retired to the street outside, chatting quietly together.

When they left, I asked Fanshaw if he minded discussing Vera Oblomov in front of Virginia and he said sheepishly, 'If she's anything like my wife she'll have it all out of you five minutes after I'm out of the door, anyway.'

It took no time to bring Virginia into the picture. She gave one of her lucid summaries. 'She has suspicions and she's nervous as all hell.'

'I'm afraid it's not a matter of her having suspicions,' I said. 'Charlie Phipps mentioned to all of us the other night that it had come out that Oliver and David's father had been in intelligence together.' I paused. Something else had just occurred to me. 'But there is one thing she couldn't possibly know unless Russian intelligence told her; the fact that Charlie Ivor killed her father. It was kept very quiet at the time at this end. You saw to that, Oliver. And the Soviets had no reason to tell anyone.'

Oliver nodded.

'But why would they tell her now, after all these years?' Fanshaw asked.

Nobody had an answer.

Oliver said, 'Well, suppose Virginia's right. Mightn't we just tell her that that's what we suspect and ask her what the trouble is? I mean, if she's innocent, surely we can persuade her that it's better to tell the truth; and if she isn't, we can probably catch her out in a lie.' He didn't seem very confident of his proposal.

'Peterson has got clearance to check her mail,' Fanshaw said quietly. 'So it might be better to wait a bit and see what turns up. It's always easier to confront someone if you've got some hard evidence.'

And we had precious little of that.

# 17

I awoke late the next morning to find that Virginia was already up. There were bustling sounds of life in the kitchen, and the aroma of bacon and eggs wafted temptingly up the stairs. I dressed and shaved quickly and trotted down to join the others. Virginia and Claudia were in the kitchen having breakfast with a fresh-faced young policeman, while Paddy snoozed in his pram. As I entered, the policeman made to rise.

'Don't get up, officer,' I said somewhat belatedly. 'I'm Patrick Scott.'

'Good mornin', Sir Patrick.' He offered me a hand. 'I'm Constable Hedge, sir; Bill Hedge.'

'Well, you and your predecessor have allowed me my first good night's sleep in several days. I expect Paddy didn't let *you* sleep quite so easily, Claudia?'

Claudia beamed at me and gazed proudly across at the pram.

'Well, what shall we do today? Shall we take a picnic somewhere out of town?' Virginia said.

I had an idea. 'Claudia, did Jinny tell you that Godfrey Stanley's expecting us to come over for dinner this evening and spend the night?' Claudia nodded. 'Well, there's a marvellous stretch of woodland on his estate, where he has some shooting. I'm sure he'd be delighted to have us picnic there.'

'And we can let Bill go and do something more important than watching over us.'

'Oh no, sir, Inspector Fanshaw said I was to stick with you,' Hedge said.

'In that case,' Virginia said, 'today your job is to go on a picnic.'

I telephoned Trinity – it was now about eleven – and asked to speak to Godfrey. 'He's left the college, sir. Won't be back until dinner on Monday.'

This time, when I dialled his number in the country, somebody answered the telephone at once.

'Heston House,' said a familiar female voice.

'Ah, Mrs Porteous, is that you? It's Patrick Scott.'

'Oh, Sir Patrick. Professor Stanley told me you was coming to stay. You and Lady Scott, is it sir? And a Mrs Phipps what has recently lost her husband. Professor Stanley told me about that, sir. It's a shocking thing. And the baby? He was complaining about having a baby in the house, and I told him that if he asked me it was the best thing that could happen; bring some life to the place.'

'And I expect he said he didn't ask you.'

'How'd you know that?' she giggled. 'Yes. I should be used to his ways by now, but he's always teasing me, is Professor Stanley. But he is so kind. I just got back from a little holiday with my sister in Bournemouth last week. I've been a bit poorly so Professor Stanley told me to go off for a few days rest.'

'Well, Mrs P., I called to ask Professor Stanley a favour. I thought that I would bring the party out for a picnic in the woods.'

'Oh Lord, you don't need to ask him about that. I'll tell him. Just you come.'

'We'll see you late this afternoon, then.'

'That *will* be nice. My best to Lady Scott.'

I drove the five of us out of Cambridge in Virginia's ageing blue Volvo along the Ely road. We said little. Claudia cooed at Paddy from time to time and eventually persuaded a bashful Bill Hedge to join in.

Heston House, a grand, largely eighteenth-century affair, stands alone in its own acreage, a few miles north of West Wratting towards Newmarket. The drive takes only about half an hour and we were soon at the gates of the park. I drove up the long elm avenue, past the main house, with its elegant Georgian façade, and along the narrow track that runs by some farm buildings into the woods. As we came round the back, I saw Godfrey's enormous old Bentley pulled up beside the stables.

'Tha'ss a lovely-lookin' car,' Bill Hedge remarked to no one in particular.

It was Virginia's decision that we eat more or less at once, seated in the shade of a copper beech with a view across meadows and fields towards Newmarket. 'Then we can go into the woods and see what we can find.'

After a lazy picnic, we packed up the rugs and the remaining food and loaded it into the boot of the car. Then we set off into the woods. Claudia had brought one of those contraptions that allows you to sling a baby in front of you and, once he had settled into it, Paddy promptly fell asleep. I must say that I rather wished I could follow his example; but Virginia in her active mood will brook no resistance.

A couple of hours later, as we were making our way back, drained, from a vigorous trek through the woods, we heard the sound of a car horn.

'Sounds like our car,' I said, and Virginia nodded.

Bill ran ahead to see what it was. 'I'll look a bit of a fool if somebody runs off with your car while I'm s'posed to be guardin' you,' he said.

When, not long after, we all arrived back by the Volvo at the edge of the woods, Bill Hedge was talking to Godfrey and another policeman.

'Ah, Patrick.' Godfrey took me by the arm. 'I thought a quick toot on the horn might do the trick. This is my guardian, Constable Wilkins. Inspector Fanshaw called. He's rather eager to talk to you. Wouldn't tell me what it was about. I promised to try and find you and get you to telephone him. Virginia, how splendid; and this must be Claudia Phipps.'

After our introductions, Virginia said, 'You and Godfrey and Constable Wilkins take the car up to the house, the rest of us will walk. Bill can be our minder.'

As we drove away, Godfrey enquired whether I had any new

ideas about David's murder. 'Who could have sent those sinister notes?'

'If the notes were sent by the murderer – and remember they were both found in pigeon-holes where they could have been left any time until yesterday morning – then he or she has some pretty distinguishing characteristics: knowledge that David and Charlie were members of the Society, knowledge of David's allergy, the ability to slip in and out of Charlie's lab unobserved, knowledge of Latin . . . On the other hand, there is the remote possibility that they were sent by one of those cranks that always gather around any murder that reaches the press.'

'Most cranks presumably do not have a knowledge of Catullus,' Godfrey offered drily.

'That would be a safe assumption elsewhere. But most Cambridge cranks are members of the university. And every one of them has to have known enough Latin once to matriculate.'

'Alas,' Godfrey said, 'no more. Latin is no longer a condition of admission, Patrick. Now, you can get away with a modern European language. Soon, no doubt, a knowledge of Urdu will be held to be sufficient evidence of familiarity with our national traditions. Still, I'm afraid you're right. We can suppose that most of the people we should think of as potential Apostle-murderers would know enough Latin to modify a line from Suetonius and repeat one of Catullus's best-known couplets.'

When we reached the house, there was a large car in the drive, and standing next to it were Hugo McAlister and a large-boned, copper-haired woman I assumed must be his wife. 'Hallo,' Hugo said genially. 'We were on our way back from an afternoon in Suffolk, and we thought we'd pop by and see how you were, Godfrey. But I see you've got Patrick with you. Patrick, I don't think you've met my wife.'

Introductions completed, Hugo said, 'It's rather convenient that you're here, Patrick, I had something I wanted to discuss with you. Would you mind awfully, if I took Patrick off for a moment?'

We wandered together across the lawn.

'A couple of things, Patrick. First of all, are you sure you'll be up to addressing the annual dinner? You know I'm presiding this year, and I could easily fix up for someone else to do it.'

'No, no. After all, the least I can do is tell the Society what I know about these ghastly murders of our young Brethren.'

'Good, good. But you need only telephone if you change your mind. Any news on that front, by the way?'

'Not really.'

'Ah well, let's hope you have some news for us on Tuesday.' He paused for only a second before going on. 'Now the other thing is, I've been meaning to get in touch with you for some time now about a tax matter and seeing you the other day put me in mind of it again. I expect you know that I bought some property in Mayfair from the Society in the thirties?'

'No, I didn't know, actually. I didn't know the Society ever owned any property.'

'Well, this might interest you, then. A small cul-de-sac in Mayfair – Beeston Place, it's called – was left to the Society in about 1929; and by the time it was all out of probate a couple of years had passed and there was some worry about what to do with it. I mean the Society isn't set up to manage property. Well, it happened that at about that time I came into my grandfather's estate and so I offered to buy it. That way the Society could put the money in the bank or spend it rather than trying to manage the place.'

'And now there's a tax problem?'

'No, not yet. But the thing is I've decided to sell it. And I understand that I should think about the best way to handle the tax consequences of the sale; I mean it's probably worth twenty-odd million.' Hugo's offhand tone seemed mildly artificial in the circumstances. 'Of course,' he went on, 'I'd rather you didn't mention this to anyone. You see, it might be thought to display a lack of confidence in my biotechnology business if I were known to be "going liquid" just at the moment. Still, I know I can rely on a Brother Apostle to be discreet.'

'Well, I'd be delighted to see what I can do. Give me a couple of weeks to think, and I'll be in touch.'

Once Hugo had left, Godfrey led me into his study. 'There. You can commune with Fanshaw undisturbed in here. Wilkins and

I are going to evensong in Weston Colville. It's a hideous church, of course, but duty calls.'

Fanshaw had given Godfrey a number for me to telephone. He answered almost at once.

'Ah, Inspector, it's Patrick Scott.'

'Sorry to disturb you, sir, but Peterson's people have come up with something I thought you ought to know about. Dr Oblomov went up to London this morning, early, on the train. Then she took a cab from King's Cross to Millionaire's Row in Kensington.'

'My God. Did she go to the Russian embassy?'

'Exactly, Sir Patrick. She was there about an hour. They let her out a back door, obviously worried that she would be seen. But by then Peterson's man had alerted the people who watch the embassy. So they had all the entrances covered. Sir Oliver Hetherington and I are going over to talk to her in about an hour. But Sir Oliver wanted me to make sure you didn't think it was too soon.' I took it that what Oliver really wanted was to give me an opportunity to invite myself along to the interrogation. Curious as I was, there seemed no reason to go. Between them, Oliver and Inspector Fanshaw would do very well. Out here, at least, I could hope to keep Godfrey out of the way of the murderer.

'Can't think of any reason to hold off now. As you said, yesterday, you needed evidence to confront her with. Now you've got it. Do phone when you're done.'

'Very good, sir, we'll go ahead with that then. There's one other thing, sir. We've been making a little progress by more conventional police methods as well. We've got an undergraduate from King's, who saw Charles Phipps talking to someone by a car outside Memorial Court on Thursday night. She doesn't have much idea about who it was – actually, she doesn't seem to have seen his face – or what kind of car; but she recognized Dr Phipps from lectures – she's a medical student.'

'Thursday night . . . not Wednesday?'

'No, so far nothing on Wednesday. But it's a start. If we can find out who was in that car, we can find out more about what Dr Phipps was up to that night. Might provide some sort of a lead. Anyway, we'll keep at it. I'm doing a spot after the television news this evening, asking anyone who can tell us more about that car to come forward. We may even get the driver offering himself. But it looks as though we don't have to worry about other people being attacked, doesn't it? I mean, if Dr Oblomov is our murderer, she can't get near anyone without being observed; now that we have her under surveillance.'

'We can't be sure, though, until you've pinned it on Dr Oblomov for certain. And if she *is* working for the Soviets, then she might have some help. I'm sure they have people who know how to poison someone quietly.' I didn't really want to encourage the notion that Oblomov was guilty. At the same time, I didn't want Fanshaw to become sanguine. Once he made up his mind she was guilty, he might lift the protection from the rest of us: and, if – as I believed – it wasn't Oblomov, that could prove dangerous.

So I was relieved when he said: 'You're right, Sir Patrick. We should still be on our guard.'

I made a few desultory enquiries about Hippo. They were still trying to find some independent check on his financial resources. 'If it comes right down to it, I should be able to get a warrant to see whether he's had any unusual transactions through his bank accounts recently,' Fanshaw said. But the truth was that whatever Hippo had been up to, I had lost interest in him. Even if it wasn't Vera, I couldn't imagine Hippo being resourceful enough to contrive two murders in a couple of days.

I sat for a while in Godfrey's study. On the desk was a collection of pens, laid out neatly above the blotter by a glass ink-pot; a glass paper-weight; a set of pipes, all of them well broken in, next to a box of tobacco; and a few pipe-cleaners. Apart from these few objects, there was only the telephone and a few dictionaries standing between book-ends of blue-veined marble.

I thought about Fanshaw's call. Was I, perhaps, too dogmatic in excluding Vera from consideration? Perhaps Fanshaw might eventually be able to link her to the murders. If Oliver's theory was right, it was a sad story. If he were right, Vera would essentially have given up her life to avenge the death of her father. Now in her late fifties, by the time she came out of prison she would be past retirement age. Her career would be over; and she would have lost much of the comfortable pension she could have expected in the normal course of things. She had already given up one life in Russia, when she defected. Now she would have been throwing away another.

It was true that the circumstantial evidence did seem to support Oliver's theory. I was frankly uneasy about the details and I knew I would be happier when Fanshaw produced something more substantial. Still, as I say, we were safe enough out at Heston: if Vera wasn't the murderer, I suspected that whoever it was was the kind of killer who operated best in the crowded world of Cambridge.

My reflections were disturbed by the sounds of the arrival of the walking party. I got up and left the study and walked along the corridor to the hall to greet them.

'What did Fanshaw have to say, Patrick?'

'It looks as though we may have our murderer. Oliver Hetherington and Fanshaw are going over to talk to Vera Oblomov this evening.' I kept my doubts to myself.

'Vera Oblomov?' Claudia said. 'I can't believe it. Why?'

'It's a complicated story, Claudia my dear. If Fanshaw's suspicions prove well founded, I shall explain it over dinner.'

Mrs Porteous appeared from the kitchen, wearing an apron that was lightly dusted with flour. 'One of your delicious pies in the making, I see,' said Virginia. 'Now, Mrs P., this is Claudia Phipps, the infant is Paddy, and our guardian is Constable Bill Hedge. So just you tell us where we're to settle in and we'll let you get back to the kitchen.'

'You and Sir Patrick is in the Green Room, as usual. And I put Mrs Phipps and the baby at the opposite end of the corridor from Professor Stanley. Otherwise he'll be fussing all night every time the baby so much as yawns.'

Bill Hedge announced that as it was now nearly six, he would soon be collected and replaced by another officer. 'Where's Constable Wilkins?' he asked.

'Gone to evensong with Professor Stanley.'

'They'll be back by half-past six,' said Mrs Porteous. 'Professor Stanley always arrives back a good hour before dinner. But if you're going off soon, perhaps I could give you something for tea, Constable?'

# 18

As Mrs Porteous had predicted, Godfrey and his policeman were back by half-past six. A police car had arrived at about six with Anscombe, the officer who was going to replace Constables Wilkins and Hedge.

By seven o'clock, Virginia and I had gathered with Godfrey in the drawing-room. 'Claudia will be down in a moment,' Virginia said. Godfrey offered us drinks and then moved us out through the French windows on to the lawn.

'Our Constable Hedge was admiring your Bentley, Godfrey,' Virginia said. 'But isn't it a rather *noticeable* car for driving around Cambridge?'

'Now you mustn't tease an old man, Virginia. I know it's not the most practical means of transportation, but I like it. And you can always hire a car if you don't want to be noticed. There are car-hire people all over the place nowadays; even down here in the country. Now our friend Hugh Penhaligon, for example, is always hiring cars for his little trips. Says it's impractical to keep a car if you live in college.'

'I suppose he's right, really,' I said. 'He's within five minutes' walk of practically everything he needs to do.'

'I expect if I gave up Heston, I should give up the car, too. But in the meantime, I enjoy it. Of course, I don't drive myself on longer journeys any more. There's a young man in the village who drives me up to London when I need to go. Ah look, there's Claudia.'

Godfrey was on excellent form, charming the ladies and telling tales of the Cambridge past. He was sweetly solicitous of Claudia, and, once he realized that she was keen to talk about Charlie, he told her about their recent discussions. 'He was absolutely fascinating about his work. I expect he told you that he had been seeking my help these last few weeks. I was so pleased when he sought me out – it was a really fascinating little problem. I've always had an interest in neuro-physiology. I knew they'd need some serious mathematics in the end. But what Charlie was doing was really quite outstanding. He came to me with a little mathematical problem, oh, about six weeks ago, and, naturally, I asked him to explain to me what it had to do with. Well, he was due to talk to the Society about it a few weeks ahead, and he was keen to know what others might find interesting. So, with many apologies and much warning me that I would probably be bored, he gave me the most enlightening account of what he was doing. Truth to tell, I think he was slightly anxious at the prospect of giving an informal presentation of his ideas in front of Hugo McAlister.'

'Hugo and his wife dropped by this afternoon. Julia Wratting had said how charming they were; she *is* awfully nice, isn't she?'

'Indeed,' Godfrey said. But he was keen to go on talking about Charlie; it was his way, I think, of helping Claudia, and I thought, once more, how often Godfrey's basic decency slipped out from under his crusty carapace. 'I think it was because he was so nervous about having Hugo in his audience that Charlie was trying his ideas out on anyone who would listen. He even grabbed our new American friend, Mr Bishop, as well; that paper two weeks ago must have had the best audience research of any paper at the Society in history. And he asked us both to visit his laboratories . . . which, as I'm sure he told you, Claudia, I did several times. Amazing work he was doing. First-rate.'

We moved into the sitting-room, and Virginia said, 'Godfrey, Patrick tells me that David was investigating the papers of Gregory Ransome. Do you know much about what he'd found?'

'Well, as I told Patrick the other day, the main outlines were quite familiar to me. It was I that went through his papers first when he died. But David had been following up on Ransome's personal dealings with various interesting figures – Keynes, Ramsey, Russell – a whole host of Apostolic luminaries. I was hoping to find out more when we next met.'

'Perhaps if I went to see Mrs Ransome, I could find out a little more about David's work. It would be nice, as I think I told you the other day . . . or was it Oliver?'

'Probably Oliver,' Godfrey said.

'Nice to get something published, if David had done enough. It's odd that there were no notes in his room.' It was the first time the thought had struck me. As I spoke, the phone rang in the hall.

'Don't worry, Mrs Porteous will answer it,' Godfrey said.

'Could he have kept his notes somewhere else?' I continued.

'Very possibly,' Godfrey said. 'Perhaps even in the study at Margery Ransome's house where he was looking at the papers. I can telephone her for you and ask about it in the morning. She's always pleased to have visitors . . . ah, now, I think I hear Mrs Porteous treading the corridor to announce the feast she has no doubt prepared.'

Mrs Porteous's cooking belongs to a genre that is widely believed to be non-existent – the genre of fine English cooking. She manages to make even the most ordinary of dishes – roast chicken, for example – into a feast. So I was particularly cross when Mrs Porteous announced that dinner was ready but Inspector Fanshaw was on the phone for me.

'I'm afraid this may take a little time. Perhaps you should get on with dinner without me,' I said with some reluctance, as the prospect of the feast receded. 'I'll join you as soon as I can.'

'Inspector Fanshaw. What's the news?'

'I'm afraid you were right all along. Which puts us back at the start, Sir Patrick.'

'How do you mean?'

'Dr Oblomov can't have done it, sir. In fact, she was very shocked at the thought that anybody in your Society even for a moment thought it could be her.'

Oliver and Fanshaw had driven out to Vera Oblomov's home in Madingley at about seven. Oliver had told her that they had come to ask her a few questions. She let them in and offered them drinks. 'Is it about David Glen Tannock?' she asked.

'Indirectly,' Oliver said. He had waded in with the hard evidence at once, hoping to make full use of its shock value. 'The truth is we're a bit puzzled about something. Why did you visit the Russian embassy this morning?'

'Well,' Fanshaw told me. 'She didn't say anything for a while; looked pale, sat down, that kind of thing. Then she muttered, "They told me I might have been followed." Finally, she got a grip on herself. "I haven't killed anyone," she said. "But I suppose I *have* done some rather suspicious-looking things recently; and, in the circumstances, you have a right to know why." Look, we made a tape-recording of the interview. Have you got time to hear it?'

I thought about Mrs Porteous's dinner growing cold. But if Vera Oblomov hadn't killed David, the trail to the person who did was also getting colder every moment. Mrs P's dinner would have to wait.

The story was like something out of a spy thriller; but Vera Oblomov had evidence to corroborate the details. It was, in the end, a rather sad tale of the exploitation of an individual's feelings for the arbitrary purposes of a totalitarian state.

'You must know, Sir Oliver,' she began, 'that my mother is still in the Soviet Union. I told your people that when I came to the West. For the first twelve years I got letters back from her regularly, and then, early last year, they stopped.'

To begin with, she had thought nothing of it. But after a couple of months, she wrote to the authorities, asking what had happened. She got no reply, of course. But the next time she was in London – "I go often to the opera" – a man, a Russian, approached her at the Royal Opera House. The stranger had told her that her mother was well and that more letters would arrive soon; provided, that was, that Vera supplied them with a little information. She said she hardly knew anything that they would find useful – and that if she did, she certainly wouldn't tell them. And then the man told her that her mother might not be able to send any more letters if she took that attitude.

'In fact, he said she might not be able to do anything. Naturally, I was frightened, so I agreed to meet him in Hyde Park the next day. When I got there, it turned out that they had found out I was a member of the Society. All they wanted was a weekly report of our meetings. I was enormously relieved. Well, as you know, Sir Oliver, there is nothing that goes on at our meetings that would be of the slightest use to them. So I agreed. In fact, I was rather pleased with myself. I made out that this was a big concession.'

And so, over the last year or so, once every so often, usually at the opera, her contact would approach and collect an envelope of information about the meetings of the Society. 'Perhaps

Philby had persuaded them that the Society was the secret heart of the British establishment. I don't know. But they must have been pleased with what I was doing. At any rate, the letters from my mother started coming once more.'

And then, a few weeks earlier, she had a letter from her mother revealing how her father had died; revealing who had killed him. 'They had given my mother David's father's name, Sir Oliver, and, of course, yours.'

Vera Oblomov had known that her father was an officer who had died in some sort of military incident on the border with China. She had not known until then that the incident involved the secret service of her adopted country. Naturally, she had been very distressed by the news – that, presumably, was why she had run weeping from her tutorial a few weeks ago. Naturally, too, she couldn't think why they had got her mother to tell her now. Then, at her last visit to London – the last one before her visit today – they had asked her to try and find something compromising about Oliver Hetherington; she realized at once that the letter from her mother had been aimed at disposing her against Oliver . . . 'I suppose they succeeded. I shall never again feel at ease with you,' she said to Oliver with her characteristic candour.

Vera Oblomov had only understood why they had been so interested in Oliver when he arrived at the meeting the night of David's death and Hugh revealed he was to be the new ambassador to the Kremlin. 'I was hoping to talk to you privately the next day – I would have talked to you that night, but you seemed so keen to go home with David . . . and, of course, I knew you were a close friend of his father's. And then, the next day, David was dead. So I thought, if I tell Sir Oliver now, he will simply think I have a motive for killing Lord Glen Tannock. It seems that in this I was correct.' Vera Oblomov's steady precise delivery was interrupted by a half-suppressed sob. 'It was stupid to lie to Sir Oliver, of course, about my knowledge of the connection between the Society and spying of one kind and another. But I was afraid . . . so afraid.' Her voice trailed off on the tape.

When she spoke again, her voice still showed signs of strain. 'When I got back from Wednesday's meeting I was very much on edge. I could not sleep. My neighbours are four graduate students who share a house. Naturally, they do not go to bed at a reasonable hour. I wanted company. I simply knocked on the door and invited myself in for coffee. They were very kind. It was three in the morning when I left.'

Her voice was stronger now.

'So you see, I could not have been in David Glen Tannock's rooms that night. And, on the morning Charlie died, I was here with Mrs Baines, the woman who cleans for me. I was here all morning. If you'd asked for my alibi two days ago, I could have told you. But it never occurred to me that anyone who knew me even slightly could suspect me of those monstrous crimes. And I suppose I thought that if Sir Patrick and the other Apostles didn't believe it, you would leave me alone.'

Fanshaw turned off the tape. Once more we had let suspicions get out of hand. I wondered if I could ever persuade Vera that I had never thought that she was the killer.

Fanshaw's voice came on the line once more. 'There's more of the same, sir, but that's basically it. She showed us the letter from her mother. Of course, it was in Russian. Sir Oliver read it. According to him, it said exactly what she'd told us. And she showed us typed copies of her reports of the meetings for the last year or so. Of course, her neighbours and the cleaning-woman confirm her account of Wednesday night and Friday morning. It all fits. Sir Oliver is here, now. He'd like to have a word with you.'

I was seated at the desk in Godfrey's study, watching the fading light across the meadows. A light breeze came in through the half-open French windows. As I waited for Oliver to come to the phone, I tried to go through the evidence we had again in my mind. We were indeed, in Fanshaw's phrase, 'back at the start'. There had to be somewhere we could pick up the pieces.

Oliver's voice was soothing. 'Well, Patrick. As you can gather, it's another cul-de-sac, so to speak. But then, of course, you warned us that it would be. At all events, I must be off to London early in the morning. I'll keep in touch, of course. Where are you going to be?'

'From sometime tomorrow we'll be back at Claudia's.'

'My regards to Virginia and Claudia. And tell Godfrey I'm sorry I didn't see more of him this time.'

I sat for a while longer, pursuing the vapour-trail of a thought that was buzzing in my head. If the Latin missives were genuine – and they were now the main lead we had – the obvious candidate was, I supposed, an Apostle or an Angel, probably one who had somehow been tipped over the edge into madness. But of the Brothers (and Sister) who had been present at the two meetings before David's death, two were dead, Vera Oblomov was ruled out, and none of the others – Hugh, James Hogg, Dale Bishop, Godfrey, Hugo, and Oliver – seemed to be crazy . . . or to have any motive for killing either David or Charlie. Hugo was out of the question. James Hogg and Dale Bishop I did not know. But Hugh and Godfrey and Oliver were among my oldest friends. And it simply did not fit that any of them should have killed one, let alone two, young men. Hugh and Godfrey were plainly fond of both the murdered boys. Oliver was one of David's father's oldest friends. Charles Ivor's life had several times hung in the balance and been saved by Oliver; why, now, all these years later should he have set out to kill Charlie's son?

And if these three were ruled out, that left only James Hogg and Dale Bishop. Hugh obviously knew James well. Surely, if there were any reason to suspect him, Hugh would have known of it. Love's passion is strong in youth. But James Hogg wouldn't have killed David just because David was in love with someone else. And what other reason could he have?

And as for Dale Bishop, he had only just been elected to the Society. He seemed an ordinary, amiable young American. We should have to find out a little more about him, now. But so far there was absolutely nothing to connect him by way of motive to either death.

But motive wasn't the only problem. There was the question of opportunity. James Hogg and Hugh had been together 'into the wee hours' of Thursday morning, Hugh had said. Unless they were in cahoots, each provided the other with a clear alibi. They were both at the meeting from after the time Joanna Ritter had delivered the new tin of milk. If they had done it they would have had to have done it after the meeting.

Dale Bishop had seemed so unlikely so far – he had said he was out of town the evening of David's death – that it was doubtful that anyone had checked on his story. Godfrey had been out at Heston, nursing a cold. And then there was Oliver.

'Ridiculous. Why would he do it?' I said out loud. But it was true that, for all I knew, he could have done it. When he walked me home on Friday night, he had mentioned that he had keys to let himself into Trinity from the Backs; and so, in theory, he could have come the other way early on Thursday morning. And, though I had talked to him on the morning of Charlie's death, it must have been well over an hour earlier. By the time of Charlie's death, Oliver could easily have gone from Trinity College to the Downing Site and made his way into Charlie's laboratories. He could, in theory, have thrown up the Oblomov business as a diversion. But, if he had, he would have known that she would probably turn out to have an alibi for at least one of the murders. Still, a murderer might want to keep the police busy for a few days, to let the trail go cold. And the Oblomov affair had put Oliver at the centre of the investigation. He now knew everything we did.

Despite these possibilities, there was no evidence at all to link Oliver to the murders. I felt, frankly, mildly contemptible for merely considering the hypothesis. It seemed oddly disloyal. Vera Oblomov, whom I knew only slightly through the Society, had made me feel remorseful when she said that she had supposed her brethren would not suspect her. Suspecting Oliver made me feel even worse.

Looked at in the best light, I suppose I could have been asking the questions that Oliver would need to answer if he was to be kept in the clear. We had simply not checked on him so far; probably Oliver was seen elsewhere on Friday morning; probably, the Darwins would have heard him, if he had left on Wednesday night. But we hadn't checked. Perhaps, if only for Oliver's sake, we should.

# 19

As these thoughts ran round in my head, I heard Godfrey coming down the corridor outside the study. He came in quietly and found me seated in the darkening room. 'We've finished eating. Mrs Porteous has left some food for you on the stove.

But I suppose that your conversation with Fanshaw has deprived you of your appetite.'

'I'm so sorry. Really very bad of me not to join you all as soon as Fanshaw rang off.' I was still distracted. Godfrey gave me a questioning look. 'I'm afraid that was a call to tell us we've lost our most promising suspect. Vera Oblomov.'

Godfrey looked frankly astonished. 'Why on earth did you ever suspect her?'

'It's a long story. But Oliver had some top-secret sources that connected her with David's father. Anyway, it was all a ridiculous mistake. She couldn't have done it: she has solid alibis for both deaths.'

'In my experience, our spies are hopelessly unreliable. I never could understand how anyone trusted our Brother Philby. Ah well; that's no reason not to have some supper. Let me take you into the kitchen and feed you some of Mrs Porteous's delicious steak-and-kidney pudding.'

'Well,' I said, as we walked down the corridor, 'at least we have one thing going for us: Charlie's killer had to get to him in a very short period of time that morning, when there were people around the labs. Somebody probably saw something.' Godfrey nodded; but he seemed to doubt what I said. And once we were in the kitchen, he turned towards me confidentially. 'Patrick, I have just had a thought. Not one I could mention in front of Claudia. We've been persuaded that David's death was not a suicide but a murder. And, of course, because Charlie was dead, we ruled him out as the murderer. But has it occurred to you that Charlie's death might not be a murder but a suicide? If Charlie felt in some way responsible for David's death, mightn't he have killed himself out of remorse?'

'But why on earth should he think himself responsible?'

'I'm not sure. But there is one possibility. You remember James Hogg said on Friday night that David might have known something that somebody didn't want revealed. I have thought long and hard about it. And I think I have found a connection between Charlie and David's work on Ransome.'

As I ate, Godfrey made the case. 'You remember I told you that Charlie had asked me for some mathematical assistance? It was basically a question in topology. The brain consists, of course, of cell-bodies – which you can think of as nodes in a graph – connected by nerve-fibres, which you can think of as lines connecting those nodes. Since elementary topology is essentially about the interconnectedness of nodes and the relationships between the areas bounded by the lines that connect them, you can see there might be many useful applications of topology to the study of neural networks. Now one of the things that led Ransome to take an interest in topology in the first place was an idea he had about the organization of the brain. He spent a good deal of time in the early thirties talking to Adrian and Hodgkin, who were beginning the modern electrical study of the neuron. I don't yet see how this connection would have led Charlie to think he had played a part in David's death. But if David's death had to do with the Ransome work, it is a possibility.'

It was an interesting hypothesis. It was also completely preposterous. 'Godfrey,' I began, restraining myself from an outburst of irritation, 'twice, so far, in this case, I have allowed people to be accused whose characters and motives were entirely unsuited to murder. I didn't know Tredwell, but David did. And I should have known that David would not have been having an affair with a cold-blooded murderer. As for Vera Oblomov: the supposition that she had done it would have required her to be mad, which she plainly is not. This time, I am going to rely on my knowledge of Charlie's character. I've known him since he was a young man, almost a boy; he was Sebastian's best friend; he spent many of his holidays with us. I knew him nearly as well as I know my own son. And I can tell you one thing for certain: nothing of that sort would have led Charlie to suicide. For one thing, if he knew something about David's death that he didn't want to tell the police, he would certainly have told me.'

Godfrey said nothing for a moment. Then he sighed. 'You're right, of course. But I suppose it *is* worth considering every possibility,' he added apologetically.

'Of course, Godfrey. But there's one thing I think you may be right about. Somehow, David's work on Ransome may have something to do with it. I suppose I shall have to go and see Margery Ransome as soon as possible.'

'I suppose you will just have to go through David's notes and try to piece together what he had found out?'

'Indeed. And I may have to ask your help with that later, Godfrey. But the police will now be taking the Apostolic connection very seriously. They'll probably regard all of our currently active Brethren as suspects. Of course, Godfrey, it hardly needs saying that *I* know you had nothing to do with it. But I'm afraid they might not stand for it if one of our number was left to follow what is now our most promising lead. So I shall have to consult you privately, so to speak.'

All he said in reply was, 'Of course.'

'I'm afraid you and Hugh and Oliver will have to start answering questions about where you were when all of this happened.'

'Well, now, let me see. Didn't you say Charlie's killer had to get to him in the short period while he was alone in the lab on Friday morning? I was at a college council meeting from nine until half-past eleven. I think I could assemble the most intellectually distinguished group of witnesses in the history of the criminal law. Oliver's movements I know nothing about. Hugh, of course, has the misfortune to live round the corner from Charlie's labs, and only a few minutes walk from David's rooms. But I rather suspect that he may be able to get James Hogg to corroborate his alibi for almost any time of the day or the night.' He broke off. 'Really the whole idea of dear Hugh killing either of the boys is too ridiculous.'

'Still, it's not a matter we can afford to make light of any longer.' I spoke severely. 'Hugh and James are nothing more than friends, we both know that, and Hugh has specifically assured me of it. But the fact is that we really can't have the police even for a moment suspecting that there is anything to go on. As it is, James Hogg by himself would be worthless as corroboration – any prosecuting barrister with half a brain would make exactly the insinuation that you did. So I hope, for Hugh's sake, that he's better covered than that. Anyway, tomorrow, I shall have to go through the unpleasant process of asking him.'

Godfrey was obviously chastened by my tone of rebuke; and he stood quiet, fiddling with a fork that lay on the table in front of him. I realized almost immediately that my reaction to him was fuelled by the anxieties that had been troubling me when he found me in the study. His levity about Hugh and James only reflected his certainty that Hugh could not be our killer. And, since, as he had just proven, we could easily persuade Fanshaw that Godfrey couldn't have killed Charlie, at least I didn't have to lose his friendship. I decided I had better patch things up at once.

'Look here, Godfrey, I'm sorry to have taken that tone with you, just now. It's just that this investigation isn't going at all well, and I really don't relish having to keep open the possibility that Hugh – or Oliver, for that matter – is our murderer. It's really very upsetting.'

Godfrey laid a hand gently on my shoulder. 'My dear Patrick, no offence taken. None at all. This whole business has been horribly upsetting for all of us. But it can't be one of us. You and I both know every one of them. Some of them we have known most of our lives. It makes no sense. And yet the wells are poisoned. None of us will be at ease until the monster is brought to justice.'

I had finished my pudding. Godfrey offered me a slice of apple charlotte, and I suggested that I take the plate into the drawing-room. 'The others will be dying of curiosity.'

Godfrey walked along the corridor with me and stopped at the door of the drawing-room. 'I must collect my pipe and tobacco from the study.'

'Well, Patrick,' Virginia said as I entered the drawing-room. 'Do tell. What did Fanshaw have to say that took so long?'

'Not good news, really. His most promising lead has dried up. All we have now is a vague suspicion of anybody connected with the Apostles, and some puzzles about the financial dealings of Hippo Buckingham.' I gave them a rundown of the conversation with Fanshaw, and passed on Oliver's good wishes. As Godfrey returned I said, 'I propose to try and follow up the work David was doing on the Ransome papers, tomorrow. I'll ask Godfrey to reintroduce me to Mrs Ransome.'

Godfrey bowed half seriously in acknowledgement of the request and we sat down. He got up again almost immediately to offer us drinks and, once Virginia and I had accepted a brandy, and Claudia had turned one down, he settled back in his chair with a small glass of Talisker. He fiddled for a while in the pocket of his dinner jacket, retrieving, finally, the pipe and tobacco he had collected from the study.

About a minute later, I noticed that Godfrey was having difficulty lighting his pipe. 'That's odd,' he said, 'won't light and tastes funny. And it's one of my best briars.'

For a moment none of us said anything. Godfrey set the match to the bowl yet another time, and drew in deeply. Then, he spluttered and raised his left hand to his throat. His face looked flushed. Virginia and I leapt, almost at the same moment, towards him. 'Godfrey!' Virginia screamed. 'Put down that pipe!'

He did as he was bidden and stared at us in mute incomprehension, coughing still, and massaging his throat.

'Don't you see?' she said. 'It might be poisoned.'

But we were already too late.

Godfrey's face had gone a strange purplish colour and beads of sweat were forming on his brow. While Virginia tended to him, I ran out to telephone an ambulance. Constable Anscombe, who had been patrolling the grounds, arrived through the front door as I reached the hall. 'Professor Stanley's been poisoned; something in his pipe. I'm calling the ambulance.'

# 20

By the time the ambulance arrived, it looked as though we might have caught Godfrey early enough. His breathing was shallow but he was conscious. On the trip into Addenbrookes, he held Virginia's hand and said over and over again, 'Never repay you. Saved my life.' I hoped to God he was right, that we had stopped him in time.

I thought, as we waited outside the cubicle in the emergency room, about how the assassin who had killed David and Charlie and who had now had a go at Godfrey could have got at the tobacco. Unfortunately, it seemed easy enough. The pipes and the tobacco were on the desk in the study. Almost any time during the day, anyone could have slipped into the room through the open french windows and spiked Godfrey's favourite pipe. And, while Wilkins and Godfrey were at church, Virginia, Claudia and I had been changing for dinner, and Mrs

Porteous was busy feeding Bill Hedge in the kitchen. No one would have noticed. The murderer, whoever he was, could rightly assume that we felt safe out at Heston.

Once we'd done all we could for Godfrey, we asked for a police car to take us back to Heston. 'We can't leave Claudia alone tonight,' Virginia said.

As we walked out into the hospital car-park, Fanshaw joined us. 'My people have been out at the house. We've taken prints all over the study. We may come up with something. There's a couple of officers outside the house to reassure Mrs Porteous and Mrs Phipps. And I've warned the others to be extra careful – Sir Oliver, Dr Oblomov, Mr Penhaligon, Mr Hogg, Mr Bishop. Mr Penhaligon has Mr Hogg camping on his sitting-room floor. The boy's scared stiff.' Fanshaw looked at me with a look of candid despair. 'I don't suppose you have any more ideas about who could have done this?' His tone was hopeless.

I shook my head. Virginia placed a hand gently on his arm. 'You're all doing your best, Inspector. We must just wait and see if we get a note in the morning. Then we'll know whether we're looking for the same person.'

'By the way, our people have gone over the two notes. The paper doesn't tell you much. It's sold in four or five shops in the centre of Cambridge. The words were done on a computer printer, as you suggested. At the moment we don't have much idea where that could have been. We've asked the University Computer Centre to see if they can identify it. I'll keep you in touch, if we find anything out.'

I placed a protective arm round Virginia's shoulders in the back seat of the police car that whisked us back to Godfrey's house. As we reached the gates of the drive, I said, 'I think I shall telephone Hugh, and tell him a bit more of what's happened. I need to ask him about Dale Bishop and various other things. We're rather stuck for where to look next.'

We said hallo to Claudia and Mrs Porteous. The strain on Mrs P.'s face eased visibly as we gathered around the kitchen table and told her and Claudia that Godfrey would be all right.

'Cocoa, anyone?' she said. 'And I expect you could do with some of my apple pie, Sir Patrick.'

'Mrs P.,' I said, 'I'm afraid we probably shouldn't risk eating or drinking anything in the house that isn't sealed. Throw out today's milk and clear the rest of the fridge. You can restock in the morning. But don't you worry,' I added, 'whoever it is isn't after you. Once we leave tomorrow, there'll be no more interruptions here; we won't let Godfrey back until we know who the murderer is. And we'll be safe tonight. Inspector Fanshaw has the place surrounded by policemen. Let's all try to get a good night's sleep.'

Once we had got the others off to bed, I rang Hugh and told him what had happened to Godfrey. 'You realize this means you're going to be one of Fanshaw's number one suspects, Hugh,' I said.

'I'm afraid that, apart from James, no one can corroborate my claim to have been here when David was killed; and I expect I was here alone in my rooms when Charlie died.' Hugh did not sound at all cheerful; and this revelation confirmed my own worst fears.

'Cheer up, Hugh,' I said, hoping I sounded more optimistic than I was feeling. 'The only way we can get you out of trouble is by finding out who did kill the boys . . . and then tried to kill Godfrey. We've got to go over everything we know again and again until we come up with something.'

'How *is* Godfrey now?'

'He's going to pull through. In fact, when we left he seemed inclined to move back into college in the morning. But it was a near thing.'

'Any sign of a note?'

'No.'

'Anything from the forensic analysis?'

'Not really. Fanshaw says they've asked the University Computer Centre to try and identify the printer.'

'I've got James here, he knows about these things. Here, I'll put him on this line and go and get on the other phone in my study.'

After a moment, James Hogg's voice said. 'Good evening, Sir Patrick.'

'Hallo, James. Very wise of you to stay with Hugh, I think. It seems there may be some sort of maniac on the loose. Hugh tells me you know about the university computers.'

'A little.'

'Do you use them yourself, I mean?'

James was unaccountably laconic. 'I do a fair amount of simple-minded econometric modelling.'

'How would you go about using it to print those notes?' I asked.

'The easiest place to get access to a terminal, if you have a User ID – that's an access code which you get once you register with the people who run the system – is probably in the Old Cavendish site.' Once he started, James proved overflowing with information. 'There's a large room with a couple of dozen terminals in the third-floor computer lab, in a modern building in what used to be the courtyard behind the Cavendish Laboratory. And downstairs, there's the Mond Room. Anyone can have a key that allows you in there any time of the day or night – and there aren't any operators, just an hourly visit from a security guard at nights. It's often empty in the early afternoon and during dinner. Of course, once the site is locked at ten in the evening, there are people about in various engineering labs, but the Mond Room is usually empty.'

'How many people would have keys to get in after hours?'

'There must be hundreds; maybe over a thousand. And you could borrow a key, if you didn't have one. Anyway, practically anybody with a User ID could walk in at any time of day; and there are literally thousands of User IDs.'

'So that wouldn't be a way of tracing someone,' Hugh said.

'Wait a minute. That's not quite true,' James said excitedly. 'There is one possibility. It depends on exactly when and how the printing was done. If the messages were composed and edited as data files, they might have been stored on disc. Then, whoever wrote them would have deleted the files and that might have been the end of it. But once the files were stored on disc, erasing them from the terminal wouldn't necessarily actually destroy the data. I mean the machine doesn't literally erase the files at once; they just become inaccessible from your virtual machine.'

'Virtual machine?' Hugh and I asked in chorus.

'Never mind, it's not worth explaining just now. The point is, it could still be on a disc in the system somewhere. And if the files were on disc during any one of the periods during the day when they back up the whole system – putting everything on tapes, which they store in case anything goes wrong – then somewhere there would be a copy of those files on tape.'

Hugh interrupted. 'Remember this is all new to us, Jamie. Are you saying, simply, that there may be a tape recording of these messages somewhere in the computer centre?'

'Yes.'

'How would that help?'

'Because the tapes would tell us the User ID of the person who created the computer files. Of course, as I say, I don't know enough to tell you how likely it is that there is a back-up. And even if there were, it would be an awfully difficult job to look through all the data tapes for a day, let alone a week. Even using all the computer's resources to do the searching it could take a very long time.'

'How long do they keep these tapes?' I asked.

'Probably at least a year. But if the only trace is a disc file, it may already have been cleared by now. You'd have to ask the experts.'

'I think I'll try and get hold of Fanshaw now and tell him to talk to the computer people about this first thing in the morning.'

'There'll be someone there now who would probably know. They have technical people there twenty-four hours a day. If you like, I could go over now and talk to them. I've got a key.'

'Isn't it rather late?'

'I've not been sleeping very well,' James said; and Hugh added, 'Nor I. So we shall both go and take the lovely Constable Hope, who stands guard at the door, with us. And I shall finally have a chance to see the future. Charlie once tried to explain it all to me, but it didn't sink in much.'

Methought, just for an instant, Hugh protested too much. It was, after all, quite a moment to be insisting on his ignorance of computing. But it was preposterous to start suspecting Hugh simply on the basis of one of his characteristic gestures of self-deprecation.

'Well, you do as you think fit. I'll leave a message for Fanshaw to call and make an official enquiry in the morning. I'm glad we had this little chat. Perhaps, at last, we have a way to nail our killer.'

'Especially', James said, 'if there's a letter for Godfrey in the morning.'

'That's certainly true. Before you go, Hugh, there are a couple of things I wanted to ask you about. One thing that's been puzzling me is how widely known it was that the chemicals Charlie worked with were so toxic. Did he ever say anything about that sort of thing?'

'Oh yes, indeed.' Hugh laughed a humourless laugh. 'Of course, he was extremely coy about it. Ever since he told Oliver once and Oliver started quizzing him about possible uses of the poisons in assassinations and such. Charlie was appalled. Said he was not going to be involved in anything of that sort. I'm afraid that after all those years in intelligence running agents, Oliver thinks that all chemicals ought to be divided into poisons and truth drugs. All the same, it did seem rather naïve of Charlie. Anyway, once he realized people might think of nasty uses for his work, he hardly ever mentioned it to anybody. Even at the Society discussion, he made it plain he didn't want it to go any further. No, I'd say that apart from those of us at the meeting the other day, when he did talk about some of the dangerous sides of what he was up to, and a few people in his department . . . and Claudia, of course . . . it was a pretty well-guarded secret.'

'I wonder if Vera mentioned this stuff to her Russians?'

'I doubt it. But even if she did, you don't think they'd send someone up here to kill off Charlie and kill David first just to sow confusion?'

'No, that hadn't occurred to me as a possibility. I think that we can assume that our killer was one of the people you mentioned or someone they trusted well enough to mention what Charlie had said. Which brings me, in a sort of way, to my second question. Can you tell me a little more about Dale Bishop? He's the one person I don't feel I've got a fix on.'

'You don't really suspect him, do you? There isn't the vaguest reason to think he had anything against David . . . or Charlie . . .'

'I know. On the other hand, he's the only currently active member of the Society about whom I know practically nothing.'

'Well, let's see. He was only elected a few weeks ago. Charlie's paper was his first meeting. He'd been suggested by

David, originally. They'd met at dinner somewhere, and David had been impressed by him. Then David had him to one of those drinks parties we have to look people over; you know, where we all pretend that it's perfectly natural that half a dozen people of all ages who seem to know each other quiz a complete stranger. All of us came.'

Dale Bishop's father was a well-known American journalist. 'One of those investigative journalists that make it impossible to keep a political secret in America. Dale is frightfully proud of the fact that his papa revealed some nasty goings-on involving the CIA in Bolivia. I asked him if he didn't think national security required secrets. He said he thought that it was a journalist's job to find out and the CIA's job to try to stop them. Made a great speech about freedom of the press and how secrets were a great threat to democracy. Then, of course, I asked him what he would think of an Apostle who broke his word not to reveal Society secrets, because he became a journalist in later life; and he was frightfully embarrassed.'

Dale had been an undergraduate at a small liberal arts college and then, after a master's degree at Yale, had applied to Cambridge to read English for a PhD.

'He's at Darwin, I think you told me.'

'Yes. And, apart from a tendency to write everything you say to him down in a little black book, he seems a perfectly normal, intelligent young man, with a suitably Apostolic range of interests. He's a great interest in the history of the Society, for example. Always popping round here to talk about it. And at the first meeting he spent the time after we stopped discussing Charlie's paper quizzing us all about our work. Strangeways, who's supervising his dissertation, says that he's the cleverest student he's had in years. He seems to be busily revolutionizing our ideas about aesthetics before Kant. But I've told you all that before.'

'Still, I don't see how he can have done it,' James put in. 'Killed Charlie and David, I mean. He's terribly nice and hardly knew any of us yet. So it's hard to see how he could have a motive.' James fell silent as he remembered something. 'David said Dale'd offered him some cocaine the first time they met; so you can see he's still a bit unused to our ways. I mean, David was terribly anti-drugs. And David was really the one of us he knew best.' He paused. 'Besides,' he said finally, 'he wasn't in town the evening David died. That's why he didn't come to the meeting.'

'Do you know where he was?'

'In London, having dinner with some friend of his father's.'

It was beginning to look distressingly as though I was going to have to start investigating Oliver Hetherington. I put the facts to Virginia as I lay in bed, nervous and unable to sleep. Her response was characteristic.

'You should check, I suppose. For Oliver's sake. But if you think he actually did it, you should have your lovely old head examined. For one thing, he's been busy in Cambridge all evening. How could he have got the poison into Godfrey's pipe? Now go to sleep. We've got plenty to do tomorrow.'

Not long after dawn, however, Virginia shook me awake. 'Patrick, I've been thinking. About Oliver. Wasn't he involved in the Society when Ransome was alive?'

'Yes.'

'And then he was in MI something or other after the War?'

'Yes,' I said.

'And now he's going to be ambassador in Moscow?'

'Really, Jinny, what is all this about?'

'Ransome knew Philby, didn't he?'

'Extremely well.'

'And he was frightfully left-wing, wasn't he? Ransome, I mean.'

'Not exactly. He just didn't approve of class distinctions much. My impression was that he was a lot more interested in Spain and that sort of thing than in Soviet Russia. More practical-minded than ideological, you see.'

Virginia paid no heed. 'Just suppose Ransome was somehow persuaded, by Philby, say, to do something for the Russians as part of the anti-Fascist thing in the period leading up to the War. Couldn't he have involved Oliver? I mean, if David found evidence of that, wouldn't Oliver have a terribly strong motive to get rid of him?'

'Virginia, sometimes your imagination quite runs away with you. Oliver is Eton and Trinity, tremendous war record, brilliant reputation in the FO. He's absolutely the most respectable person you could imagine.'

'They always are,' she said darkly. 'Look at Philby. For all we know, Oliver is the Fourth Man.'

'Look here, Jinny. The Fourth Man has to be in the intelligence establishment. Oliver hasn't done anything of that sort for twenty years.'

'Are you sure? I mean where did this Peterson person come from? Do all ambassadors know how to whistle up their own Special Branch officer when the mood takes them?'

'Really, Jinny, I'm not going to argue with you. It's just too silly. Do let's get some more sleep.'

# 21

Next morning we called the hospital, to discover that Godfrey was making a great fuss about being let out. When we finally got through to him he instructed us firmly to visit him in college at lunch-time. He was uncharacteristically down-to-earth. 'I've had a terrible fright, Patrick. I've never before thought I might die.' Then his voice brightened a little. 'I shall have the college arrange as delicious a lunch as we can manage in my rooms.' He was obviously well on the road to recovery.

When the post arrived, we went through it very carefully under the watchful eye of a couple of policemen. But none of the envelopes was of the familiar bond paper. I didn't have to read the contents to see that none of them was in the right typeface or on the right paper.

It was a frankly depressed party that made its way back in our Volvo to Cambridge. Virginia obviously felt that I had been less than fair to her when she had her bright idea in the early morning and she was not terribly inclined to talk to me.

'Look, darling,' I said to her when we got to Claudia's, 'you're right. I really ought not to rule Oliver out. I'll put Fanshaw on to him, after I've found out if he has anything from the forensic work on the tobacco and the pipe.'

When I got hold of Fanshaw, he told me that Godfrey's

poisoning was a pretty professional job according to the forensic types. The chemical used had been one of Charlie's neurotoxins, though different from the one that actually killed him. 'My people seem to think that if the killer wasn't a professional scientist, he must have been pretty well informed. This is one of the few neurotoxins that doesn't break down immediately when you heat it. And it's not so easy to get hold of. Could have come from Dr Phipps's labs, of course; but if it didn't, the boffins suggested it might be someone with connections in intelligence.'

'I don't know, Inspector. I mean, suppose this stuff was stolen by the killer when he got Charles Phipps. It could just have been luck that he picked something that wasn't going to be destroyed by heating; or perhaps he saw Charlie heating it in a test-tube or something. I don't think anyone who knew what they were doing would use a pipe at all; why not simply lace a drink with the stuff? I still think it all fits with the picture of an opportunist who happened to find out about Charlie's neurotoxins and David's penicillin allergy, but didn't have a chance to use a more obvious method to poison Godfrey.' As I spoke, I realized that I didn't know whether Oliver knew about the penicillin; nor, as I thought about it, would Oliver have been in a good position to use the university's computers to print the messages.

Virginia notwithstanding, it was not yet time to suggest that Fanshaw checked on Oliver. 'Anything on the notes?'

'They were done on a printer in the Mond Room. We've identified the printer. Hundreds of people use it so there's no question of getting any fingerprints. By the way, did you know that Dr Penhaligon had suggested to somebody over there last night that there might be a tape of the messages stored somewhere?'

'Yes,' I said. 'Actually it was James Hogg's idea. They said they might go over there together last night, so as to set the experts looking as soon as possible.'

'Well, they had a look at the accounts of all the members of the Society – them as have them, of course. And Dr Tredwell. Nothing. But then they told us it could have been done directly from the terminal without ever being stored. They said there was no storage of the print queue. I asked them to have a quick sort through their files anyway, just in case the notes turned up on somebody else's account. They thought that was very funny. They said that without a few hints about where to look and whose files to look in, it just wasn't feasible. Aside from that, it seems anyone who knew what he was doing would never have stored the files on disc, and there's a good chance they wouldn't have been copied to tape even if they were. And then, according to them, you don't need to know much to put your files into some sort of code, so they wouldn't ever be found by a computer search anyway. So, all in all, they seem to think it's a very long shot. Needle in a haystack, is what they said, Sir Patrick.

'Of course, I can see why they're not exactly enthusiastic about having to look. It turns out these computers run practically everything round here; the university's accounts, scientific experiments, that kind of thing. All the students use it for writing their dissertations. And right at this moment all the exam results are being stored and worked out on it. Now, the only way they can search quickly is to shut off the lot. So it'd be like shutting down the whole university. Even then, it would take weeks, *if* it's there and *if* it isn't coded, unless we can tell them more about where to look.'

'All the same, if we *do* ever have any ideas about who did it, it may be a possibility to take up. Unfortunately, there was no sign of a note in Professor Stanley's mail this morning. So the whole business of the notes may have been a distraction.'

But it seemed I had spoken too soon. Not long after, Godfrey rang in a state of high excitement.

'A note has arrived, like the others. It was in my pigeonhole.'

'Have you told Fanshaw?'

'No, I thought I'd leave it to you. Would you like to hear what it says?' he asked. But the question was rhetorical. '"*Epistula tertia. Godfrey Stanley. Tales angelorum in caelis decet esse cohederes.*" I recognized it at once, of course. It's from Bede's *Ecclesiastical History*: part of Pope Gregory's joke about the Angles being like angels.'

'I'll be over in a minute, as soon as I've called Fanshaw. And . . . Godfrey . . . don't throw away the envelope.'

*

'It is fitting that such people should be co-inheritors with the Angels in the heavens.' Fanshaw read the translation I had given him back from his notebook.

'I haven't mentioned it before, Inspector, I don't think, but senior members of the Society are called "Angels". So, you see, it fits with the pattern of someone who knows about the Society.'

'What we have here, sir, is a grade-A lunatic with a classical education.'

'I fear, Inspector, that in this fair city that is a description that applies to rather a large number of people,' Godfrey said. His enjoyment at occupying the centre of attention was wonderfully transparent. As he sat propped up in bed, receiving the ministrations of the college nurse and the attention of Inspector Fanshaw, he put me in mind of a naughty child enjoying the release from criticism that comes with illness.

Virginia had come over with me, since it had been very nearly lunch-time when he had telephoned. It was a jolly lunch party, and Godfrey was delighted with his succession of visitors. 'I shall have to be poisoned more often,' he was saying, as Hugh and James Hogg arrived. He received them grandly, offering them places in the circle of chairs he had had collected around his enormous four-poster bed.

It seemed a sensible moment to pull out. 'Godfrey, old chap, I'm afraid we should probably set off, now. I'm so glad you're feeling better. Could I ask you a favour?'

'Anything, Patrick, dear boy, anything. For God's sake, you and Virginia probably saved my life.'

'I wasn't thinking of anything on quite that scale,' I said, laughing. 'But you did offer to put me in touch with Gregory Ransome's widow.'

Godfrey telephoned Margery Ransome and explained that I should like to come and talk to her about David's work. She suggested that I come around at about half-past four.

'Ask her if I may bring Virginia,' I murmured at Godfrey's free ear.

'Oh, and Margery, Sir Patrick would very much like to bring his wife. She was especially close to the dear boy.'

It had been easily arranged. I thought that Virginia's presence might emphasize the family character of the connection. If I came along simply as an unofficial policeman, Mrs Ransome might be less forthcoming.

As we left, another visitor arrived: a young man in his early twenties, dressed in an extraordinary ill-fitting suit. 'This is my protégé, Andrew Phillips, from Trinity,' Godfrey announced, beaming with satisfaction. 'He's nearly as clever as I was at his age. And he knows how to humour an old man by letting him pretend to help him.'

The presence of Dr Phillips made me feel even warmer about Godfrey, even more delighted that we had not lost him. Phillips said nothing much until he noticed the note on Godfrey's bedside table. 'This looks as though it was done in the computer labs,' he said. 'What does it mean, Godfrey?'

Godfrey raised his eyes to the heavens and then looked at me. 'Urdu,' he said. 'What did I tell you?'

'Not Peter Tredwell. Not Vera Oblomov. Not Hugh or James, unless, for some bizarre reason, they did it together . . . No, even then, it's not in Hugh's character, is it, my darling? Of course, he has penned some rather murderous reviews in his time, but that's not quite the same thing.' Virginia ran her finger across the page as she skimmed through my notes.

We had finished our lunch in Godfrey's rooms at about two, and were back, now, in Claudia's sitting-room. 'As you say, it can't be Godfrey, surely.' Virginia continued her catechism. 'Of the Apostles, that leaves only Oliver, which you say is absurd; and Dale Bishop, about whom we know practically nothing. And the only outsider you have any reason at all to suspect of anything is David's friend Hippo Buckingham.'

'Well, I can't believe Oliver did it. There's no evidence and no motive. But Hippo's still a possibility; even if he didn't do the killing, he seems to be trying to hide something. Knowing *what* might help. And I should also find out more about Dale Bishop. But first of all, we must try to make sense of David's researches into our illustrious predecessors.'

The telephone rang in the hall. It was Oliver.

'Patrick,' he said. 'Anything new? How's Godfrey? I didn't want to telephone him at the hospital, in case he was still in a state.'

'He'll be as good as new in a couple of days. But whoever put that stuff in his pipe knew what he was doing. It seems that in a few more puffs, there'd have been no more Godfrey.'

'And how about your investigation?'

'Not much further forward. There was another note, of course. And, like the others, it was printed in a room in the university's computer laboratories to which the whole world seems to have access. I'm just off to see Margery Ransome, to see if there's anything David might have found in her husband's papers that could help explain why someone should want to kill him.'

'Well, if there's anything I can do . . .'

'There is one little thing Virginia and I thought of. Of course, we don't wish to seem to be interfering in your affairs, but you might want to volunteer an account of your movements during Wednesday night and on Friday morning. Fanshaw's bound to check on all the members of the Society who were around; but he may be a bit embarrassed about asking you, after all that work together on Vera Oblomov.'

'Good idea. Actually, I'm rather short of alibis on Wednesday night; unless the Darwins heard me coming in. *And* on Friday morning, come to think of it, after I talked to you. I spent an hour with Alan Blumberg at about midday. When was Charlie killed?'

'Between half-past ten and eleven.'

'Well, I'm in trouble on that one then. One could probably get from Trinity to the Downing Site and back quite easily from here in half an hour. So far as Wednesday's concerned, perhaps I'll suggest to Fanshaw that he asks the Darwins if they heard anything. Though, come to think of it, I was on the scrambler for a good while after coming in on Wednesday night, trying to dig up the info on Oblomov. I'll see if somebody down here has a telephone log that covers those conversations. I wasn't keeping an eye on the time, but I suspect I may not have finished talking to them until a good deal after one in the morning.'

'Splendid, Oliver; I know Fanshaw will be happy if you can get him some solid evidence you were clear at the time one or other of the boys was killed. You might as well give him all you can.'

When Oliver rang off, it was nearly time to leave for Mrs

Ransome's. 'Odd,' I said to Virginia, 'Oliver doesn't seem to have a clear alibi for either killing.' She gave me her most angelic smile. 'That look wouldn't by any chance mean "I told you so," would it?'

'No, darling. That would be childish. But you'll just have to work extra hard proving that Oliver didn't do it, won't you?'

Margery Ransome had had nearly four decades as the widow of Gregory Ransome after a mere five years as his wife. Outside Cambridge, she was best known as a fine sculptress; certainly, not yet with the reputation of Barbara Hepworth or Elizabeth Frink, but spoken of in the same breath as them by the *cognoscenti*. From time to time an article in a Sunday colour magazine would show her with her work: a fine woman, younger than her years to look at, with a beautiful face of the sort that people unaccountably call 'spiritual'. But in the university, Margery Ransome was still Gregory's widow. It was hard to tell whether she resented it. She shared, apparently, the general view that Gregory had been a genius, and that he had mattered to her deeply was plain from her two years of grieving. And the fact that, though widowed before she was thirty, she had never married again.

As we drove out to her house in the High Street in Coton, with the magnificent wild garden behind her studio that we had seen in a dozen photographs, Virginia and I wondered what she would actually be like. 'In my experience,' Virginia had pronounced, 'these people you read about in the magazines are simply never like their public images. She's probably frightfully jolly and unpretentious and expects everyone to take her as they find her.'

Margery Ransome's welcome strengthened my resolve to practise a suitable deference to Virginia's superior knowledge of the human personality. She didn't actually say, 'You must take me as you find me,' as she guided us through into her sitting-room, but she was, indeed, marvellously unpretentious.

'So, Sir Patrick, I don't suppose you remember me. But I recall meeting you with Gregory a couple of times before the War.' She moved on swiftly, offering us tea and crumpets and a cake.

'Well, you've come to talk about young David Glen Tannock. A remarkable boy. It was horrible to hear of his death. I still can hardly sleep for thinking of it. He was so beautiful. I did drawings. I mean, on the surface, he was a handsome boy, anybody could see that. But if I had had time to sculpt him, you would have seen what real manly beauty is. Of course, one would have loved him just for his thoughtfulness. David's thoughtfulness had nothing to do with conventional manners. I mean, for example, I had one of my strong feminist great-nieces here a few weeks ago, when David was visiting. And when we came in from the garden he was talking to me. Now, if she'd been a girl of a different stripe, he'd have waited to let her pass through the door. But David knew instinctively that that would be wrong in this case. He followed me in and she came after. Most people don't notice such things.'

It was a wonderful eulogy. Virginia's eyes were getting misty as Margery Ransome finished. I tried a gruff, 'We were very fond of him,' which produced from Mrs Ransome only mild surprise. 'Fond?' she said. 'You couldn't be fond of David. You could love him – the way you and I and Lady Scott did. You could desire him – the way the papers says his tutor did . . . quite understandably: there was a lot of sex in him, if you know what I mean. But "fondness" is too flabby a word.'

'How much time did he spend here?' Virginia asked, trying, I thought, to set off on the path to the interrogation we had intended.

'Lots. He was riveted with Gregory. He knew next to nothing about mathematics – about as much as you or I, I expect – but he could recognize the extraordinary feel of Gregory's mind. GR was terribly involved in all sorts of things; but the really exciting thing about him was the way he *thought* about everything. The war in Spain, class, sex, everything. All those other Bloomsbury types were rather too inclined to posturing: but not GR. Everything he did was supremely honest; that's why he never understood politics. I knew that one day someone would come who would know how to read Gregory's papers. Godfrey Stanley went through a lot of the mathematical stuff before the War; but I didn't show him any of the personal correspondence, or GR's little essays on various topics. He wouldn't have appreciated it. Between ourselves, I think Godfrey always resented Gregory just a tiny bit. I told Gregory that, once, a few years before he died. He said, "We have no right to expect him not to resent us. Everything he has struggled for, we were simply handed on a plate." But, you know, I think it wasn't our social position that Godfrey resented; what irked him was simply that Gregory had the superior mind. Gregory always spoke so highly of Godfrey's mathematical accomplishments that I didn't know that for a long time. And then, one day after the War, Crispin Redgrave-Smith, who was a mathematics don at King's, told me that everyone's estimation of Godfrey absolutely soared when he produced that theorem. You know it's called the Ransome-Stanley theorem, because the conjecture that Godfrey proved was first made by the two of them, even though Godfrey actually did it, in the end. Still, Godfrey's always been very good to me, you know. Helped me out in all sorts of ways. Even buys my sculpture, which he obviously hates.' She laughed. 'I expect you'll think me frightfully snobbish, but I do find all that fake grandee lark terribly funny. Whenever I see Godfrey and I remember what he was like when he first came up – ungainly child, trousers too short, ghastly haircut – it's all I can manage not to fall on the floor and laugh. God, how I do talk. Have some more tea.'

She bustled off into the kitchen, and returned carrying a folder. 'These are the notes. Godfrey – the old fraud – says that you are interested in them because you don't want David's work to go to waste. Presumably you actually want them for the more pressing purpose of seeing if there's anything in here that would give someone a reason to kill him. I haven't looked, myself. I told him he could keep the notes here and that I wouldn't look at them. But I'll tell you one thing. If anything I can do finds you his murderer, Margery Ransome will die happy.'

The folder was full of David's careful notes; page after page. 'I wonder if we could take these away and have them photocopied? Of course, we'll return you the originals. I'm sure David would have wanted you to have them.'

Margery Ransome did not reply immediately to my request. Instead she pondered. 'I wonder whether he really wouldn't have wanted the originals put in the Ark,' she said finally. 'He told me once he wanted to do something that was worth putting in there. I didn't like to tell him that Godfrey once told me that Richard Butterthorne went through it all and declared all but a few papers of Ramsey's to be worthless. I suppose Godfrey shouldn't strictly have told me about that, should he, Sir Patrick? But I was curious about whether there was anything more of GR's in there.' She smiled at us both. 'All these secrets. It's no wonder we're all in a mess.'

After a moment's pause, she returned to her earlier thought. 'I think it might be right for the Ark to contain such an homage from one generation of the Society to an earlier one, don't you, Lady Scott? At all events, we don't have to decide now. I had two copies made in town the day he died. One is in my bank. I just felt certain the only reason to kill David Glen Tannock would turn out to be something he found in Gregory's papers. So I thought someone might come after them. And d'you know – of course it was probably a coincidence – but someone had tried to break in here early the very morning David was . . . I had the police around in a flash, but whoever it was had gone. As I say, it was probably a coincidence, of course. There've been a lot of burglaries around here recently. But I had the copies made all the same.'

'Nothing was taken?'

'Lord, no. I turned all the lights on upstairs and telephoned the police as noisily as I could. No, he didn't get beyond scraping at the windows. I'm a light sleeper at the best of times.' She paused. 'You know, I'd have started trying to understand the notes myself if I hadn't made that promise to David. But I told him I wouldn't look at them and I won't. I've been waiting for you to come and work it out. I knew you'd be here eventually. Your copy is in the envelope by the door.'

'Did David ever take any of your husband's papers away with him?' I asked. It was the only question I had planned to ask that she hadn't answered unprompted.

'Sometimes he took things to be copied. But he always returned the originals. So far as I know, nothing is missing. He was quite meticulous, you know. He kept records of everything he was doing. I told Godfrey a few weeks ago that David put *his* work on the papers to shame.' She laughed again.

In the course of an hour and a half Virginia and I said only a few dozen words. Margery Ransome spoke passionately of the past and its shadow in the last few months of David's life. Despite the huge part that the Society had played in her husband's life, Godfrey and David seemed to be the only Society connections that she still had.

It was six o'clock by the time we got up to go.

'By the way,' Margery Ransome said as we stood in the porch saying our farewells, 'one of your Brethren was here before you, looking for David's notes. I knew at once that he was not someone to trust. He was too anxious to please me, and too ignorant of David's real interests. So I sent him packing. An American. He said his name was Dale Bishop.'

# 22

Our visit to Margery Ransome left me with plenty to do. And it all had to be done soon. The annual dinner of the Society was now only a day away. If I could not solve the remaining puzzles before then, I wanted, at least, to have enough information to present to the Society, enough facts to be able to answer their predictable questions. That would give them the best chance of helping me to a solution.

And to three of these questions, I had very little so far by way of an answer.

First – and, now, probably least important – what was the truth about Hippo? Might there not be, buried somewhere along with the truths Hippo was hiding, the key of the identity of David's – and Charlie's – killer?

Second, what explained the extraordinary curiosity of Dale Bishop? Twice he had visited Claudia, whom he did not know, on the basis of a relationship with Charlie that was only a couple of weeks old. He had called on Mrs Ransome, whom he didn't know either, in search of David's notes, and she had sent him packing. He had even gone to see Vera Oblomov, before Hugh and Oliver's first visit, in search of what, I did not know. He seemed always to be just at the point where he could disclose the next clue – and thus, of course, at the point where he could conceal it. Whether or not he had the motive or the opportunity for murder, Dale Bishop's behaviour was, as Virginia said, 'hideously fishy'.

But the third, and most pressing, question was whether there was anything in David's notes that might offer a clue to the motive for his murder. I should have to spend the evening going through those notes.

When we got back to Claudia's house, she proposed a light supper.

'That's a lovely idea,' I said. 'I'm afraid I've a certain amount of telephoning and, perhaps, a visit or two to make this evening.'

Virginia and I sat in the sitting-room, David's notes and mine piled up before us.

'I suppose I should check in with Inspector Fanshaw, to see if he's got any more news,' I said to Virginia.

'But first let's make a little plan of action. What are the urgent questions?'

I gave her my list of three.

'Well, Fanshaw should have been working away at the first two questions. He must have interviewed Hippo again and one of his people must have talked to Dale Bishop. Your real contribution is going to have to be working through those notes of David's.'

'If I'm to be ready for the dinner tomorrow, I shall have to move swiftly. And I probably won't be able to make sense of these papers of David's without help. Godfrey's too out of sorts to be bothered with it, now.'

'Why not ask Peter Tredwell? He obviously knew David rather well.'

'Perhaps. But I wonder if he knows enough about Cambridge before the War.'

'You'll have dozens of old boys longing to talk about *that* at the dinner tomorrow. What you need now is someone intelligent who knows how David was thinking.' Virginia took my hand and looked, smiling, into my eyes. 'You've got to see him sometime, darling. It'll only be embarrassing for a few moments.'

'I really wasn't thinking about that. Just about whether he's the right person.' But it's not a good idea to lie to Virginia about my feelings.'

'Hokum,' she said. 'Go and telephone him now. If you don't call him soon, he'll have gone to dinner in college. And then you won't be able to get hold of him for another couple of hours.'

I rang through to the college and Tom Mitchell answered the phone in the porter's lodge.

'Dr Tredwell, Sir Patrick? Hang on. I think he just went up to his rooms. By the way, there's a note here for you, sir, left by one of our students, Miss Ritter. What would you like done with it?'

'Well, I'm hoping to persuade Dr Tredwell to come and see me this evening. If he agrees, I'll ask him to pick it up on his way out. Otherwise, I shall collect it in the morning.'

'Very good, sir. Now let me see if I can put you through.'

Peter Tredwell's tone was not exactly friendly. 'Ah, Sir Patrick. Busy finding murderers?'

'Look . . . Peter . . . I meant what I said in my note. I am truly sorry. And now I need your help.'

I explained to him quickly about the papers that Margery Ransome had given me. 'I'm sure you can help us understand them. You knew David very well.'

'If you think it will help, of course I'll look at them.'

'It's an awful imposition, I know, but could you come over this evening? We need to act fast.'

'Would now do?'

'Have you eaten?'

'No.'

'Well, it won't be fancy, but I'm sure Mrs Phipps could fit you into our plans here. We're at 62 Portugal Place. Oh . . . and I have one small favour to ask.'

Tredwell's 'Yes?' was on a rising tone. He was obviously sceptical of my notion of what was a small favour.

'There's a note for me in the porter's lodge. Could you bring it with you?'

There was an audible sigh of relief at the other end. 'Sure. See you in fifteen minutes.'

I told Virginia that Tredwell was on his way over and we asked Claudia, rather belatedly, if she minded. 'Not if *he* doesn't mind a nursery supper,' she smiled. 'It's going to be scrambled eggs, bacon, sausages . . . that kind of thing.'

'I'll give you a hand, Claudia,' Virginia said. 'Patrick has to talk to Inspector Fanshaw.'

'A little ordinary police work sometimes pays off,' Fanshaw said. 'You can set your mind to rest about Mr Buckingham. It's not a very nice tale, but it doesn't have much to do with murder.'

Fanshaw had gone back to see Hippo himself. Discreet enquiries had revealed that Hippo had gambling debts – probably a couple of thousand pounds – which he owed to various bookies in town. Armed with this information and Caufield's report that Hippo's Pitt Club bill had already been paid before David gave him the cheque, Fanshaw had decided to adopt a less gentle approach.

'"I've applied for a warrant to search your banking records," I told him. "In my opinion," I said, "you needed money badly enough to blackmail Lord Glen Tannock. You obviously owed money to other people too – your so-called friend who turned up the other day, for example."'

At this point, Hippo had capitulated. The cheques from David were given to cover Hippo's gambling debts. Hippo had not told David how much he really owed; but when David had offered him a couple of hundred pounds earlier in the term, he had accepted. But he swore he hadn't been blackmailing David.

'I asked him about the cheque Lord Glen Tannock wrote the night he died, and he said, "I'd borrowed some money from the May Ball committee. I needed to pay money to repay the loan: the bills were coming due. If I hadn't paid, the others would have found out." I asked him what he would have done if Lord Glen Tannock had not coughed up the cash. And he said he was expecting some other money. So I said, "The money that covered the cheque you wrote last time I was here?"'

Hippo had nodded and so Fanshaw had asked, naturally enough, where *that* money came from.

The answer was something that Hippo had even more reason to be ashamed of. Despite David's subventions, he was still very much in the red. And so he had come up with a scheme to make a little extra money. The idea was simple and unpleasant. The Pitt Club contained most of the undergraduates with well-known names – the children of bankers, the odd viscount, like David, an earl and a score of 'hons'. Rumour about these people was a commodity that could be sold to the gossip columns. So Hippo and the friend whom Jamie had heard in his rooms on Friday night had contacted a couple of newspapers and offered to be anonymous sources, provided the price was right. To cover his gambling, Hippo was going to publish the private lives of his friends.

'Did he sell that story about Peter Tredwell and David to *Private Eye*?' I asked Fanshaw.

'Not exactly. He tried to. But it seems they don't pay. So his friend sold the story to another gossip columnist who wasn't allowed by his editor to use it. And this journalist passed it on to *Private Eye*.'

'That's how they get a lot of their stuff,' I said. 'We've a man in our chambers who does a certain amount of libel work in connection with *Private Eye*. He says any journalist who can't get his editor to run a story, pops into one of those Fleet Street pubs and passes on the glad tidings to someone from the *Eye*.'

'Anyway, the young man who came in when Mr Hogg was there was after his share of a cheque that they'd had for some stories in the last few weeks.'

'Have you been able to confirm any of this?'

'He showed me invoices from various newspapers . . . and copies of some typed "stories". Mostly about people getting drunk at parties and taking off various items of clothing. We'll be getting in touch with his accomplice to confirm all this; but this time he's told us something we can check on. I don't think he's lying.'

'So now we know why he wanted the truth kept quiet. It's pretty sordid, in a trivial kind of way. He was even willing to sell the story about David and Tredwell. What did he tell you about the evening that David died?'

'More or less what he told you, without the nonsense about Tredwell and Lord Glen Tannock in the garden.'

'So that's one puzzle solved. Any news on other fronts?'

'We've put together lots of bits and pieces from people who were on the Backs on Wednesday and Thursday. That little appeal on television paid off. It looks as though Dr Phipps was there both nights. Various people saw him between midnight and about one on Wednesday, and a little later – probably nearer two – on Thursday night. He lectured to the first-year medical students, so a lot of people knew his face. Now, you remember I told you a young woman saw him talking to someone by a car on Thursday night? Well, she couldn't really describe it, as I said. Just said it was a biggish car. But various people saw a Rover drive out of the road up to Thirkill Court on Wednesday night; and when I showed her a Rover, she said that was probably it. So what we have is: somebody in a Rover was visiting Thirkill Court on the night Lord Glen Tannock died. I've checked with the college, by the way. The only Fellow with a Rover is someone called Dr Bainton, who was away at a conference in Leeds last week. This person in the Rover may have come back for some reason the next night; and he was then probably spotted by Dr Phipps, who talked to him.'

'Any description of this other person?'

'No one – so far – except Dr Phipps, of course, seems to have seen him.'

'Or her,' I said routinely.

'Oh no,' Fanshaw said, 'it was a man, all right.'

'Why would anyone have gone back to Lord Glen Tannock's rooms the next night? They were locked, weren't they?'

'Indeed, sir. But didn't I mention to you that we hadn't found any keys in the boy's room?'

'No, Inspector, I don't think you did.'

'Sorry about that. It slipped my mind. I didn't think it was very important until we got these stories yesterday about the Rover coming twice.'

'I don't suppose anyone saw a strange Rover near Heston late last week? Professor Stanley was at Heston on Wednesday and Thursday nights; but he was away from the house much of the time in the last five or six days. We should probably ask him when he last used that pipe; but I suspect it could probably have been poisoned at practically any time in the last week.' I paused. 'Sorry to ramble on like this, Inspector. Hadn't occurred to me before. Did anyone in fact see the car out Heston way?'

'No, Sir Patrick. Mrs Porteous says she probably wouldn't hear a car that was driven to the end of the drive and parked there, especially during the day. She would have heard anyone who drove up the drive in the middle of the night, though. Nobody on the estate seems to have seen anything either night. And Professor Stanley doesn't remember anything odd when he was out there. Of course, we're still asking.'

Fanshaw paused and when he proceeded it was with a good deal of uncertainty. 'There is one other thing, Sir Patrick. It's about Sir Oliver. We had another report from someone who was on the Backs on Wednesday and Thursday nights, jogging. And he says he saw someone who fits Sir Oliver's description both nights just after midnight. Of course, it's only a rough fit – these things always are. But I wonder if you think I should ask him.'

'Well, I'd say it might be best to keep that information back for a while. It's a long shot, in my view, but *if* Oliver's our man, we'll want to keep him offguard as long as possible.'

'Good. That's what I thought, too,' Fanshaw said in a rather concluding sort of a tone.

'Before you go, Inspector, I've got a bit of news in exchange for yours.' I told him about the visit to Margery Ransome.

'Dr Tredwell and I will be going through the notes this evening. Do you have anything much about Dale Bishop? He's been poking his nose in all over the shop.'

'No, sir. We've checked his alibi for Wednesday night, though. He said he was dining in London with a friend of his father's and stayed overnight. Well, the friend in question was an American publisher by the name of Schwartz, who was staying at the Connaught Hotel. And he confirmed, over the phone from New York, that he had dinner with Mr Bishop until about ten that evening.'

'Hold on, Inspector,' I said. 'There's someone at the door.' It was Tredwell. 'I'll only be a moment,' I told him. 'I'm talking to Fanshaw. Run along to the kitchen at the end of the corridor and introduce yourself to Claudia Phipps and my wife.' He handed me the note he had collected from the lodge.

When I got back to the phone I said, 'Carry on, Inspector, that was Dr Tredwell arriving.'

'Bishop says he got back here on the milk train, in the early morning, after having a few drinks and a dance in a disco in central London. Scotland Yard says that nobody there remembers him – but they probably wouldn't. We've also got our people asking if any of the cab-drivers remember picking him up from the station that morning. So far, no luck.' He paused.

I had unfolded the note that Tredwell had handed me while Fanshaw was speaking. Now, I looked down at it.

*I think another man visited our staircase on Thursday night/Friday morning after you. I'm sorry I didn't mention it before, but when Michael Mallory-Browne told me on Friday that he'd seen an older person disappearing down the stairs from his rooms on the first floor early on Friday morning, I assumed he had seen you. But at dinner tonight he mentioned that the man went down into the basement, below the staircase, which means he must have been going out. And, of course, I knew you were staying in the college. So, if you didn't come back that night, maybe you should tell the police that somebody else did.*

*Jo Ritter (U 3)*

'Listen to this, Inspector,' I said. I read it to him.

'Very good, very good. I'll go over for a word with Mr Browne in the morning.' He sounded merrier than he had since I met him.

'We're close, aren't we, Inspector?'

'You know, I think we are, sir, I think we are.'

Peter Tredwell and I read David's notes for several hours, occasionally speaking to each other, occasionally jotting down a note of our own. Because of his work on probability – a subject on which our Brothers Keynes, Braithwaite and Ramsey had done important work beginning long before the War – Tredwell had taken an interest in the published literature on their circle, and he seemed to be able to make sense of a good deal more of David's notes than I could. Virginia's instincts had once more proved reliable.

She and Claudia chatted in the kitchen and came in from time to time to offer us more coffee. As I watched Virginia refill my cup for the umpteenth time, something clicked in my brain. I didn't rush about shouting 'Eureka.' I simply savoured the awareness that I had been liberated from something that had been clouding my vision. I went on reading. By about a quarter past ten, Tredwell and I had been through the file.

'What do you think?' I asked him.

He pointed to a sheet of paper. 'I think this may be the key. But we ought to show it to someone to be absolutely sure.' It took him only a moment to explain what he thought he had found. I thought I had now seen the solution: Peter gave me what I needed to prove it.

'Can you do it tonight?'

'Yes. I'll telephone you with the answer.'

'Any time. I'll be waiting. And Peter . . . thanks.'

When Peter left, I rang Hugh and asked him if he could arrange for all the currently active members of the Society to meet in his rooms before the annual dinner the next evening. 'I'll ask Oliver and Hugo to come as well,' I said. 'I want everyone there who was present at the last two meetings before . . . Will you ask the others? It's important that everybody comes.'

'What's all this about, Patrick?'

'I'd rather not say till I'm certain. But I think that I may know before we meet who killed David and Charlie . . . and why.

'Is it one of us?' Hugh asked.

'I'm afraid so, Hugh. But oddly enough, I'm not yet quite certain which. Can I ask you to do one more thing for me? Do you know where James Hogg is?'

'He's here. Do you want a word?'

He handed over the phone.

'James, the people at the computer centre won't look through their back-up files without a User ID – is that what it's called?'

'That's right.'

'Do you know how to look up a User ID?'

'Yup. It's easy. It's useful to be able to check if anybody you know is on-line when you are. You can send them messages.'

'Could you show me how to do it?'

'Sure. When?'

'Tonight.'

'What time?'

'I'm not quite sure yet. It depends when Peter Tredwell gets back to me. Why not come over here in an hour or so and we can wait for Peter to telephone together.'

'All right,' he said. 'Shall I bring Hugh?'

'By all means, if he wants to come.'

All I had to do now was to phone Hugo and Oliver and wait for Peter Tredwell's call.

'Hugo,' I said, 'I know it's late and I'm so sorry not to have called earlier, but I wonder if you could do me a favour.'

'You've decided to pull out of your talk tomorrow evening. I quite understand.'

'No, not at all. It's just that I'd like you to join the active members in Hugh Penhaligon's rooms in Corpus for a drink before dinner tomorrow night.'

'Does this have anything to do with Glen Tannock and Charlie Phipps?'

'It does.'

'Do you know who killed them?'

'No. But the meeting tomorrow should allow us to discover.'

'When should I arrive?'

'Let me collect you at about a quarter to six. And thank you.'

'Not at all, old boy. I'm sure you have good reason.'

I hoped he was right.

'Oliver, sorry to call so late. It's Patrick. Are you still planning to come up to the dinner tomorrow?'

'Of course, wouldn't miss it for the world.'

'Splendid. Would you meet us in Hugh's rooms in Corpus at about six? I need to gather everyone who was at the last two meetings one last time.'

'What do you have in mind?'

I told him.

When Hugh and James arrived at Portugal Place it was about a quarter past eleven. Peter Tredwell had already phoned. Naturally I was rather tense. Now I was almost certain I had our killer. But I tried to keep calm as I walked with them over to the computer laboratory. I needed just one more piece of evidence to convince myself. Perhaps the massive memory of the computer would produce it.

James led us in through the iron gate of the Old Cavendish. 'It'll be locked at midnight. That's why you need a key.'

We walked into the courtyard, with a huge modern building towering over it. 'The Mond Room is round the corner to our left,' James said. 'Let's go there – it'll probably be empty.'

It was.

James pressed a key on one of the printer terminals. It invited him to enter a User ID and a password. After a second the terminal printed 'Logging on to Phoenix'. The typeface looked familiar: it was the sort of printer that had been used to print the notes. Now the system was spewing out various messages about the computer. Finally it said when the account was last used.

'Phoenix is the operating system. The USER command – you just type USER followed by a name – gives anyone's User ID, once you have the name. You can see when Hugh and I came in here last night, because it gives the time the account was last used.'

'Ask for Hippo Buckingham's User ID and Peter Tredwell's,' I said.

The printer responded: *JB22, PT13.*

'Could you ask it for the User IDs of all our active members?'

James obliged. His own name, Charlie's, and Vera Oblomov's produced responses. David's name and Hugh's and Godfrey's produced: *User not known*.

'I'm afraid we haven't been introduced,' Hugh said.

'I suppose', James commented, 'that Professor Stanley must use the machine in the Applied Maths Lab.'

'How about Hugo McAlister?'

James entered the name. 'Ah ha,' he said, 'a real bigwig. He's got two.' The IDs clattered out at the printer.

'And now how about asking for the User IDs of a group? For example, all Fellows of Trinity.'

James typed HELP USER and read the message that filled the page. 'Yes, you can. Here we go.'

As the printer spewed out a great list of names and the associated User IDs, I asked James whether you couldn't use somebody else's User ID.

'Only if you knew the password. There are a few hackers around who might be able to do it. But you'd have to know your way around the system very well. In fact, I doubt there are more than half a dozen people – apart from the people who run the system – who could get away with it. The weakest point in the system is just that people type in their passwords when other people are looking over their shoulders. Of course, it doesn't show up on the screen as you type it, but you can perfectly well watch somebody's fingers on the keyboard. Still, even if you did get on to somebody else's virtual machine, there'd be traces: you see, when an account is used some of the resources allocated to it disappear.'

I looked puzzled.

'When you're given a User ID, they tell you how much you can use in the way of computing resources. The units are a complicated measure that takes into account things like how much time you actually use the central processor – that's the main computer – how often you use the discs, what time of day it is, what other people are using the system, and so on. If somebody uses the machine while you're away, you should notice that some of these units have been eaten up. And anyway, as you saw, it tells you when the account was last used each time you log on.'

James gathered up the paper from the printer. 'Here, you can have this print-out as a memento.'

I walked Hugh and James back to Corpus.

'Till tomorrow night,' Hugh said, 'when we and our Brothers shall feast.'

When I got back to Claudia's, I called Fanshaw. 'Sorry it's so late, but you remember that the computer people said they'd check their back-up files if they had a User ID?'

Fanshaw remembered.

'I'd like you to call and ask them to do that, as early in the morning as possible. I gather it may take a good while, even *with* an ID.'

I scanned the print-out as I spoke to him, running my finger over a page. 'Here it is.' I gave him two User IDs. 'You know what they should look for.'

*

It was late; but not too late, so it seemed, to telephone Godfrey. He had left a message with Virginia saying I should call whenever I got in. It was just as well. I had been planning to call him early in the morning.

'Patrick,' he said, before I could say more than my name, 'an astonishing piece of intelligence has reached me by a rather odd route about Dale Bishop. You may find it useful in a negative sort of a way if you're still not sure who did it. I mean, it would certainly explain some rather evasive behaviour on the part of our young American friend. You see, I had a telephone call from Ronald Stoddard earlier on this evening. Did you ever know him?'

'Not very well. He's an Angel who specializes in publishing rather unrevealing books about the security services, isn't he?'

'That's the chap. Well, he was calling because he'd been visited this very day by our young friend Mr Bishop with a proposal for a book and a request for a substantial advance. It seems that Mr Bishop has rather American ideas of the profitability of publishing. Hugh tells me his father makes a respectable living betraying his country's secrets.'

'And . . .?' I said.

'He's hawking a book called *Inside Secret Cambridge*, and guess whose dirty laundry he's offering to hang out on the line?'

I'm afraid I gasped. I hadn't intended to give Godfrey the pleasure. But I had never, not even in my wildest dreams, imagined a member of the Society doing something quite so . . . The words that came to mind sounded, on the whole, rather old-fashioned: caddish, unsporting, dishonourable.

'It explains all that taking of notes, of course. And that endless round of questioning; visiting Claudia, Vera Oblomov, Margery Ransome . . . chatting up Hugh. I suppose that he thinks he's got a best-seller on his hands because of the murders. How frightully shabby.'

'Is he one of your suspects?'

'Not really. I was about to start sounding him out, though. He's been chasing David's papers, for reasons I now understand, of course. Well, at least if he acts shifty with me, I'll have a reasonable explanation. But it makes it rather unlikely that he actually killed anyone, doesn't it? It would take a pretty cool customer to try to sell the story of two murders he's committed himself, a few days after committing them. So that's very useful, Godfrey. I have some rather troubling news to give you in exchange. It's about Oliver, I'm afraid. How much did you tell him about what David had been doing?'

'I didn't tell him anything much. Good Lord, surely you can't think . . .'

'I'm afraid so. I think Ransome may have involved him somehow in some dealings with the Russians. Fanshaw has someone who saw a person fitting Oliver's description on the Backs near Clare both nights. I'll know more tomorrow, but I'm pretty sure we've found evidence in David's notes.'

By about half-past midnight, Virginia and I were ready for bed. When I told her the results of my evening's work, she seemed more than mildly surprised.

'But how are you going to prove it?'

The truth is, I wasn't sure I could.

# 23

I had a relatively peaceful day on Tuesday after the rushing hither and thither of the last five days. I telephoned Godfrey to ask him how he was doing and he and Virginia had a few words.

'It is a matter of one's priorities,' he said. 'I told my doctors that I was coming to the annual dinner whatever they said and that I would rather change my doctors than my plans.'

I gave him a brief rundown of my plans for the evening.

'I'm counting on you to help sort out the final details,' I said.

I called Hugo and Oliver, too, to make absolutely sure they were still coming.

And a few other telephone calls were necessary to collect the final confirming pieces of evidence. In the early afternoon, I had a chat with Joanna Ritter and Michael Mallory-Browne on my way back from seeing Peter Tredwell in his rooms after luncheon.

A little after tea, Fanshaw called excitedly with the news that the computer lab had found copies of the notes in the back-up files belonging to one of the User IDs I had given him. 'Actually, what we found was in some kind of code, but young James Hogg was able to break it.' Fanshaw's grasp of theatre was rudimentary, but he knew to pause before his next remark. 'You'll be interested in this,' he added. 'They found one more note: it was addressed to you.'

Inspector Fanshaw came round, and we did a little conferring and planning. And, as usual, as each fact came in, I tried to imagine the crime with every detail I knew sketched in. It's the only way. By the time I had finished, the story I told convinced even Virginia.

The annual dinner was to be in a small dining-room at Peterhouse. It was a pity that after the events of the last week, it could hardly be a festive occasion. I was due to meet the others at six in Hugh's rooms. An hour and a half later we would take the two-minute walk over to Peterhouse and the dinner. Unless something went wrong we should be sure by then who had killed David and Charlie and who had poisoned Godfrey. And my paper would be neither an account of the law of trusts, nor a series of amusing legal anecdotes: I would owe my Brethren and the two Sisters who would be present an account of my last week's labours.

'Hugo,' I said, as he opened the door of his rooms in Peterhouse. He waved me in.

'Nasty business, all this. What's your plan of operation?'

'Oh,' I said vaguely, 'I just want to go through the evidence in the company of our Brethren. I am sure that we can work out who it was. The key thing is going to have to be where people were when the boys were killed.'

'Seems to me extraordinary that nobody saw anyone on the Backs the night David Glen Tannock was killed. I mean, I was out there walking, as I do every night, and I saw a whole host of people. At this time of year the undergraduates never go to bed before two or three in the morning.'

'Well, someone *was* seen; or rather one or two people.' And I explained to him about the sighting of someone Fanshaw thought looked like Oliver.

I arrived at Hugh's rooms, as I intended, a little earlier than the others, at about ten to six, with Hugo in tow.

'Sorry to come a little early, Hugh, but I wanted a word before the others arrive. I hope I can count on your support this evening for a rather unusual proposal. I've tried it out on Hugo, as this year's President, and he's willing to go along with it if you are.' Hugo nodded. 'You see, I want to constitute this gathering as an official meeting of the Society.'

'Nothing to object to in that.'

'No. But I want to propose and admit a new member.'

Hugh raised a questioning eyebrow. 'May I know who it is?'

'Peter Tredwell.'

'Well,' Hugh gulped theatrically. 'Make your pitch.'

'This is not a sentimental gesture, Hugh. I worked with him last night on David's papers. There is absolutely no question but that he has an Apostolic intelligence. And an astonishing breadth of knowledge.'

'Not', Hugh put in, 'that we have ever insisted that our Brethren *know* anything.'

'He is also, as you would expect of someone that David admired, an extremely congenial conversationalist . . . provided you are not engaged in accusing him of murder. I admit he didn't behave very well at the start of this business; but he did have every reason to worry that he was an obvious scapegoat.'

'The truth is, old thing,' Hugh said, smiling, 'that you want him in for David's sake. He just happens to be suitably Apostolic as well. And, speaking as a sentimentalist to a crypto-sentimentalist, you shall have my support. Still, as you know, the custom is that we have unanimity. I can't vouch for all the others. I don't think anyone can object on principle, though, provided we are convinced he is suitably Apostolic.'

'Thank you. I'm most grateful.'

'Think nothing of it, my dear. What are old friends for? And now I insist you have a glass of this delicious sherry.'

The others arrived in quick succession a few minutes after six. First Dale Bishop.

'Don't you dare take out a notebook this evening, young man,' Hugh said, 'or you will be cast into the Outer Darkness.' For reasons I now understood, this remark produced rather more embarrassment than Hugh had anticipated.

James Hogg and Vera Oblomov arrived together.

'You are owed an apology,' I said to her.

'You were all doing your duty,' she said, as grand as a Romanov. 'It is forgotten. I am in fine spirits. James, here, has come and he has fetched me and he has chaperoned me over through these festive streets and I was as proud as the silliest girl on her way to a dance.' Vera Oblomov had clearly been preparing for the evening with a little spirituous sustenance.

Finally Oliver and Godfrey arrived from Trinity.

'Full house,' said Oliver as Hugh poured the last arrivals a drink.

Godfrey raised a glass. 'I should like to begin the evening with a toast: David Glen Tannock and Charles Phipps, may they rest in peace . . . And now, Patrick, to your business.'

'First of all, I should like to suggest that we constitute this as an official meeting.'

'Hearing no objection, it is so ordered,' Oliver said in his best Robert's Rules manner, after glancing swiftly around the room.

'Good. And now I should like to propose that we admit Peter Tredwell of Clare College to the Society.'

'And I', Hugh said, 'should like to second the proposal.'

'And I,' Hugo said, 'as an Angel who has no rights in the matter will observe only that Patrick and Hugh deserve the most serious consideration.' It was not the most spirited support that I had ever been offered, but pronounced in Hugo's languidly assured manner, it was somewhat reassuring.

I made to the astonished company a suitably elaborated version of the case I had made to Hugh. When I had finished, Vera Oblomov was the first to respond. 'The quality of his mind is, of course, quite beyond question. But he was having sexual relations with a student.' Hugo's eyes widened only the slightest bit. This was not one of the things I had felt I needed to tell him. But he said nothing.

'My dear Vera,' Hugh said, 'if that had been grounds for refusing admission to this Society, we should have had to close down years ago.'

'Anyway, he wasn't strictly a student of Tredwell's,' James said. 'I mean your tutor doesn't teach you or even choose who does.'

Vera plainly thought this a piece of casuistry.

'I should probably not butt in,' Oliver said, 'since I am the most Angelic of the Brethren present and it will affect me very little. But it seems to me that a little private indiscretion is not a matter for us to concern ourselves with. There is only one question; there has only ever been one question: Is he Apostolic? Hugh and Patrick say he is. Is that not enough?'

I relaxed inwardly. With Oliver on my side, I knew I would have my way unless Godfrey objected; and he had seemed less disturbed by the proposal than any of the others. I waited for Godfrey to speak.

'Patrick, I agree with Oliver, subject to one caveat. Are we absolutely sure that Tredwell did not kill David or Charles? An Apostolic intelligence is one thing, but a murderer is a murderer.'

'Not only am I sure that Peter Tredwell did not do it, it was his Apostolic intelligence that detected the final piece of evidence.'

'You have my vote,' Godfrey said.

I walked out of the room and down the stairs into the court. I had asked Tredwell to come there at six fifteen. As I entered the court he emerged from beneath the arch that leads below Hugh's rooms into Benet Street.

'Ah, Peter, I'm afraid I couldn't tell you what it was about before. It would have been embarrassing if my Brethren had not agreed. You have just been elected to the Apostles. If you come upstairs now, I will introduce you to the others and we will induct you. And then we must tell them what we know.'

He looked at me in silence and said nothing as he followed me up the stairs. Peter Tredwell was beginning to take his shocks rather sanguinely. As we reached the top, I turned to him. There was one more shock to prepare him for. 'One more thing. One of the people in there is the killer. Please don't let him see that you know. He knows that we think we know who the murderer is. If you treat him coolly, he'll be put off balance. Remember we still haven't enough proof to convict him. And, above all, whatever you do, back up anything I say about the notes.'

Peter Tredwell was inducted into the Society by the age-old ritual. Hugh read the letter which had been sent expelling the first – and, so far as I know, the only – member ever to be thrown out of the Cambridge Conversazione Society. It is a rather over-elaborate Victorian joke, a curse couched in the language of Kantian metaphysics: the world of the Society is real – 'noumenal' – the world outside is merely illusory – 'phenomenal'. The penalty for failing to keep the Society's secrets is set in these words: 'and, thus, forever, to be utterly cast into the Outer Darkness of the phenomenal world.'

When I heard it the first time, I had had an almost irresistible urge to giggle. But I had not now been present at an induction for more than three decades. I could not have known how moved I would be by the associations of the formula. I wondered if Peter Tredwell was thinking of Russell, Keynes, Ramsey and Moore – or trying, instead, as I had done, to think of anything that would stop him laughing out loud.

'With your training,' Hugh said once he had finished reading, 'you are likely to regard the noumenal world as unreal and the phenomenal one as real, Vera tells me. But in case you think that threat idle, let me report my own view that the real penalty for breaches of our code of secrecy is that if you let it be known you are one of us, you will be pestered by every pretentious brat who ever wants to become a member. Welcome, Brother Tredwell.'

'I'm extremely grateful to you all. It's a great honour.'

'And now, since we have only a little time before dinner, Patrick will deal with the second order of business.' Hugh spoke firmly. 'The question for discussion is: Who killed our Brothers Glen Tannock and Phipps? Our Brother Scott has the hearth rug.'

I had jotted down a few notes. I wanted to begin, as much as possible, in the style of an ordinary meeting of the Society. 'The heart of our problem has been secrecy. Precisely the sort of secrecy we have imposed upon our own dealings. Hugh is right. Our secrecy has one advantage. It means that we cannot be pestered by the importunate. But the compact each of us made with the others is worth keeping for another reason:

because it is one of the few things that binds together Angels and those who are currently active. In that sense the ceremony we have just witnessed is more than the re-enactment of a Victorian prank. Apart from the life of reason, it is our only tradition.' I hoped that Dale Bishop was not too busy memorizing the proceedings, now that Hugh had banned the notebook, to grasp the relevance of these remarks to his own situation.

'There are other secrets that are surely worth keeping. Our Brother Tredwell rightly thought it proper not to tell me that our late Brother Glen Tannock was homosexual. In the ordinary course of things, such matters are not the business of the world. In defining a sphere of privacy – whether it be in the bedroom or in the meetings of a society, such as ours – secrecy has its proper place. So, as I say, there are surely honourable secrets.

'But David Glen Tannock and Charles Phipps died,' I continued, 'because they each uncovered secrets that were not honourable, secrets that cried out to be made known. Unfortunately, David did not know that he had uncovered such a terrible secret. If he had known, he would have told most – perhaps, eventually, all – of us in this room, and there would have been no hope of killing the secret with him. But it was only last night that someone other than the murderer discovered what David had found. That person was, of course, our newest Brother. In a moment, I shall ask him to explain. But before I do, let me tell you briefly what I know of what happened to David Glen Tannock and Charles Phipps.

'On Wednesday night, after he left Oliver Hetherington, David went back with Hippo Buckingham to his rooms and gave him a cheque. Hippo then left. David had an exam the next day and he was planning to go to bed soon. You were wrong when you said that he had an appointment later that evening, Oliver. He was keeping an eye on his watch, I suspect, because he wanted to find Hippo, whom he had missed outside Corpus, and get to bed not too late. But someone had followed David and Hippo. And when Hippo left, that person climbed the stairs to David's room. I imagine he found Dvid making himself some cocoa – David often took a cup of cocoa before bed. Someone downstairs heard them talking.

'The killer told David he had come to see him because he was very interested in some of the things David had discovered about Ransome. He knew, you see, that David had found something in Ransome's notes that severely compromised him; he also knew that David had not yet realized how compromising it was. Peter Tredwell and I found that evidence – a photocopy of a page of Ransome's notes, along with a note in David's hand saying he had sent a copy to the killer – in the file of notes Margery Ransome gave me yesterday. I think he may have hoped to find Ransome's original papers in David's possession and somehow get them away from him. But David never took any papers away from Margery Ransome's house, all he had were copies. And so our killer, who knew about David's allergy, decided he must kill him.

'Somehow, he slipped the penicillin into David's cocoa. Somehow, he also managed to pick up David's keys. He needed them so he could come back later, when David was dead, and look for David's notes. Then, knowing that David would soon be dead, he left.

'His car was parked outside on Queen's Road. And he left thinking no one had seen him. But Charlie had been walking along the Backs, thinking, working out some puzzle in his mind, and saw the car. Now Charlie thought nothing of it that night. He probably didn't even see the driver. But the killer saw him as he drove off, and he did not want to be recognized.

'He had not found the papers in David's rooms. Now he had killed David, they were the one link between him and the murder. So, in a desperate move, he went out to Coton to see if he could break into Mrs Ransome's house and steal the papers he wanted from there. But Margery Ransome is a very light sleeper. She heard him, and she turned on the lights and called the police. Then she went down to investigate and the killer ran off.

'The next night he came back to Clare, probably some time after one in the morning. He climbed once more up to David's rooms. He unlocked the door with the keys he had stolen and searched the rooms for David's notes. What he didn't know was that his guess of the night before was correct: David did indeed keep the notes at Margery Ransome's. I imagine he may have thought that the notes were taken by the police. At any rate, after searching carefully, he left. The same undergraduate who had heard the killer talking to David the night before saw his retreating back descending into the cellar of U staircase, when he left.

'But as bad luck – Charlie's and, I suppose, the killer's – would have it, Charlie was out on the Backs again, pondering; and this time he saw the killer unlocking the car – perhaps he was putting the keys to David's rooms in the glove compartment – and came up and spoke to him. He probably asked him what he was doing and whether it was he that Charlie had seen the night before. The killer wouldn't have murdered someone who didn't connect his coming out of Thirkill with a visit to David. But once he realized what Charlie knew, he had to kill him too. Charlie's secret was that the killer had visited Thirkill Court two nights running. Hardly a secret to die for, you might think.

'And here we come to a problem. Why did the killer not follow Charlie back to his labs and kill him then? I confess that, for a long while, I was stumped by this question. Fanshaw and I both assumed that the killer watched Charlie's lab the next morning, waited for the lab assistant to take his mid-morning break, went in, and poisoned him with some of the neurotoxins he was working with.'

As I spoke, I was thinking, How long will it take? I had to keep telling the story until he revealed himself. To accuse him too early would risk his realizing we had too little evidence. It would encourage him to brazen it out. But I was going to be at an end soon of the evidence I had. He had to speak soon.

'The solution to this problem, an obvious enough solution, like so many, once you see it, is simple. *The killer did not go to the labs the next morning*. He did the obvious thing, going with Charlie back to his labs that night. Because he was one of us, this was a natural enough thing to do. He knew, as we all do, about the neurotoxins; and sometime that night, perhaps when Charlie slipped out to go to the loo, he laced Charlie's cup with the stuff, assuming that Charlie would do what he often did: go out to the machine in the hall, collect a can of Coca-Cola and drink it from the cup. But then our killer had a bit of luck. Charlie did not drink from the cup. Since the neurotoxins are transparent and lethal in minuscule doses our killer had only used a drop – quite invisible to the naked eye. The cleaning woman thought his cup was clean. And so she did not wash it.

Charlie died the next morning because that was the first time after the killer left that he used the cup.

'I only realized this last night. I suddenly saw that it could have been not the Coca-Cola but the cup that was poisoned. And then, since the police had only been looking for alibis for Friday morning, practically all of us became suspects again.

'So now I had a wider group of suspects, I had to think through the whole thing again. One thing I knew. These murders were committed by an opportunist; someone who thought fast and acted decisively when he had to. And now, after poisoning Charlie, as he thinks, on Thursday night, he wants to complicate matters a little for those of us who are trying to find him. So he goes to the Mond computer room, probably early on Friday morning, and prints the notes that he then slips into the pigeon-holes at Clare and on the Downing Site later the same day. The notes were meant to suggest planning, to muddy the waters by concealing the fact that the murders were opportunistic. As soon as I saw them I knew they were only meant to distract us. I encouraged Fanshaw to take them seriously, to put guards on all of us, because I thought that that might keep the killer believing that we took the notes seriously.

'Looks easy, doesn't it?' I continued. 'Someone who knows David well enough to find his rooms in the middle of night, who knows Charlie well enough to want to follow him back to his labs and cause no surprise. Someone Charlie recognizes. Because of the way the Society brings together people from different circles in the university, that can't be too large a group. Indeed, it has to be someone now in this room.' I paused and took a sip of sherry.

'And so, I regret to say that at various moments I have had to suspect almost everyone here. I must apologize to those I have dealt with unjustly. But until we had the last piece of evidence, the note of David's that Peter uncovered last night, I was unable to rule out the younger members, those of you who did not know Ransome.

'And so we must ask: who in this room might be compromised by a forty-year-old note of Gregory Ransome's? There are only four of us: Hugo, Oliver, Godfrey and me.'

The only person who displayed unalloyed astonishment at

this remark was Hugo. But he kept his peace. Godfrey merely nodded contemplatively, as if encouraging a student in a supervision.

Oliver, however, appeared irritated. 'Really,' he said. 'This is ridiculous. You yourself pointed out that I said goodnight to David in full view of Hippo Buckingham.'

'But you could easily have slipped out of the back of Trinity later. You told me that you would probably be able to get someone in London to confirm that you had been talking to them at the time that David was poisoned. But you can't, can you? Fanshaw says you've offered him no such alibi.' Oliver said nothing.

'No, the first real puzzle was why you would have hired the car. But, of course, you had come up by train; and you needed to be able to get out to Coton to find the Ransome papers. Even then it didn't make much sense. Why would you have got into the car after the murder? Why not go straight back to Trinity? And why would you go back to the car on Thursday night, after your second visit? But then Mrs Ransome told me yesterday that early on Thursday morning somebody tried to break into her house; and on Thursday night, according to Fanshaw, the killer was only seen *by* the car with Charles. You could simply have been hiding something in the car – the keys, say – before going back to Trinity.'

'I wish somebody had asked me about all this,' Hugo interjected. 'I thought I saw Oliver that evening along the Backs on one of my midnight rambles.'

'What does that prove? I won't deny I went for a walk late that night.' Oliver hesitated for a moment before continuing. 'What about the notes? I couldn't have done those. I didn't have access to a computer account in Cambridge.' Oliver was now shouting – if that is not too unrefined a word to describe the activity of a senior member of Her Majesty's Office of Foreign and Commonwealth Affairs.

'Indeed you did not. But Blumberg did. And, as James pointed out to me last night, one would only have to look over a person's shoulder to see the password they were entering. So you had all the opportunity you needed.'

'But the killer also printed a third message, addressed to Godfrey,' James said excitedly.

'Yes, why would he do that?' Godfrey said in a puzzled tone. 'If his motives in killing had nothing to do with the Apostles, why set out to kill me next?'

'Indeed. Why *would* Oliver set out to kill you, Godfrey? That was a problem for my theory. I said the notes were obviously a distraction. But if Oliver did want to kill someone else, to create a false pattern, why not pick on someone more easily accessible: Hugh, say, or James, or Vera? Why pick someone who was often away out in Heston, difficult to get at? The answer was in David's notes, wasn't it, Peter?'

'Yes,' Peter said confidently.

'What we found was a note from Oliver to Ransome, written late in 1937, discussing a contact with the Russians that Ransome had arranged. I imagine that David asked you about that on the way back to Trinity, didn't he?'

Oliver was still silent.

'And that', Godfrey said, 'would explain why I was next on his list. David had probably also told him that he had mentioned his suspicions of Oliver to me. We were going to meet to decide what to do on the day David died. I remember seeing that note, when I looked through the papers in '38. Of course, in those days one didn't think much of it. And when, later, Oliver disappeared into intelligence, I assumed – as we all assumed about Philby and the others – that he had simply given up his leftward leanings. It seemed unfair to mention it when all that Fourth Man stuff appeared again. I may not be sympathetic to all that socialist nonsense, but I don't believe in witch-hunts.'

The trap sprang shut.

# 24

I gazed at Godfrey in silence. There was a deathly hush. Godfrey looked slightly smug, now, with a trace of a smile. The others were staring at Oliver. Godfrey was the very picture of *gravitas*, concerned but not disconcerted by the idea that our next ambassador to Moscow was a murderer and, perhaps, a traitor. Finally, when the silence had stretched almost to breaking-point, I shook my head mournfully and spoke.

'There's no such note, Godfrey,' I said. 'But then, Margery Ransome never let you look at the private papers, only at the mathematics.'

Godfrey exploded. 'Now that is just preposterous. Are you suggesting *I* killed David and Charles?'

'Didn't you, Godfrey?' Oliver said quietly. 'Didn't you?'

'Do you think I . . .' For the first time he faltered. 'Do you think I . . . risked my own life on a gamble that you and your wife would stop me smoking too much of the poisoned pipe?'

'Why not? You needed to draw suspicion away from yourself; what better way than by appearing to be the next victim. You'd talked to Charlie so you knew a good deal about the toxicity of the different compounds. That is the answer to the question why the killer printed a note to you, Godfrey: you were the killer and it was the obvious way to distract attention from yourself. You printed the extra note as insurance. And when I told you on Sunday night that we knew it wasn't Vera Oblomov or Peter Tredwell, you simply put the next stage of your plan into operation. It was a magnificent performance, by the way, Godfrey. Magnificent.'

'What evidence do you have for any of this?' Godfrey asked quietly. 'I was wrong to say that it was an utterly preposterous theory. But let us treat the issue Apostolically. Let us review the evidence.' He had calmed down completely. He sat very still. Godfrey was going to make me prove it. One had to be impressed.

'Let me start with the simplest elements of the story. When I first began to suspect you I was worried by a number of things. First of all, you have notoriously never taken an antibiotic. So you wouldn't have any old penicillin about the house. And you wouldn't have been silly enough to get a prescription just for killing David. But Mrs P. told me the other day that she had been "poorly." It didn't ring a bell at the time, but when I phoned her this afternoon, I enquired after her health. "A little women's trouble," she said. "But Dr Smedley gave me some penicillin and I'm right as rain." So that dealt with my first problem.'

'My dear Patrick, you aren't going to condemn me because

my housekeeper has a tendency to urinary infections.' Godfrey smiled. And the smile meant: you'll have to do better than that.

I decided it was best to continue without reacting. 'The second problem, of course, was the car. But Inspector Fanshaw's people called a few car-hire firms in the neighbourhood; you hired a Rover in Royston a few days ago, one that fits the descriptions given by half a dozen people who saw it parked on the Backs on Wednesday and Thursday nights.'

'Circumstantial. I told you, sometimes I hire cars because the Bentley is too ostentatious. And I'm sure nobody claims to have seen a car with the right number plates.'

'That's true. So far. I only mention it because it was a piece of evidence that weighed very strongly with me. I had to ask myself why you would hire a car twenty miles away, when you could get one round the corner in Newmarket.'

'The dealer in Newmarket I normally use didn't have a Rover at short notice.'

'Very inventive, Godfrey. But it won't do. You see, we can prove you sent those notes.'

'Of course, since I did not send them, I doubt that very much. You said they were produced at the Mond Room in the Old Cavendish. I don't even have an account at the computer centre.'

'I know. That stumped me for a bit. And then I remembered Dr Andrew Phillips. He came to see you in your rooms when we were there after your note arrived. You introduced him as a Trinity maths don and said that you worked with him. From the way that you treated him, I had a hunch you could ask him for any favour you wanted. So last night I got James to produce a list of the User IDs of the Fellows of Trinity. His was *AP14*. Does that ring a bell? This morning I asked Fanshaw to get the university computing service to check back through the archives to see if they had stored a copy of any files of about the right size for *AP14* last week.'

'But you didn't find them, did you?'

'No, you're right, we didn't. But they did find some files of about the right size that had been encrypted. Phillips told me this afternoon he never stores text files and certainly never encrypts them. He also said you had asked to borrow his computer account about a month ago; and he hasn't changed the password since because he hasn't used the account. Anything in his files is somebody else's.'

'Still terribly circumstantial. After all, you can't infer anything much from a file that's in code.'

'There, I'm afraid, Godfrey, you are not quite right. James here saw these encrypted files as a challenge. You were right, Hugh, James is very clever. Late this afternoon he broke the code. Those files contain the notes.' James nodded. 'There is also a fourth note,' I continued, 'addressed to me. I confess that was something of a shock. What were you planning for me, Godfrey, if your own faked posioning did not divert me?'

'My dear Patrick, I assure you that until this evening it had never once occurred to me to cause you any harm.' Godfrey sounded angry now. His jaw muscle tensed and untensed as he glared at me.

'But now, Godfrey, we come across something of an irony. I asked James how he did it. And do you know what the answer is? He tried some standard encryption algorithms that he'd learned from you. He used one of the strategies you sketched in your paper in February.'

'It was an elegant variation on the Rivest-Shamir-Adelman encryption algorithm,' James said. 'It took me a while to see what you'd done.'

Godfrey smiled a tired smile. 'A most Apostolic deduction, Patrick, I congratulate you. And James. You are wasting your time with the dismal science. You should apply yourself to real mathematics and not to the games economists play.' He looked at each of the others in turn before he went on. 'I wonder if Patrick could prove any of this in court.'

'To know that, of course, it would help to know what secret you were protecting,' I said. 'Peter, why don't you tell them about what you really found in David's file.'

'It was a sketch of a proof. I didn't know enough about topology to be sure, so I took it back with me to talk to one of the maths dons at Clare: a topologist. He took one look at it and said it was the outline of a proof of the Stanley-Ransome theorem.'

'A theorem which, as Godfrey has often told us, was not proved until after Ransome's death,' I said. 'You see, there was nothing at all about Oliver in those notes. And so, Godfrey, I knew it had to be you.'

All eyes turned towards him.

'So your theory is that I killed David to protect the guilty secret that I had stolen the theorem.' Godfrey's voice was quite steady. He spoke deliberately.

'Plagiarism, Godfrey, is a matter of intellectual property,' I said. 'It's not a criminal matter.'

Godfrey snorted. 'It doesn't matter now whether you can prove I killed David and Charlie. You see, whether or not you could prove it, my reputation is ruined. The Ransome papers prove that I *stole* the theorem, do they not?' As he stressed the word 'stole', he looked at me scornfully. 'It hardly matters whether I am a murderer as well. Did you know I was to be in the Birthday Honour's list, Oliver? Sir Godfrey Stanley. That would have been most satisfying. And now, of course, it will not happen.

'I am truly sorry I had to kill David. But you do see that my whole life depended on it. Such an honest, engaging, intelligent boy. He would have been very shocked, wouldn't he, if he had realized that my intellectual reputation was based entirely on somebody else's work? I don't think he would have let me get away with it, do you? At all events, I couldn't chance it. Forty years, everything I ever achieved, every scrap of recognition, all gone. None of this would have happened if Margery Ransome had allowed me to see all of Gregory's papers. I destroyed all traces of the proof in his mathematical papers; even the first inklings of it. But Margery didn't like me much. So she insisted on showing me nothing that was, as she said, "personal". GR must have left a copy of the proof among the deep thoughts in his commonplace book.'

Godfrey's manner now became brisk, almost dead-pan. 'But I am sure you, Brethren and Sister Oblomov, will want to know how much of what our Brother Scott has deduced is correct.' He was my old mentor guiding me through a problem as if it had nothing to do with us personally. 'Much of what you have worked out is right, Patrick. I am pleasantly surprised. I never thought much of your mind: you were so pedestrian at Bletchley. Nevertheless, I must congratulate you. You caught me out with that nasty trick. And as for Oliver; well, I feel sure that the

Russians will have a worthy adversary in their games of bluff.' We watched as Godfrey finished the remaining sherry in his glass.

'A brief synopsis of the facts is in order,' he continued. 'When Hugh mentioned to me last winter that David was taking an interest in the Ransome papers, naturally I offered my assistance. I was hoping to keep him away from danger. And I was able to keep an eye on him by the simple device of returning from the Angelic realm to live among the ephebes. Sadly, it became clear several weeks ago that I had failed to divert young David.' He smiled nervously at all of us. 'It was such a difficult decision. His young life or my fulfilled one? There is a puzzle that would have kept our Brother Moore busy.'

Godfrey's hand travelled to his waistcoat pocket and he drew out a small silver fob-watch. He looked at the time, before continuing. 'You mustn't be late for the dinner. That would never do.' He was speaking quickly now.

'You were planning to kill David with some of Charlie's poisons, if he got too close to the truth, weren't you?' I heard my own voice sounding softly curious, unreproachful. 'That was why you were spending all that time in his laboratories on the Downing Site.'

Godfrey nodded. 'It would have been quick and painless.'

'But then at the meeting in David's rooms a fortnight ago, you heard about the allergy. You probably noticed the powdered milk then, too. And you thought you might be able to persuade the world that it was an accident, that way. With Charlie's poisons it would look like murder from the start.'

Godfrey looked at the others. 'A mistake to be taken in by the fuddy-duddy upper-class manner. You do get there in the end, don't you, Patrick? . . . Now, let me see.' Godfrey had obviously prepared his story. When he started again, it was in the same clipped delivery. 'On Wednesday night, I brought along a glass jar like David's, filled with a healthy mixture of penicillin – borrowed, indeed, from dear Mrs P – and milk powder, and simply substituted it while David was at the meeting of the Society. When I left, David had already made his cocoa so I replaced his jar as I walked out. I was going to come back later to look for the notes; but, as you say, Charlie saw me, so, after my little visit to Margery's, I drove back to Heston and waited till the next night.'

'How did you keep Mrs Porteous from hearing you?' I asked.

'I parked the car in one of our fields, a quarter of a mile from the house, and walked back. Even if she had heard me, she would only have thought I was going for a midnight walk. But poor Mrs Porteous's hearing is not what it was . . . Now, where was I?'

'Thursday night.'

'Ah yes, while you were meeting here. I thought it best to come a little after midnight, so as to avoid such unfortunate encounters as the one with Charles the night before. But, as you say, Patrick, he and I had the awful luck to bump into each other again the next night, as I was on my way back from not finding David's notes. Naturally, he asked what I was doing. And I had the bright idea of telling him that I had been visiting you, Patrick. So then, of course, I had to kill him before he saw you again. Charles was not a very suspicious person. I regret to say, I cannot report the same of you. Of course, I knew every detail of his laboratory habits; his taste for Coca-Cola from the slot machine. Such a sweet tooth, Charlie. Once the mug was lined with the poison, it was only a matter of time. As you say, Patrick, it was the merest good fortune that Charlie waited so long to slake his thirst. That – and Fanshaw's dim-witted assumption that the drink not the mug had to be tampered with – gave me the best alibi in the world.'

Godfrey got up and went over to where the sherry bottle stood on a small side-table. 'May I?' he asked Hugh. He did not acknowledge Hugh's slight nod of assent. 'The irony, of course, is that David found no evidence of the *real* crime.' Godfrey was very tense now, his voice was hard-edged. 'Yes, I killed two of our Brethren in order to keep secret my theft of the theorem. And, dear Patrick, you found me in less than a week. But no one ever found any evidence of my first murder – which took place on April the eighth, 1938, to be exact. That, I got away with for nearly forty years. More than two thousand times as long, as if the time one gets away with it is inversely proportional to the significance of the murder. Wonderful as David and Charles were, neither of them would have made more than a blip on the intellectual horizon. But my first killing . . . now that really made a difference. So you see, dear Brethren, it all goes back such a long way. Right back to the day I pushed Gregory Ransome over a cliff in the Alps in the spring of '38.'

The effect of the revelation on our party was of course startling. Several of us – under our breaths – called on various names of Our Lord. Hugo finally gave up all attempts to preserve a dignified manner, clapping his hand to his forehead and puffing in a gesture of horror and distaste. Mr Bishop's offering was particularly savoury. 'Jesus fucking Christ!' he muttered and then, 'God . . . sorry.' Godfrey seemed uninterested in the effect he was having on us.

'I should like to make a toast. Can I fill anyone else's glass?' He turned back to the drinks tray, his body between us and the bottles and glasses.

I said, 'In the circumstances, Godfrey, I don't think that it would be safe to drink from a glass you had had a chance to tamper with.'

'That *is* amusing, Patrick. What a pity. It is such an excellent sherry. You will find, I think, that it is only mine that is dosed with one of poor Charlie's neurotoxins. To Brother Ransome. A genius even among Apostles.' He raised his glass and knocked back its contents. 'This was to have been David's dose.'

Godfrey Stanley never spoke again.

Fanshaw had, of course, been waiting in the wings. It did not take long for him to collect our statements and arrange for the removal of the body. I wondered if Godfrey had really thought as ill of me all along as he had suggested. Had he been just lashing out in his distress or had he always thought me a fool? I had to admit that it was a strong possibility. After all, in a sense his whole life had been an elaborate lie. Once he had covered a murder and the theft of a career, concealing his real feelings about me, about all those around him, would have been a simple task. The performance when he was poisoned was only the finale in a life of staged pretence.

I had told Fanshaw before the evening began that the evidence we had would not convict Godfrey; that I wanted to provoke a confession, if I could. And I knew that if I made out the case against Oliver in front of him, Godfrey would be unable to resist the opportunity to hammer the final nail into Oliver's coffin. If Oliver were accused, Godfrey would escape: his two – now, three – Apostolic murders could remain his own secret. And Professor Sir Godfrey Stanley FRS could retire to Heston House and die in the grand style, as he had lived.

When I had put the plan to Oliver, he had said it was 'fiendish'. And Hugo had agreed, as we walked together to Hugh's rooms, to back up the story by claiming to have seen Oliver on Thursday night. I had realized in the course of our conversation that it must have been he that Fanshaw's informant had seen walking along the Backs on Wednesday and Thursday nights. Since I'd already let Godfrey know that Fanshaw had a witness who had seen someone like Oliver, I thought Godfrey might really believe he had had the good fortune to have found at least a circumstantial scapegoat.

I must candidly admit I had not intended that the confession should come attached to Godfrey's corpse. I had rather densely assumed that he couldn't have more of Charlie's poisons after he had used the stuff in the pipe. But Godfrey's manner of parting certainly had its advantages.

Even Fanshaw immediately grasped the point: 'I don't think we need to mention the actual Society itself to the coroner. "A group of friends" should cover it.' Since I had recorded the meeting, Fanshaw was also willing to let us go on to the dinner and sign our statements later. 'If you can stand eating after this sort of thing.'

'I don't suppose I shall eat much. But I do owe my Brother Apostles an explanation of the deaths of four of their number.'

'A very congenial chap, Inspector Fanshaw,' I said to the assembled group as we walked over, slightly belatedly, to Peterhouse.

'I should think so too,' Hugh said. 'After all, you solved two murders he was looking into – and one he didn't even know about – for him.'

'I must say I still can't quite believe it,' Vera Oblomov said. 'What persuaded you it was Stanley?'

'It was very hard even coming round to considering the possibility. I've known him all my adult life and he's always been a great friend. Or so I thought. But, as you said, James, on Thursday night, it had to be something that David knew. And once Peter found the Ransome proof, we had, for the first time, a really powerful motive for murder. After that, it was a matter of blowing away the smoke screen Godfrey – and various others like Hippo – had left. But it wasn't until we got him lying about Oliver I was absolutely sure. Godfrey would never have done such a thing if he hadn't got something to hide.'

'So all these years, Godfrey made it out that Ransome and he were like Watson and Crick, when it was really like Mozart and Salieri,' James said.

'What a charming analogy,' Hugh offered. 'We shall make something of you yet, my dear, we shall make something of you yet. And now we must all be sweet to the Angels.'

I need hardly say that the dinner was not exactly a roaring success. I don't even recall the wines. The convention is that the newest member gives a report on meetings he – or she – has attended. It did not seem fair to insist that Peter Tredwell continue this tradition. But the Angels wanted to know about the deaths of David and Charlie, which they had read of in the newspapers. They had not expected to hear of another death, nearly forty years earlier, or of the suicide of a Brother whom they had been expecting to see that very evening.

Hugo McAlister presided in grand style and thanked me graciously 'both for your work and for your account of it'. I suspected that what he was most grateful for was that I had described to him a little scheme – perfectly legal, you understand – involving various banks in the Canaries that was going to do the Revenue out of a fair whack of his Beeston Place capital gains. Hugo's little speech ended with an Apostolic sting in its tail. 'In conclusion, I have to say that the only thing I didn't like about the way our Brother Scott has proceeded is that he never suspected me! I may be an Angel, Patrick, but, like Berkeley's God, I am always about in the quad.'

Richard Butterthorne joined in the murmur of appreciation that went around the table and then pronounced: 'Never could understand how Godfrey produced that theorem. I mean, he was clever enough, but he didn't have an ounce of real mathematics in him.'

'Hindsight', Dale Bishop whispered in my ear, 'is 20–20 vision.'

'Will you publish your book about us?' I asked him, still looking at my plate. I thought I might do best if I caught him offguard. As I turned to face him, I could see he was quite utterly speechless. *'Inside Secret Cambridge.* Such a sensational title. If it's all the same to you, I'd rather you didn't. Unlike the CIA, we're a private club and nothing in British democracy depends on our being exposed. It's not like your father's Bolivian business.'

Dale Bishop was suffused with embarrassment. 'How did you know?' he stammered.

'Would you believe: someone in British counter-intelligence told me?' It seemed the most helpful gloss to put on the facts.

'After tonight, I would. Look, I'll call them tomorrow and ask them to return the proposal. I mean it.'

'I don't think that will be necessary. The proposal has already been destroyed. But I think it would be wise not to offer it anywhere else. Inspector Fanshaw mentioned to me yesterday that he had found a certain amount of white powder when they were routinely searching your rooms. Naturally, they analysed it – it might, after all, have been penicillin – and it seems to have been cocaine. I fear that Fanshaw was rather inclined to take the view that this was a straightforward criminal matter. I persuaded him, however, that I was in a position to influence you for the better and, since he is feeling generous towards me, he agreed to have the matter put aside.'

'What's the deal, Sir Patrick?' He spoke calmly now but it was obvious that he was apprehensive.

'Perhaps you would allow me to have a signed confession?'

'You can trust me, Sir Patrick.'

'In the circumstances you will have to allow me to treat that claim with scepticism.'

There was a long pause. Finally, he said the one word, 'Deal.'

I was enormously relieved. The story I had told was not entirely true. Fanshaw had not searched Bishop's rooms and so, naturally, had found no cocaine. But it had struck me as we walked over that James's tale of Bishop's offer of drugs to David provided the opportunity for a little creative invention. Of course, nobody who knew anything about the British police would have believed a word of it. But to judge by the programmes one sees on the television, American policemen are always coming to such arrangements. I thought it was worth a try: it was worth seeking for the Society a guarantee of privacy, at least in the medium term. And, since all this happened some time ago and Bishop has kept his part of the bargain, I think I can claim to have been proved right.

I put to him my side of the bargain. 'I shall arrange for the document to be kept securely in my bank. We can agree that it should be destroyed in, say, ten years.' Bishop wiped his brow with his napkin. 'I think by then,' I went on, 'the more sensational interest of your book will have substantially diminished. I shall leave instructions with my executors in case I should die in the interim.' I turned to him with a sickly smile. 'You can trust me.'

He laughed anxiously. '*Touché*.' For a moment he said nothing and I resumed my perfunctory picking at the food on my plate. Finally he said, 'You must think I'm a real shit.'

'No, I think you're just a young man trying to make his way in the world. I should have thought that what mattered was what you thought of yourself.' Remorse, as one learned in confession, is always to be encouraged. If that cannot be managed, I suppose a little embarrassment comes a serviceable second best.

'Anyway,' he laughed nervously, 'if I published the truth, nobody would believe it.'

'I'm afraid,' I sighed, 'that if it's about the Apostles, people will believe almost anything.'